WE

DISAPPEAR

4.8.08

for Charlotte
with thanks

Scott Heim

Also by Scott Heim

FICTION
Mysterious Skin
In Awe

POETRY
Saved from Drowning

WE
DISAPPEAR

a novel

SCOTT HEIM

HARPER PERENNIAL

NEW YORK ● LONDON ● TORONTO ● SYDNEY

HARPER ● PERENNIAL

This book is for my mother.

ACKNOWLEDGMENTS

FOR THEIR ASSISTANCE, patience, and understanding, I'm grateful to Michael Lowenthal, Dorian Karchmar, Alison Callahan, Jeanette Perez, James Ireland Baker, Maura Casella, Christophe Grosdidier, Tamyra Heim, Carolyn Price, and Michael Borum.

I'm also indebted to John Hampson and the London Arts Board for assistance during the early work on this book, and to Abraham Lowenthal and Jane Jaquette for granting me necessary time and space to finish.

Go, Youth

I was in a dreamstate and this was causing a problem
with the traffic. I felt lonely, like I'd missed the boat,
or I'd found the boat and it was deserted. In the middle
of the road a child's shoe glistened. I walked around it.
It woke me up a little. The child had disappeared. Some
mysteries are better left alone. Others are dreary, distasteful,
and can disarrange a shadow into a thing of unspeakable beauty.
Whose child is that?

—*James Tate*

ONE

THE LITTLE GIRLS who found the body of the missing boy were not angels, although that is how the newspaper described them, the following morning, beneath the headline. I saw the photo, after all, and the seven girls were only girls. They had no haloes or transparent wings. They had no heavenly warmth or sweet, scarless faces kissed indi-

vidually by God. What the girls did have were muddy pant-
legs and boots; bright jackets buttoned against the wind of a
Sunday hiking trip; name tags in crooked calligraphy made
just that morning by their Lutheran youth-group sponsor.
Teresa and Joy, Maura Kay, Mary Anne. Two Jennifers and
a Missy. When I close my eyes, I picture the girls stepping
back, a warped semicircle, as the body of the murdered boy,
his bones and tattered flannels, alters their lives forever. Their
hands folded clumsily for prayer. Their seven mouths a silent
chorus of ohs.

My mother woke to her room, her hushed house at the end of
the street. It was newly morning; she sensed the threat of rain
in the bleary sky. She made the walk to the kitchen to pour
weak iced tea into a smudged glass. Through the sounds of
wind and the sparrows in the trees, she listened for the paper-
boy, his determined grinding rhythm, until finally, through
the swelling silence, came the circular clack of gears, the spit
of gravel, the paper's thud against the screen.

She carried the *Hutchinson News* to her morning bath. The
clawfoot tub . . . the Victorian washerwoman prints she'd
found at the junkyard . . . the pink towels bordered with roses.
She twisted the faucet as hot as she could stand and, lowering
herself through the layer of water, unrolled the front page.

My mother saw the headline and photograph. At last: the
missing boy.

Henry Barradale, the words said. For the past three days,
since reading about the body, she'd been tracking the progress. She had called the police offices; searched for articles

on her slow-speed, secondhand computer; stayed up late within the tolerant television light. And now she knew. She raised the paper above the bathwater and ran her fingers along the words. FAMILY IDENTIFIES PARTRIDGE BOY: a father, mother, and two younger sisters still lived, left behind, in tiny Partridge, Kansas. My mother noted the funeral date. Henry Barradale would be laid to rest at Rayl's Hill cemetery: the same that held her parents, her older brothers and sisters, and even her first husband, the father who'd died only weeks before I was born. Rayl's Hill was the same where, only fourteen months earlier, my stepfather, John, had been buried beside her own empty plot. Yes, my mother knew the cemetery well.

She took her pills with the tea, sitting at the table to sketch her plan. At two o'clock she dialed my number in New York. "Finally he has a name," she said into my machine. She pronounced each word as though he were royalty. From bed I heard her breathless voice, but was too tired to answer. "Hope you're thinking seriously about coming home. I'll call again when I know more."

She found the road atlas, torn-cornered and coverless, among a stack of hospital bills in the hall closet. Partridge, faint point on the map, was only twenty miles away. My mother ripped the atlas pages, figuring she'd never visit those other states again. She tucked Kansas into her purse and began to dress. I imagine she wore her tortoiseshell glasses. I imagine she dabbed some red on her lips, pausing to decide between the wig and half-folded scarf. The straggle toward the antique mirror. The uncertain smile, lights off, the same I'd caught on the day of John's funeral, before Friday-morning treatments, times she thought no one could see.

The rain was soft; she could walk to the pickup without getting too wet. Henry's picture stayed sheltered in her purse, alongside the pictures of John, of my sister Alice and me, the atlas pages, the orange prescription bottles. My mother spread the map on the seat, turned the key, and silenced the pedal-steel ballad on the radio. She fixed her eyes on the rainy road, steering John's pea-green Ford along the highway toward Partridge.

All week, she'd called as often as four times a night. In a hesitant, almost childlike voice, she'd urged me to leave New York, to return home. We could play detectives, she'd said. You and me, just the two of us, like we used to do. Come home and we'll learn everything about the missing boy.

The two of us, she'd said. In truth, it was my mother, not me, who'd willingly traveled this world before. Her obsession began the autumn I turned ten. During those chilly, copper months, a boy named Evan Carnaby had vanished from our hometown. He was a boy of fifteen, just like the later Henry; he had identical boredoms and daydreams and after-school slammed doors. MISSING, said the flyers Evan's family posted along our streets. MISSING, warned the newsmen on our radio and TV.

At first, Alice and I were stunned. We felt we'd known Evan personally: we'd seen him hurling backyard baseballs with his dad; we'd watched from our window seats as he'd boarded our bus. But our strange thrill was no match for our

SCOTT HEIM

mother's. She'd recently accepted a job at the Kansas State Industrial Reformatory, the maximum-security prison in nearby Hutchinson, and was now our authority on any trickles of knowledge about Evan. She became an insider, a specialist. Evenings, I'd watch proudly as she unbuttoned her walnut-brown uniform and took her hair from its bun. I'd stare at her gold badges and KSIR patches, the belt on which hung a gold-knobbed nightstick, and, most astonishingly, a gun. Perhaps I believed our mother could save Evan Carnaby. Perhaps she believed it, too.

The boy had disappeared during the time our mother was drinking, those weeks and months so long before her *real* disease, and soon she began staying up, quiet leaden midnights and beyond, to search for information on Evan and more missing souls. I remember hunkering downstairs to find her in the darkened kitchen, absorbed in her new undertaking. The staggered breathing, the rustle of newspapers, the sudden glint of scissors. And the slow, narcotic linger as I watched her slump across the table, hair fanning across the bourbon bottle, ice melting in her favorite green glass with the palm trees on the side. In the mornings, Alice and I would wake to find all the faces watching us, Evan and his vanished companions, their photographs taped and pasted and pinned to our kitchen walls.

Pictures from the sides of buses, from highway posters, grainy gray from cartons of milk. To me, their names seemed like song lyrics or lines from poems. George Jordan, Penny Paulette Myers, Clyde Heiding Jr. I remember the weary-eyed, nightly-on-the-news Cantrells, residents of nearby Abilene, whose daughter Gina had disappeared one Christmas Eve. Or Inez Eberhardt, a Coffeyville librarian, whose coworkers reported her missing. Or the runaway Douglas Francis Minahan. The decade-without-a-trace Christopher Kemp.

Alice and I watched and worried. Sometimes our mother would stand in the center of a room, staring blankly, staring at nothing. We watched her pin photos to the wall, inspecting her like we'd inspected our substitute teachers at school. We remembered stories we'd heard about our mother's teenage years: wild tantrums and blackouts and attempted overdoses of pills, magnificent bouts of depression. At seventeen, she'd spent two weeks in what she called a "sanitarium," although she never clarified the details. Was she somehow shrinking into that former afflicted self?

For a while, those new nights of her woozy kitchen-table enterprise, we tried to assist or federate. But neither my sister nor I could match her compulsions. October droned by, November and December, and Alice eventually withdrew. Since I was younger, I didn't mind laboring onward, even as Evan's mystery remained unsolved; I sat with my mother late into the night, organizing pictures in her scrapbooks. I remember her explaining, in her Jim Beam voice, how badly she wanted to meet the deserted ones, the innocents left behind by those who had vanished. The wives and husbands; the distraught, insomniac parents. She wanted to ache with them. To get as close as she could, to understand the victims "gone without a trace," those saints for whom the earth seemed to yawn its bleak and blackened throat and swallow whole.

Then things got better. During the spring and the sum-mer that followed, my mother's nights of drinking gradually ceased. She removed the pictures from the walls; like so many other fancies, her interests began to wane. It wasn't that she stopped caring. It wasn't that her sources, those tragic chil-dren and women and men, had stopped disappearing. She simply slipped into other unwelcoming worries. In a few more years, Alice would leave home for college; a few after that, I would follow. For my mother, another marriage, a move to a new town. Eventually I left for New York. Eventually she became sick.

Sometimes, all these years since, I'll read a missing-persons report or catch some late-night crime show on TV, and my mother's words will flood forth. I'll imagine her sitting at the table, her officer's uniform, her twinkling green glass, and I remember her utter devotion. Back then, each detail of each disappearance was her essential clue, tucked away with the promising hope to develop, someday, into meaning. The snagged and bloodied sleeve of the blouse. The cellophane sweet-candy wrapper. The chain with its lockless key.

It didn't take long to find his house. She felt an almost crimi-nal thrill, and then, a numbing sorrow. She eased to the ditch and parked. Rain rolled across the windshield and smeared her view, but she could see the silver mailbox with the final ALE broken from the family name, the black angled roof, the blue shutters and hail-battered siding, the fence that ringed the flower beds. She could see the empty tire swing, lazily swinging from the branch of a mulberry tree. She imagined a younger Henry playing there, his lanky denimed legs kicking from the rubber, the rope rasping and branch bending on his upward soar.

Nothing about the Barradale house seemed to invite what had happened. She watched the front door with its surprising cobalt paint; the scarred screen door before it. The doorknob seemed the same type as hers, back in her own small town of Haven. She thought of its familiar sound, the echoing buckle as the latch uncaught. Entering could be so simple. If only she possessed enough energy—but how would she escape if they arrived home? She thought about the mom and dad and two sisters. "Whatever happened to our little Henry," she said, as though they all could hear.

She kept her sentry in the Ford, warmed by the heater's silky huff, the nubbled seatback marking her skin. Finally she drove the length of Partridge's central street until she found a pay phone. When I answered, she blurted, "Nobody's at his house." Thunder shuddered through the breaths between her sentences. "I got a little lost but then I figured it out. I'm sopping wet!"

"What? Where are you?"

"Right down the street from Henry's house. Been waiting and waiting in this storm. But it's like everybody's vanished. Have you made your decision about coming home?"

"I don't know. Haven't said anything to my landlord. You drove all the way to his *house*?"

"It was a nice drive. I wanted to see where the dead boy lived."

"I've got stacks and stacks of work at the freelance job," I said. "I'm still not sure I should come."

"Please. I really need you here."

What she forgot to describe, I composed on my own. I know she drove back to the Barradale address and lingered, caught in the storm, until twilight. By now she must have been so tired. Surely she forgot to eat dinner or take her meds. Her scarf leaking rain; her clothes a mess. My mother might have cried a little, a dislocated suffering for Henry and those he left behind. She stayed to watch the house, the tree with its tire like a blinded eye. I believe she pictured him again and again, leaving for school, slamming the bright blue door, running toward whatever waited for him. Against the sodden skyline drifted a thin collar of geese, and my mother followed them so far she had to squint, and then her gaze returned to the empty house, which she watched until her hand dropped from the steering wheel into her lap, and she closed her eyes.

How many times, in that stretch of days, would she stare at Henry's photograph? His uncertain smile, the ridge of his clavicle, the modestly mussed hair? The newspaper article filled four columns, with six more on page three, its focus so careful and deep that my mother wondered if a relative had written it. I remember her reading it, more than once, over the phone.

Henry Harris Barradale was only fifteen, born December 23, an A and B student, so kind to his sisters, his German shepherd Shasta. He'd been missing nearly a month. He left his summer-session football practice that Wednesday night, all shower-damp hair and soap-scrubbed skin, rushing to meet a cluster of friends at a diner. But Henry never showed.

When we reviewed the article, my mother and I found every detail so perfectly pat and American, so generically teenage and clean. I helped her embellish the scene: the unfilled space at the café booth, the plate without the usual Henry hamburger, Henry fries; his friends' letter jackets, the maroon P pinned with each football and basketball, each winged shoe; the boys' red-white-red straws in their root-beer foams as they waited and waited.

The medical examiner speculated that Henry had been murdered nearly three weeks after he'd disappeared. He'd been lying in the field five days. Pressure to his throat had snuffed his air and crushed his hyoid bone. Henry had been stabbed, although the paper did not specify where. Both his wallet and letter jacket were missing. There had not been, as the author of "Family Identifies Partridge Boy" noted, any "sexual foul play." Mr. and Mrs. Barradale had identified their son through dental records. They recognized the size and brand of his T-shirt, his red high-top sneakers. And the friendship bracelet circling Henry's wrist, a gift from a girl, violet and forest-green threads with delicate egg-shaped beads.

For days afterward, my mother would marvel at this final, focused image, the beaded bracelet connecting her irreversibly to his murder. At her prodding request, I helped her elaborate on the reporter's story. We decided that for Henry, the eggs on the bracelet meant something special. According to the article, his grandparents kept a farm just east of Partridge, and we guessed Henry often worked in the hatchery, the chicken coop with its aisles of white warmth, of red-beaded eyes. Each autumn, he helped his grandfather incubate eggs—his cau-

10   SCOTT HEIM

tious, touchdown-tightened hand beside the old man's speckled knuckles—twisting the heat-lamp bulbs in their sockets, preparing the beds of hay and cedar chips, bunching gunnysacks against the feverish chicken-wire corners. Yes, Henry had joined this ritual every year his grandparents could remember. But this fall, this terrible fall, Henry would not help.

Together we focused on the flickerings, the accidentals most others would miss. I remembered this practice from before, all those years ago, whenever she'd come to me with the details of some new disappearance. Because I couldn't mirror her fascinations, I'd keep her satisfied by embellishing. Now, with Henry, we fabricated a boy who must have smoothed each eggshell against his cheek; a boy who stuck dandelions in the gaps between the eggs. A boy who, left alone, sang hymns to the pullets and hens. In our visions he stood in the blood-scented shadows, no relation to us, yet somehow *ours*, Henry without a thought of the future or the field with its waiting demon. Henry, poised beside his grandfather's incubator, letting lamplight warm the eggs, shudder them, until, at last, some miracle evening, when a single shell cracked and the firstborn head emerged, damply dazzled thing, breathtakingly alive.

On the phone, my mother's enthusiasm began to worry me—it was excitement, after all, over a murdered boy. Then again, after so many stories of her doctors and therapies and pills, I found it refreshing to hear some zest return to her voice. So in these new conversations, I let her speak solely of Henry. I avoided talking about myself, trying to conceal what she doubtlessly knew: that my depression hadn't improved since I'd last come home; that I still hated Pen & Ink, where I sometimes freelanced, writing copy for school textbooks. Worst of all, that I hadn't stopped abusing the drugs she'd often begged me to quit.

The day after her Partridge trip, I received an Express Mail envelope on my apartment doorstep. Inside were clippings from five separate Kansas newspapers. To my surprise, they weren't further articles about Henry. They were classifieds she'd placed in the *Hutchinson News*, *Wichita Eagle*, *Salina Journal*, *McPherson Sentinel*, and *Emporia Gazette*. Each of her ads read the same: "MISSING PERSON? Upcoming book about disappeared people. Conducting interviews w/loved ones left behind. Share your story!" Following that was my mother's address and phone. Lastly, in boldface, "ASK FOR DONNA OR SCOTT."

My week had been reckless: two days at Pen & Ink, followed by five of getting high. My studio apartment stank of chemical sweat. Dust had settled across the piles of clothes, the glasses of water, and the framed photographs on the mantel, now facedown as though toppled by some surprise wind. The branches outside made shadows on my walls, and I watched their shifting blacks and grays. A headache was spurring at my temples, and my hands and feet were cold. I thought about my mother and Henry Barradale. About each word in the newspaper ads. Finally I rose and picked my clothes from the floor, sniffing to find a shirt clean enough to wear. I needed to leave, to get high again.

I rode the grumbling subway into Manhattan. Random images layered in my head: Henry's angle as he lay discarded, forgotten; the eyes gone gray as paraffin; his pale ears filling with sounds from the surrounding field and the woods beyond. Perhaps he hadn't suffered long. Perhaps in death he'd heard the whispers of animals; the twist of night-bloom ivy; the rowdy struggle as the hands stopped his throat.

The subway riders quietly crowded the train. There was the blank-eyed old man, reading and rereading a page of a movie-star magazine. There was the stout, ambiguously female Chinese vendor who shuffled between cars, amassing dollar bills in her fists, selling miniature plush penguins and bears, batteries and ballpoint pens, dainty bracelets and handheld face-fans that no one would need. And the little girl across the aisle, likely returning from some party or street fair, sitting apart from her mother and a man decidedly not her father. The adults traded bites from a white-pink whorl of cotton candy but offered the girl nothing.

It was almost palpable—there within the old man and the luckless vendor and the marooned girl—this urban loneliness shared by so many, yet still distinct, so hers and his and ours. For months I'd been learning its nuances. All the dinners I'd botched or burned, amounting to more than a single plate, dinners dropped in the trash. All the soured bottles of wine. The drifts toward sleep while the TV droned, the quiz shows with easy answers, correct and correct until victory, with no one there to marvel or congratulate.

Sometimes, to cut the underlying dread, my mother and I would joke about the loneliness. I'd hint at mine; she'd illustrate the facets of hers. She said she'd learned to recite nutrition facts from the panels of frozen dinners. She'd gotten skilled at imitating the voices of each late-news anchor; she'd dallied at her computer screen, reading through other women's testimonials on the cancer-survivor Web sites. And as my mother reported these things, I'd realize my despair was minimal in comparison. All the radiation and chemotherapy had weakened her blood and taken her strength. Throughout the years of disease, she'd managed to endure the deaths of friends and family and, just months ago, her second husband.

On my previous trip home, she'd asked about my addictions. She'd been drowsy and nauseous, just finishing another round of treatments, but seemed far more troubled by her son: my forgetfulness and mood swings; my itchy skin and bleeding, receding gums. The sleeping pills she understood, but the crystal meth she didn't. *Methamphetamine*, I'd pronounced for her. I tried to describe the highs, the resulting smother of emotions. I avoided any specifics about the early days, when the drugs made me confident and seemingly invincible, when I'd used it to meet friends or go searching for sex. I could only explain how I felt now. The diminishment, the depression. I remember claiming how I no longer used because I *wanted* to; now, my body needed it to survive. At this, my mother stared without speaking, and then she grasped my hand.

Through the subway window I watched the stations move in ribbons until the train reached my stop. I ascended to the street and headed for the target apartment. Gavin buzzed me in, and I hiked the stairs to the fifth floor. He stood waiting, squinting from his open door, certifying I was indeed one of his regulars.

I let him lead me inside. "Two times in one week?" he asked.

"I might be going away for a while. Can't take the chance of not having enough."

Gavin lived in the dirty studio walk-up with his equally addicted younger brother Sam. Although we called one another "friends," we clearly were not; they were only my dealers. Their place showed all the inattentive hallmarks of the addict: the piles of unlaundered clothes; the burn-scarred tables littered with glass pipes and tightly rolled bills; the unfinished, crudely painted walls, part blue, part gold, part antacid-pink. There was the smell of cheap vanilla incense and, beneath it, the acidic scorch of the meth Gavin and Sam smoked daily. They even stank of it. One night after I'd arrived, another fellow buyer had mentioned how much I resembled Gavin—the strawberry blond hair, the stubbly chin, the vintage button-down shirts—and I felt sick at the suggestion. I hoped my speech hadn't assumed Gavin's bleary slur, or my body hadn't turned as feeble and pale as his.

I pulled my wallet from my back pocket. Gavin opened his silver box; I said I wanted four times my regular amount. His fidgety hands prepared the order, the knuckles pink and scraped, the cuticles torn. As always, he coughed and swiped at his runny nose. He was so wed to the drug he'd started wearing a half-snipped straw behind his ear, the way my Pen & Ink cowriters wore pencils or ballpoint pens.

"Where's Sam?" I asked, the usual bit of small talk, hoping he'd offer a freebie, a jolt to get me high.

"Don't know. Don't care."

I handed Gavin the bills, two weeks of freelance earnings. "And Ambiens—please, as many as I can get with all this."

He counted the sleeping pills and dropped them in an unmarked prescription bottle. He measured the right amount of meth with his shaky hands, then sealed it in a tiny black translucent pouch. "*This* stuff—it's particularly potent."

The drug felt flawless in my palm. I held it heavenward, letting light catch the plastic and the shiny, promising grains. "Smoke or snort?" Gavin asked as always, and I chose the latter. At the table he prepared two thick lines; I felt my brain shudder with need (crush it *now*, arrange it *now*, breathe and feel its kick *now*). He slid the fast-food straw from behind his ear—stripes of yellow, white, and red—and delivered it to me.

"If you're heading all the way back home, you should take the bus," he said. "Avoid the airport security."

I bent to the table and deleted the two lines, then smiled as the drug hit my brain. "Hadn't thought about that."

He nodded. "You're going back to care for your mom?"

I couldn't recall telling him anything about home or my mother's health. I'd gotten high with Gavin and Sam countless times—we had never seen each other clean—yet I had to distance them, to distort any truths. I thought of the most recent lie I knew. "I haven't told anyone this, but the big news is that she and I are writing a book. Accounts of missing people. These mysteries, all these unsolved cases. Tons of research we need to do."

"Really. Well, it's terrific if that means her health is better." Gavin scooped some meth with the straw, then tapped it into the pipe, its glass warped and blackened. "Have to do it this way. Too many nosebleeds." He held the pipe over his lighter, waited as its tiny belly swirled with smoke, and gave it to me.

I took a long pull and handed it back. *He looks nothing like me,* I told myself. As I pocketed the pills and the meth, I vowed to speak nothing more about my mother. Soon I would stand and leave, head down the street, board the subway back to my apartment. I wouldn't go out tonight; wouldn't call other friends to see who else was high. Instead, I promised myself I would use the drug's energy to prepare for the trip home. I would pack and plan the methods for helping my mother— how the two of us might outdistance the detectives as we discovered the secrets they'd missed. How, together, we might fill the fading parentheses of our days.

In those childhood months after Evan Carnaby disappeared, Alice and I grew content believing that our mother's strange hobby had generated simply from our small-town mystery. Later that winter, however, we learned that a deeper secret, even deeper than her stay at the mental hospital, might have been responsible for her recent behavior. We might never have learned this secret, had it not been for my own disappearance.

As a boy I was perennially damaged: scabbed elbows and knees, chipped or loosened teeth, blooms of bug bites and poison ivy. I was scrawny and my eyesight was bad. At school I was constantly teased, and my mother, again like a detective, searched for some solution. The upcoming January 29 was Kansas Day, and when teachers pinned notes to our shirts—CELEBRATE OUR STATEHOOD! PLEASE DRESS STUDENTS TO FIT THE DAY'S THEME!—my mother saw my opportunity to make friends.

The week before the celebration, an uncommon conviction seized her. Together we unwrapped Hershey bars, gifts I could deliver to my classmates. We nibbled their upper right corners, then held them toward the kitchen light: rows of chocolate miniatures of our state. Next, she opened a library book filled with costume ideas: boys dressed as bison, girls decked out as shocks of wheat, a flock of yellow meadowlarks with black-bibbed chests. These ideas, she decided, were just too complicated. Instead she fashioned stiff yellow petals from rag-rug fabric and wire. She dyed my white corduroys the green of a stem. In our bathroom mirror, I watched her unwrap chocolate kisses and glue them to my cheeks and chin, studding me with the fragrant seeds. "The world's loveliest sunflower," she announced. The glue stung my skin, but I didn't care. My mother had remodeled me; she had proven herself.

The next afternoon, the Kansas Day party was crowded with kids. To my disappointment, I saw eleven, then twelve, other sunflowers. None of my teachers or friends seemed to notice my costume. Did this make my mother a failure? Did it make *me* a failure?

I retreated to a corner of the room. The day was nearly over; from a window I watched the hood of clouds that covered our dismal town, the church steeples and wind-worn grain elevators, the patches of snow across the dulled wheat fields. I fingernailed the kisses from my face and swallowed them, glue and all. I knew that if I slipped out the door, not a single soul would notice. I could shuffle petal-and-stem from school. I could simply disappear.

That evening I took a different route home, plodding through the muddied snow, wasting time. Would anyone notice if I failed to return? I made my way along the roads that bordered town, the barbed-wire fences and flat, windy fields. I waited for the shadowing skies, the soft buzz of streetlamps, keeping my gaze at the ground whenever a car slowed or braked. It was nearly seven thirty when I reached our house, three cheerless hours later than my usual arrival.

When I stepped into the hall, both Alice and my mother were waiting. My sister seemed frightened; I couldn't pinpoint my mother's emotion. She was, however, undeniably drunk. She grabbed Alice and me by the hands and led us to the living-room couch. "Neither of you will make me worry like this again," she said.

She went to the kitchen for her bottle, then stumbled back and knelt before us on the floor. "The time has finally come to tell the story," she said.

To this day I remember each detail: perhaps it was the lamp's fiery gold on her face, perhaps the frenzy in her eyes as she spoke. We couldn't interrupt, she said; we couldn't ask a single question. *Just listen.*

When my mother was a little girl, her parents were much too busy to bother with her. She was the fifth of six kids; along with her younger brother, Dan, she was forever finding trouble. Together they'd throw rocks at neighbors' windows. Roses uprooted from trellises; hand-dug holes in the city park. And then, one afternoon, my mother said, *something bad* happened.

Something terrible. A black car pulled close to the Hutchinson park playground where she and Dan were playing. She stood to investigate, still holding her crayons, her coloring book with its pictures of dinosaurs. A tall man in dark clothes got out of the car. She said she couldn't remember his face. Yet she remembered the way he smiled, the way he hobbled toward them. Dan panicked and ran, but my mother stayed calm, standing at the playground's edge, waiting as the man lurched closer.

"But here's the funny thing, the *horrible* thing. I don't remember what happened after that." She took a sip from the bottle. "Maybe the man drugged me or hit me over the head. I don't know. It's just empty now, it's all a big blank. An entire week later, I woke on the front porch of our house. I didn't know where I'd been. Didn't know what happened to me. I'd just disappeared, and to this day no one knows who, or how, or why."

Alice stammered, wanting to speak, but our mother raised her hand. "Don't say a word," she said. "Shush. I'm telling you this because I was lucky. I could have been killed. Strangled or stabbed or something worse. Whatever happened during that week, I was lucky enough to survive it. Others aren't so fortunate. Others turn up dead—just like poor Evan Carnaby might be dead."

For a moment it seemed she would cry. She tipped the bottle to her lips and spoke again. "Now think about this. Do either of you want that to happen to you?"

Her story was finished. We waited, but she only closed her eyes and kept her hand in the air, prolonging the room's stillness. *Something bad.* Alice looked at me, and then toward the floor. We weren't allowed to wonder about Dan or her parents. No pressuring questions about her absence at school; the possible organized searches; the involvement of police. Why couldn't that little girl remember the face of the man, the make of his car? Who was that girl, and what had happened to her?

Later that night, after the bourbon shifted our mother into sleep, Alice snuck to my room. She sat at the corner of my bed to tally our reactions. We still weren't sure how much we could accept as fact. Maybe, if parts of the story were true, it could explain her obsession with Evan and the others who'd gone missing. And maybe—the maybe that scared us both—the story was the cause of her awkward eccentricities, her lifelong melancholy, and that secret history of hospital stays.

Or maybe, we reasoned, our mother told the story to scare us: only that. She didn't want us rebelling or running away from home. A foggy, rather generic yarn of adolescent danger to keep us obedient, attentive, safe.

Yes. Alice and I agreed to settle on this final answer. She was dizzily drunk, after all, and she'd never mentioned any piece of the story before. Together, we decided that the story was our mother's well-meaning but drunkenly misguided lie. We swore we'd never speak of it again.

After returning from Gavin's, I discovered one last message on my machine. First, the click of the phone; then a snag of static from her line. I heard her clear her throat. And finally, my mother's voice: a little hoarse, a little weary, but confident and clear.

"I think I understand now," she said. She paused for a breath, and then: "I think I know what happened when I disappeared."

Henry's funeral was scheduled for the afternoon, late that Friday so his classmates could come. She saw Dr. Kaufman in the morning, and afterward drove to the service. She must have been sitting there, prim and immobile in the cramped pew, while simultaneously I'd sat in Gavin's room, filling my lungs and head with meth.

In the casket he seemed peacefully sleeping. He was wearing his letter jacket and holding a small black Bible. My mother nodded, hummed the hymns, and rumpled the funeral program in her hands. It didn't seem right to speak to his parents or his bewildered, perfumed sisters. She avoided Henry's classmates and his football friends. At last she summoned the courage to approach an aunt: a steel-haired nail-biter named Sunny, the only woman wearing white instead of black. In fifteen whispered minutes after the service, before the drive to Rayl's Hill, my mother learned specifics from Sunny, details she'd later report to me.

Some were curious and random as miracles. In an aquarium in his room, Henry had kept a hognose snake. He'd been allergic to penicillin, but refused to wear the identifying bracelet. The week before he'd gone missing, Henry—new license placed proudly in his wallet—had accidentally sideswiped his father's car into the front-yard mulberry tree. And the murderer, according to Sunny, didn't use his hands on Henry's neck after all. He'd actually used the missing belt, looping around the boy's throat to tighten, to stop the final breath.

At the grave she stayed inside the truck. A hunched pastor murmured stock blessings; the friends and family nodded. She drove along the cemetery's edge, noting John's grave and the space beside it. Then she followed the winding road to the gate.

Halfway home, some curiosity, some desire for her day to matter, must have seized her. The funeral hymns echoed in her ears, melodies holding some coded command, and she wanted to search for the place he'd been found—that brambled field, the secret acre gone suddenly holy. She didn't care that the truck's clock read 7:15 or that, according to the article, the field lay miles and hours away.

But my mother got lost. She couldn't recall the names of the roads or towns. The pickup's feeble light tricked her eyes, and she couldn't decode the map, the skinny blue and red veins leading toward home.

She unrolled the window to breathe the air, the fields of fermenting milo and oats. A storm was coming. Lightning shot the sky in streaks that revealed the barbed-wire fences, the columns of poplars. She listened to the bump, below her feet, of another unknown road; the radio's flow of love songs. Finally a sign glittered faintly in her lights. REST AREA, it said, with an arrow below. Perhaps she should stop; she could study the map until the storm passed, then find her way home. The road curved inward, and her lights illuminated the splintered planks of a picnic table; a silver trash barrel, overturned; the dried seedpods of yucca plants. My mother parked, buttoned John's jacket higher at the neck, and looped her purse around her arm.

I think I understand now. I think I know what happened when I disappeared.

After the message replayed, I picked up the phone and dialed Pen & Ink. "I won't be coming in to work," I told the receptionist. "Not sure how long. An emergency back home." I hung up before she could question me. Next, at Gavin's suggestion, I reserved a weekend seat on the bus. One way, New York to Wichita: 159 dollars; 1,517 miles.

Then I made my final call, but my mother wasn't there. "Well, you're getting your wish," I said to her machine. "I'm leaving everything behind. Meet me at the Wichita bus station, Monday night at eight. I'm finally coming home."

As she left the truck, she found the night air swooning with pre-rainstorm mosquitoes. She didn't bother swatting them, allowing their sting and lilt and lift as she headed for the dirty restroom doors. The women's room was bolted and locked, but the door to the men's was open. Cautiously, she pushed it with her purse. She heard a cricket greeting with its black armor. She smelled the heavy antiseptic, the urine and mold. The lightbulbs had been shattered, but bright blue from the security lamp was oozing through the mesh-wire windows. My mother saw the sinks, the clouded mirrors, the urinals on the wall like limbless, blood-drained bodies.

She turned a faucet, and the cricket ceased. She splashed water on her face. Then she turned, moving toward the stalls, their broken-hinged doors.

She lowered the toilet seat and sat. Within the silence and the cold blue light, my mother thought of Henry, picturing his life as though he were her own. She thought of my sister and me, miles away in our separate cities. She thought how the ditches and roofs would soon be sleeved with snow. How winter, in months or even weeks, would blanket the other bodies, the possible roster of missing boys and girls from which Henry had risen.

My mother reached inside her purse. Deep in its lining, below her checkbook and keys and unpaid hospital bills, she found an ink marker, permanent blue.

On the stall partitions, men had drawn pictures and scribbled graffiti, a maze of limericks and jokes, knife-grooved phone numbers. She did not read the words. Instead she began to write, the oversize H and oversize B, each consecutive letter. Such a melodious name, Henry Harris Barradale, a line from a ballad. Again she thought of his picture: the sandy hair fringing his eyebrows, hair so long only the earlobes showed; the smile both harmless and handsome.

Then she wrote more names. She filled the wall's length with them, spelling all she remembered with her fragile hand, her thrill trembling the letters. She continued in slanted calligraphy, covering the rest-stop poems and dirty drawings and offerings of sex, until finished.

She leaned against the opposite stall. Aligning neatly: HENRY HARRIS BARRADALE. EVAN CARNABY. SUSAN JONES. PENNY

PAULETTE MYERS. RUBY BAILEY. RAY DEAN HUNSINGER. And others. And others.

At the bottom of the list, in letters large enough to be easily seen, was DONNA KAYE BLAKE.

Not my mother's first married name, and not the name she took when she married John. Her girlhood name. Her name when she'd disappeared.

Outside the restrooms, the night had gone gloriously dark. Her special funeral shoes slipped in the mud. It had started to rain; no drivers were braving tonight's roads. My mother looked to the poplar trees, their inky dripping leaves. Within the stutter of lightning were more clouds, moving closer, and beyond, not yet invisible, the million-and-one stars. She held her arms to them, but this time no insects bothered her skin. Perhaps she had only dreamed them. Perhaps imagined them as I imagine her now, standing patient as though in prayer. The lightning and endless sky. The stars.

TWO

I SLEPT THROUGHOUT the trip, avoiding the hoard of Gavin's drugs. For twenty hours I'd maintained my willpower. But during a passenger stop at the St. Louis station, I'd seen a lanky woman sitting cross-legged on a bench, hugging a mud-flecked backpack, waiting. She was obviously high. Somehow I knew it was meth, and knew she was waiting for more. She seemed completely taken by it. Months, or even years. Her T-shirt stained and torn, her hair matted with sweat, the teeth gone tan and soft. Yet no matter how repellent these details, the woman was filled with the drug, shuddering with its force, and this recognition consumed me. I rummaged through a station trashcan until I found a McDonald's fast-food straw like the one behind Gavin's ear. Then I reentered the bus, eager to crouch in the cramped bathroom.

I soon realized that a bus heading toward Wichita was the worst place to be high. I hoped my mother wouldn't notice. I thought about my Pen & Ink coworkers, three gossipy girls who'd surely question my empty cubicle and chair. I thought of my landlord sliding the envelope flap to find three months' worth of rent, all twenties and tens, paper-clipped to my note of lies. But New York had fallen behind me. For now there was the engine's cough; the wind at the windows in a thin shear. Already the drug was making me clammy and claustrophobic. I closed my eyes and decided to think of Evan. From one of the seats ahead came a melody, seeping from some passenger's headphones: a ballad, surely meant to be heartbreaking. But I couldn't hear the words, and my heart felt nothing.

Evan Carnaby had been a thin, blond boy with wire glasses and a cough like knocked knuckles, who rode our afternoon bus, backseat always. Alice and I had secretly loved him. Together we stared and stared, slinking low in our seats when he glared back. We loved the loop of baling twine he wore around his wrist; the ripped knees of his jeans, twin explosions of denim. We loved his shirt pockets loaded with candy:

cinnamon disks, butterscotch, anything he could unwrap to spark our craving. And we loved his sing-alongs to the music played by Susie Mayhew, our driver in hoop earrings and a red bandanna headscarf, whose tattooed husband drove a bus route, too. Susie played eight-track tapes on the rides after school—those windows-down trips with sunflowers shaking in the ditches, each thunderstorm a doomy promise toward the north—and while the bus kids enjoyed the music, even anticipated rides home, no one seemed more engaged than Evan. He sang Elton John, Steely Dan, and, in failed harmony, Simon and Garfunkel. From our seats, Alice and I crouched to listen as he belted them out. Verse, chorus, chorus. God had tuned Evan's vocal cords slightly flat, just slightly, but his fingers against his seat kept prudent, bafflingly apt rhythm. Evan.

Then one day he stopped riding the bus. At first we barely noticed his absence. He could have fallen ill, could have skipped a day. But four days passed, five, and that following Monday we heard the news.

Back then, we'd always listened to the morning radio—the novelty songs helping to wake us in the shower, the disc jockeys volleying their jokes. But that particular morning, their tone turned serious. They stopped the music for a special report. Evan's mother, Nancy Carnaby, had somehow nudged her voice through our radio. We heard her sobbing through the staticky waves. I remember Alice's eyes, their green gone dim; I remember my mother, egg yolk dripping from the whisk in her hand, as she cocked her head to hear. Evan had taken an early-evening ride on his bike. Evan had headed for the woods near Scudder Creek, to search for bluegill and bass and sapphire-backed turtles. Evan had never come home.

"The world's not right," a teacher told my class that week, and we all believed her. "Don't leave home. Never, ever get into a car if you don't know the driver."

We'd heard this lesson many times before but suddenly, dreadfully, the words carried an accompanying illustration. At bedtime, I pictured Evan sliding into the backseat of a dark Cadillac. Imagined him squinting from behind his glasses; tugging the twine at his wrist. But I couldn't imagine more. No gags or knives or nakedness, no degradation or annihilation. I was too young to know what might have transpired after that skidding bike, that sudden surprised cry.

I watched the roads unravel from the bus window. By now my mother's telephone message was a continuously echoing loop in my ears. *I know what happened when I disappeared.* If the kidnapping she'd described on that long-ago night—her drunken reprimand, her warning we'd disregarded and tagged as fake— if that story were actually true, then why had she kept it buried all these years? How did the news of Henry Barradale relate to my mother, and how did it make her feel? How had she felt back then, during Evan?

And why, after so much time, was she remembering?

Across the aisle, two women had been talking since Topeka. Something in their tone invited my eavesdropping. The older woman's voice was harsh; I guessed the lingering rosewater perfume as hers. "I give her good advice after good advice, but she just doesn't learn," the woman was saying, referring to a granddaughter whose picture she had pulled, from a maroon purse, to show her seatmate. "Those tops she wears. And you should see those little skirts! Boys that age don't know how to handle themselves. And it's not the ones *her* age I worry about."

The bus clattered along, passing a sleepy unincorporated town, the usual farms and silver-topped grain silos, the road-side barns and churches. It passed forgotten railroad cars on a forgotten track, then an orchard where overripe apples bent the trees. The gathering shadows nearly obscured the lanes peaked with sand, the patches of scrub, an abandoned apple-ladder. From the bus, all these scenes seemed artificial, like pictures from a child's book. They were places I imagined children might have recently played. Where my sister and I would have played, or, years before that, Donna Kaye Blake and her younger brother, Dan.

In the window reflection, my face looked thin, and my eyes showed more pupil than iris. *She shouldn't see me like this.* Yet I had to follow through with our arrangement. I hadn't rented a car; hadn't yet informed Alice, or anyone else, of my return. Only my mother, meeting me in the Wichita station.

The woman wrapped up her story about the granddaughter. "I never let *my* kids leave my sight," the younger woman said. She pointed to two boys in the seat ahead. They were somewhere between eight and twelve, obviously brothers, clearly not twins. Both held miniature video games, yellow plastic and red; both were sunk inside their realms of asteroid and rocketflash.

The boys' names, I decided, were Henry and Evan. The older (*Henry*: yes, more like Henry) had buckteeth and braces; he grimaced at some handheld catastrophe as a tinny warning echoed from his game. His brother's hair (*Evan's* hair) was darker and flawed with a cowlick slicked down, rather ineffectually, with glistening grease. The boys wore jackets, even in the swollen bus heat. Henry's left shoelace had loosened, and Evan's jeans were unbelted and baggy. As I studied them, the passengers and seats fell away; I thought of the real Henry and real Evan, the real Mrs. Barradale and Mrs. Carnaby, *never let my kids leave my sight,* they surely said, and with the drug in my veins I watched the brothers, the messy-haired backs of their heads, and the fingers on their sputtering games, until at last the driver announced the turn toward our final exit.

The *real* Evan, *our* Evan, had been so beautiful.

After his disappearance, the city paper printed his seventh-grade picture, awkwardly posed, taken two years earlier. It was on the front page, adjacent to a snapshot of Evan's cherry-red Schwinn, the bicycle he'd steered that evening toward Scudder Creek. I remember looking closely at the bike, its particulars blurry within the newsprint. I imagined his lanky ankles straining on its pedals; his knuckles gripping ownership on its handlebars. Then I looked longer at Evan and his lopsided grin. The scar on his right cheekbone. The teeth slightly big for his mouth. Evan was staring beyond the polished O of the lens, at the photographer's face perhaps, his expression making the picture sadder, crueler—as though he'd seen, hovering in the shutter, something terrible waiting two years away, and just then had flinched from that future. At the time I had no language for my reaction to the photo. I only shuddered and stared and asked my daily questions: have the officers heard any news, have they found him yet, could he still be alive.

Even with her job at the prison, my mother knew very little. A mailman, or so she'd heard, had found two broken bicycle spokes along his route near Scudder Creek. In a nearby ditch, police had picked up wrappers from Evan's favorite brand of black licorice (sticky prints, however, proved from fingers not his).

Nights, I remembered the Evan I'd see when I watched him on the bus. The pimples on his forehead and chin. His hair, hay-blond and oily, still tracked from the drawn comb. The delicate chain with its featherweight cross at his throat. And Evan's throat itself, so often bruised with kisses I couldn't understand.

Songs on the bus weren't the same anymore. Susie Mayhew granted our requests for a new round of eight-track tapes. Some mornings, she idled before the graveled Carnaby driveway before realizing her mistake. Alice and I saw the space, near the porch, where Evan once anchored his bike. The upstairs window; the dust-drawn sailboat curtains; the abandoned basketball net above the garage.

After Christmas that year, an ice fisherman snagged a T-shirt from the creek where Evan had traveled, that evening, hunting turtles. The shirt was medium, his size; it was Fruit of the Loom, his brand. There were no bloodstains or bullet holes. His parents tacked more posters around town; they reappeared on the radio spots, the public TV shows. Their temporal hope seemed to have dissipated: wearied crack in the voice; head lowering slowly from the camera.

By then our mother's drinking had ceased completely. Alice and I could disregard her erratic behavior; we could almost forget her suspicious story. Spring, then summer, the days before my fifth-grade year. I gained eighteen pounds, placed runner-up in a countywide spelling bee, and launched into an urgently doomed, unrequited crush on a hurdler on the school track team. And through it all, I still thought of Evan. I dreamed him in some heroic world, wandering, windy-haired, his eyes pale pieces of sky. Maybe, somewhere and someday, the policemen would find him. Maybe even my mother would find him, presenting all the pictures she'd saved, all the newspaper tales from the tattered scrapbook she'd now retired to a dark basement shelf. And Evan would take them and smile, he would laugh his lopsided laugh, no longer vanished, now alive and delivered, dirty from midday wind and midnight rain, sleepy as a breather of poppies.

The driver announced the Wichita stop. I joined the crush, debussing to retrieve our bags from the stowage compartment. In the stagnant air of the station, I parked my backpack and suitcase, while the others hurried for the vending machines, the pay telephones, the warm embraces of family or friends.

Soon I would see my mother. Soon, her expectant, hesitant grin. I swallowed and sniffed, steadying my face to erase its evidence.

For a moment—maybe because I'd been away so long, or needed a familiar face amid the strangers—I thought I saw her. In that flicker she didn't seem so sick. Her hair was busy with curls; her back had straightened from its hunch. I almost yelled to her. Then I realized my mistake: the woman in the crowd was not my mother, but instead her best friend, Dolores.

Years before, the two had worked at the prison together. They'd sometimes go out drinking, back in the days when my mother drank. They shared a love for Willie Nelson and Tennessee whiskey. Dolores later left the prison for another job, but through the years they often crossed paths at yard or estate sales, antique shops, the grocery's checkout aisles. Their friendship rekindled three years ago, one afternoon when they saw each other at a health food store. "Do any of those help?" my mother had asked, pointing to the wire basket Dolores had crowded with amino acids and fish-oil capsules. Dolores shrugged: just that week, she'd begun breast cancer treatment. "It's lymphoma for me," said my mother.

Later, both had stayed on the west wing of Hutchinson Hospital. Dolores had gotten my mother hooked on crossword puzzle magazines. She'd given her patterns and sewing supplies, and helped her make the decorative headscarves she now sewed and sold and mailed to other chemotherapy patients. Together they, as my mother said, "endured all the hospital crap."

Ultimately, Dolores's breast-cancer treatment had worked. She'd been the luckier.

She still looked relatively healthy now, I thought. She'd remained free of it. She wore the same pink-framed glasses; her hair had silvered slightly but still hung to her shoulders.

I watched her sip from a can of Dr Pepper and chew her gum with a steady jaw, and I watched her straight, clean teeth, and then I hollered her name.

Dolores rushed to me, scrambling through the crowd; her smile widened as I bent toward her hug. She muttered something I couldn't hear. She'd always called me *Scotty* and I'd always secretly hated it. As she pulled away, I saw her smile had changed, disarranged by my shirtsleeve. "She didn't come with you?" I asked.

"We have a lot to talk about," she said. I could smell her bourbon scent, which answered a question I'd planned to ask my mother.

The parking lot had darkened. Dolores led me through it, shuffling in her unlaced shoes, shaking her keys like a maraca. She dropped the Dr Pepper can and crushed it beneath her heel. "I drove John's truck," she said. "Your mom insisted." When she pointed, I could see freckles of mud on the tires, bumper, and license plate—evidence, I guessed, of my mother's prowls through the rain-smeared roads and NO TRESPASSING fields.

Dolores opened my door, then circled the truck to take her seat behind the wheel. Before turning the key, she lifted her wrist and held it to my face. "Smell," she said. "My new perfume."

"Very nice," I said. She was definitely drunk, but I wasn't any further fit to drive. I put my bags at my feet. In the lot, the boys from the bus, my Henry and Evan, were herded into a Buick's backseat by a man presumably their father.

The interior of the Ford still carried my stepfather's evidence: his smells of loose-leaf tobacco and spice-brown aftershave; three pheasant feathers jammed into the windshield's corner; and a warp-edged photo of John himself, in hunting gear, taped to the glove box. But the dashboard also showed newer pictures. A gallery had been taped across the truck, steering wheel to passenger door, the wood-grain panel now decorated with faces. MISSING, some of them said. Exactly like our kitchen walls, all those years ago. Before Dolores steered from the lot, I saw, in a stripe of streetlight, the newsprint names beneath the faces. Audrey Plumly. Ben Kent. George Johnson Lloyd. And yes, Henry Barradale.

"You never know where she gets the energy," Dolores said as she approached the highway. "She'll be real, real sick one day, but then the next she's different. Yesterday she made me take her to the library. She held a pair of scissors in her hand the whole way there. Next thing you know, *snip-snip-snip*. She'd done up the truck like that. And just wait'll you see her kitchen walls."

I leaned to squint at Henry's face. "Then this is what you wanted to tell me?"

"Not exactly, no." She frowned as though unsure where to start. I saw her working her jaw, gnawing the hollow of her cheek. I saw the rhinestone bobby pins, parallel above each ear to secure her hair. *Dolores used to be a beauty queen,* my mother had told me once. *Queen Dolores. She could get absolutely any boy she wanted. And believe me, she sure did want a lot of them.*

"I have my doubts that she's been completely honest," Dolores said. "You know, that she's filling you in on things."

"What things does she have to fill in?"

"Health things."

I felt the flutter of worry. "Lately, when she's called, we've mostly talked about the body."

"That murdered boy of hers."

"And other missing people. Cases she's been following."

"I know all about it," Dolores said. "She wants you to get back into your detective work. That's what she called it yesterday, your *detective work*. I have to tell you, I think it's just plain strange."

Some disturbance in her eyes made me look away, out to the stark sandy roads, the harvested fields. "But it's good to hear her so excited about something again," I said. "For once she's excited by something other than—oh, I don't know, whether her insurance is paying the doctor bills, or whether or not her platelets are strong."

Dolores had slowed the truck, and now other drivers were speeding past—the hay trucks, the horse trailers and rattling semis. She was watching me more than the road. "On Friday she made me drive over to that kid's funeral to meet her," she said. "Don't you think that's strange?"

I corrected a bent corner on one of the taped photographs. When I didn't answer, Dolores continued: "You should've seen that funeral. Pretty classy, overall. Except someone brought a bouquet of orange carnations in the shape of a football. Everyone's clothes and the rest of the flowers and the way they dressed him up—all very classy. Then out came that horrible ball. I left before it was over."

I tried to imagine them in that church, watching his family and friends, stilled by the organist's "In the Garden" and "Amazing Grace." But as Dolores spoke, I couldn't focus on the casket or the flower sprays or the mourners in the family room. I could only see my mother, rooted in her back-row chair. Her alien, satisfied smile; her wig, pinned back; her black sweater and both hands clamped in her lap. Surely she kept the next seat empty, as though waiting for me.

"You said 'health things,'" I said. "Does that mean it's gotten worse?"

"Scotty, don't tell her I'm telling you this. It'd make her furious to think I was worrying you kids." She paused to take an unsteady breath. "But I have to say it. Your mom just isn't fighting anymore. I think it's happening now."

"*Happening*? Tell me exactly what you're saying."

"It's so much worse than when you saw her last. She's hardly worked in her garden. Remember last summer? That's all she did. But this year, no. And she's tired all the time. She can hardly get around by herself."

With a slow swerve, Dolores moved from the highway to a narrower road. "I wanted her to call you and Alice," she said. "I told her, 'Donna, call those kids!' But she wouldn't. Now she won't tell me everything Kaufman's said, but apparently there are new tumors. I think she's reached that *point*. I think there's no remission left."

I looked across the seat at her. Really, I thought, I hardly know this woman. I knew she owned a fancy snowmobile; she had a good recipe for chocolate-chip cookies, which my mother often borrowed. She had a much older husband, named Ernest, whom I'd never met, and a Pomeranian, named Fred, whom I had. *Reached that point*. Since the time I'd last seen Dolores, her voice had become less chirpy, less childlike. *No remission*: so grave and deep. I remembered my mother relating a story of Dolores after she'd beaten the cancer: her immaturity, her girlish dresses. "She showed up at the flea market in something like a ballerina outfit," my mother had said. "Only one breast left, and a ballerina! Idiotic." That Dolores didn't seem the same as the woman beside me now.

I felt a sudden, stinging guilt as I realized I hadn't questioned my mother enough about her health. I'd been snared by her excitement over Henry, our upcoming days together. Before, there were only the misty, enigmatic words, *non-Hodgkin's lymphoma*, a vague cancer at vague crossings of her blood. But now, according to Dolores, the disease had a tangible shape.

"I have to tell you more." She pulled a cigarette from her purse and lit it with the truck's lighter. "I'm worried it's affecting her head. I know at one point Kaufman said something about possible mild dementia. But I think it's started to progress."

"Dementia? Isn't that a little extreme?"

"She's been telling me lately about this business when she was a girl. It's like this murdered boy has stirred something up in her. Do you know about all this?"

"Her disappearance," I said softly. "Yes."

"You know these things she's apparently kept secret all these years?"

"Alice and I always thought it was an exaggeration. Just something to scare us. It never seemed quite so important, really." I looked away from the window and back to Dolores. "I've only thought of it lately because she's brought it up again."

"And do you believe her now?"

"What has she been saying?"

"She's been telling me things—oh God!—these awful things. I can't fathom how she thinks them up. She told me about some horrible man who kept her locked in a cellar. Some other boy, kidnapped in the cellar with her. It's just crazy! All our years and years as friends, and she's never mentioned any of this craziness? What am I supposed to believe? Now I want to call Kaufman, because I'm worried that the sickness went to her brain. She's been following that boy's case too much, and watching too much scary TV. She's starting to think things like this really happened to *her*."

Dolores adjusted her glasses and sighed, releasing a cloud of blue, unfurling smoke. A horrible man . . . a basement . . . another kidnapped boy. I wished the spillage would stop, but knew the silence would be worse. "So you don't believe these things she's been saying," I said.

"Honestly? No, I don't." She paused. "Have you called your sister to let her know you're home?"

"I haven't."

"You should. I know it's hard to hear, but I think your mother's inventing these things to bring you home. She doesn't want you to know the real reason. There's no time left, and her doctor's given up hope. Right now she just wants her kids back here with her."

The headlights cast arcs along the road, the ditches with their fringes of weeds and stagnant rainstorm pools. Ahead, at the railroad tracks, the crossing bars had lowered: the flickering strobes of red, the bands of white and black. Dolores slowed and stopped the truck. I wanted to open the door and walk away from her words, passing the upended tree roots snarled with strips of clothing and plastic cups, with the crumpled newspapers and their indistinct headlines. I wanted to walk the final miles home to be with my mother, to hear her voice and hold her hand.

Dolores remained idling at the tracks. There were no other cars, and there was no train: no oncoming light, no whistle coldly slitting the air. Yet the crossing bars remained in place, the lights blaring red. I unrolled my window and breathed. From the dark distance came the sounds of geese: the door-hinge creak of their throats, carried closer by the wind.

Dolores lowered her own window and looked out at the night. She was still drunk. I was still high. We were less than five miles from my mother, but we weren't ready, not yet. Together we listened until the geese were gone, and then we listened longer. "It gets so quiet out here," she said at last.

"Please, just stop. Let's not say another word until we're home."

We reached the sandy road into Haven. The roads were silent, flanked by cottonwoods and elms, their shadows wavering in the streetlights. Dolores made a final turn, steered into my mother's drive, and parked.

I left her and headed for the house. Stepping onto the porch, I sensed at once that something had changed. Before, whenever my mother heard the car in the street, she would rise to greet me at the door. Now, even with the ruckus of the Ford, she hadn't yet appeared.

I leaned from the porch and looked into the living-room window. Through the curtain I could see the television's greenish light, its defective picture. My mother had never sent the TV for repair—for years, both Alice and I had smacked it ineffectually with the hocks of our hands—and it still projected its images in queasy thirds: the bottom section of picture mistakenly at the top, the top at the bottom, a black stripe separating the two. The picture wouldn't straighten or unite. Yet my mother kept the TV going, its sound turned low, often drifting to sleep in its aqueous, nerve-numbing light.

"Go on in," Dolores said from behind me. She reached to open the screen door, and together we stepped inside.

As always, when I first arrived home, I stamped my shoes on the mat, took them off, and peeled away my socks. In my drug-heightened state, the carpet felt plush and soothing on my feet. To our right, the TV displayed its marred picture of the evening news, the maps of a weather report. And within its glow was my mother. She lay on the couch, one arm crooked across her face.

"Asleep," said Dolores. And, as though that proved something, "See what I mean?"

Her breaths were labored and dense. She was wearing her scarf, but in sleep it had shifted to reveal the threads of hair, the dry, mottled patches of scalp. I stepped closer, dizzy with sudden love, breathing the sharp chemical smell, the residual Rituxan and Neupogen injections that I knew, from her explanations, now filled her sweat. I remembered that smell, even across the eight-month gap since I'd last come home.

"Mom, it's me." I leaned to touch the bare skin between her scarf and ear. She woke, drawing the arm from her face. At once I saw the truth in Dolores's words: clearly her health had gotten worse.

For a moment it seemed she didn't recognize me. Then she smiled. "I found you," she said.

"No, I found you."

From behind us, Dolores jostled the keys in her pocket. "I should get moving," she said. "Getting late."

My mother dug at the cushions, pushing herself to stand. She hadn't inserted her lower plate of teeth; I saw her trying to veil the exertion on her face. "No, stay awhile," she said. "At least have some iced tea."

Dolores said no, but my mother began moving haltingly toward the kitchen. It had only been eight months, yet at that moment I saw, more precisely than before, her aging and her illness. The deeper bend to her back, the random patches of steel-colored hair, the apprehensive dart in her eyes.

Dolores made an exaggerated sigh. Her cheeks seemed newly flushed, as though she'd secretly snuck more bourbon. She peeked to the kitchen to assure my mother couldn't hear. "Remember what I told you," she whispered as she went to the door. "Whatever you need, just call."

Any form of agreement would feel like a betrayal. I didn't want to hear any more admonishments or warnings; I couldn't wait to close the screen on her. From the fogged window glass I watched her stumbling slightly, stumbling toward her own car. I delayed until she'd driven down the street, her single unbroken taillight dissolving, and then I locked the doors.

The bronze chandelier with its drops of glass . . . the old firkin sugar bucket, clumped with dried roses . . . the Dazey butter churn. Most of the antiques had remained in our family for years. Others I hadn't seen before, her recent discoveries from junkyards and auctions. I stepped around the room, straightening the picture frames, examining the rows of dolls in the glass china cabinet. Already I was toughening to my mother's smell, the mix of medicines, the yellowed cigarette smoke, the bowls of apple-peel potpourri.

She returned, her smile realigned with the lower teeth, two mismatched glasses in her hands. "We have an appointment at the café tomorrow." And, just noticing: "Oh, I thought she was going to stay."

"Rushing to get back home or something."

"Ernest goes crazy if she's out too late. What all'd she make you talk about on the way here?"

"More about the funeral."

My mother sat again. "I thought you quit biting your fingernails."

"I tried, but I gave up."

She took a sip from the smaller glass. "Did she tell you about the football?"

I nodded, reaching to cup my hand on her knee. Even this close she seemed to be retreating, reluctant to let me sufficiently see her. This wasn't the vitality I'd imagined when I pictured her driving toward Partridge or watching Henry's house. Until now I'd vowed to be forthright and firm, to stare directly into her eyes and ask point-blank about her memories. But I couldn't stop thinking of Dolores's warnings, and that terrible word, *dementia*. As I watched my mother, I forgot all the words I'd planned to say.

"While you were on the bus yesterday, I arranged a little meeting with Sunny."

"Sunny from the funeral?"

"She doesn't live all that far away, and she plays bingo where John and I used to go. I found her name in the book and called."

Relating this seemed to perk my mother; she grabbed her purse from the floor and produced a yellow notepad. "She actually came to Haven! I wasn't feeling so hot, but she took me to the café and treated us to butterscotch sundaes." She opened the pad, and I saw scribbled notes from their conversation— "goodies," she called them, more pieces from Henry's life that she claimed I needed to know. *Loved swimming at Kanopolis Lake. Loved seafood—esp. shrimp—ate em crunchy tails & all.*

"That's nice," I said. "Butterscotch." I imagined them together in the lustrous leather booth. I pictured her taking notes on Henry's clothes, Henry's room, his love for swimming and shrimp, as all the while Aunt Sunny spoke, woe-wrecked, directionless. Perhaps these details, these "goodies," were essential clues toward Henry's murder. Perhaps they weren't. I didn't know; neither Sunny nor my mother knew. None of the "goodies" would bring Henry back.

She squeezed my hand. "You haven't given me a hug."

I'd been thinking the same thing. Somehow she could tell I needed the solace, the balm of her. Dolores's arms, back in the station, had been a poor substitute. Her skin the wrong warmth, her hands clasping at my back. So I leaned closer and wrapped my arms around my mother's shoulders. With the embrace, new fear fluttered through me. Her muscles, once taut like a carpenter's, had thinned and atrophied. She'd grown fleshier in the stomach and back, yet I could feel her brittle collarbone and ribs. I could feel the rubbery ridge of the surgical port, implanted in her chest, where her doctor injected the meds. When I looked at her again, really looked, I saw her stained, oversize pink slippers; her lavender nightgown with its neckline of purple beads. I saw the tracks and brown bruises where the needles had hit. These, I understood, were all the expected aspects and manners: a woman, sixty years old, with cancer. She'd surrendered to the pattern and mold.

For now the memories of her disappearance could wait. "You *know* what I'm going to ask," I said. "Any recent health things I should know about?"

"Oh, not really. I don't know. Last week the blood work didn't look so good."

"Be specific."

"He says I have to give myself shots again. It's all that anemia crap."

She had always used this word. Her favorite throwaway word, her breezy signal that the world was still trivial and subtly ludicrous. I remembered, as a boy, feeling a baffling pride whenever she said the word. My classmates had thought my mother slightly nutty: she worked at the prison, after all; she'd remained a widow for so many years; she always said *crap* or some further curse where other moms would have stayed silent. But Alice and I didn't mind *crap* or her other choice language. *Crap*, for us, came to mean we didn't need to worry. Our lives hadn't progressed toward anything critical or urgent. Not yet.

"But anemia—that's common, right? If the chemo makes you lose red cells and get tired, then it must be working on the bad stuff."

"I guess so. *Hope* so."

She relaxed against the arm of the couch, and for the first time I noticed the badge pinned to her nightgown. I looked closer and saw, just above her heart, the laminated photo of a preteen girl. Immediately I understood: it was another of her researched missing children.

She pulled the tiny picture forward, looking down at the grinning face. "Lacey Wyler," she said. "That's what I meant about tomorrow. I've set up a meeting at the café."

"Tomorrow? Already?"

"They're going to start thinking I'm weird down there. That waitress will see us coming and set a glass of iced tea at my favorite table. Hopefully they'll leave us alone and let us do our interview."

And so the classifieds had achieved their purpose. Perhaps I hadn't fully grasped my mother's determination. I wasn't certain she understood the gravity, the possible danger: could she actually exploit these despairing family members or friends with all her promises, her false guarantees? Would she still discuss our fictitious research and resulting book? *Her detective work*, Dolores had called it. Whatever warped strategies she'd been planning, I knew I wasn't yet prepared to join her. Before morning, I needed a bath and a warm bed; I needed Gavin's sleeping pills to ease my heartbeat.

From the badge, the girl stared out at me, her eyes blank, her face expressionless. "She went missing months ago from up west," my mother said. "Don't know much about it yet, but we will tomorrow."

"We're meeting her parents?"

"Her grandpa." She shifted, and the pain of it tightened her lips. The yellow notepad slipped to the floor.

"And he's coming all the way to Haven."

"For an interview."

"He really believed you, then." I tried to disguise my concern. "Don't you think this could potentially wreck the man? Especially if he knows you can't help him, and you aren't writing a book?"

"But maybe we *can* help him. We'll be very kind."

"You won't wear the button, will you? Won't grandpa think that's odd?"

"No, grandpa's the one who sent it. We talked on the phone to set this up, and next day, registered mail, I got pictures of her and these little pins. Apparently the people in Lacey's town go around wearing these. Maybe somebody will remember seeing her somewhere." She slid her purse across the sofa cushions. "There's an extra for you."

I put my hand into the jumble of Lacey badges and selected one. My mother clasped it to my shirt, just above my heart. She patted it twice with her fingers, then lifted her chin toward the kitchen. "Now, I bet you're hungry."

"No. Sleepy, though. I just want to get some sleep."

"But there's more to tell. You need to be prepared for tomorrow."

I stood, blocking the television light, and for a moment the room was shaded. "Don't worry," I told her. "We can wait until morning." For a moment I considered what else she needed me to say. "Tomorrow I'll do whatever you want. From now on, it's just you and me."

Already that first night, I thought about leaving. Maybe this had been an awful, imprudent idea. Her home felt spacious for one person, yet cramped for two. Despite years of illness, my mother still smoked; even though I'd sunken myself in sleeping pills and meth and would soon crave more, I'd always despised cigarette smoke, and cringed knowing it would permeate my clothes. She used the shaved-wood, apple-and-rose potpourri, but its syrupy smell, lifting from glass jars and vintage cookie tins, just depressed me further. The antiques sapped me, too. Each room was filled with them. She'd decorated the house in dull browns— chestnut-colored carpet, umbers and tans for each wallpaper and paint. Drawers, bowls, and random corners were clogged with dried flowers; the husks of tiny nocturnal spiders; old medals (Best Marksman—Women's Division) and awards (KSIR 10 Years Service). She collected a host of antique dolls and faceless, flop-eared rabbits. Her walls were busy with Victorian pictures in antique frames, distressing, blue-hued prints she'd found at junk shops and estate sales. The love-lorn Lady of Shalott. Ophelia, adrift amid the lilies. But even more wounding than the prints were the photographs. She'd hung pictures of her parents, her brothers and sisters, and John, each face positioned carefully on the walls, in upright frames on cabinets and tables. Supplementing these were the newer faces, the disappeared people she'd begun to display. That first night, whether in the kitchen or bedroom or bath, I continually felt some lost spirit guarding me.

At her insistence, she made her bed on the living-room couch, giving me the oversize mattress and graying sheets of her room. I swallowed three of Gavin's Ambiens, lay my head on the pillow, and waited. I tried picturing his slipshod apartment; his silver box of black-capped vials and rubber-banded twenties; the glistening, scattered grit of his unceasing drugs. I thought about my own empty apartment, and my empty cubicle at Pen & Ink, desk strewn with papers, notes toward assignments I'd never finish.

Inventing these things to bring you home, Dolores had said. These tactics didn't seem typical of my mother. I knew that ailing people, when they sensed the end was near, often abandoned their obsessions. Instead, my mother was reviving hers. Something in her eyes, in the tone of her voice, evoked her drunken fervor, all those years ago, as she'd hunched at the kitchen table with her scissors and bottle. Had the sickness, as Dolores suggested, now affected my mother's head? *She just wants her kids back here with her.*

Soon the pills began their soft heave and drag. I reached for the bedside lamp, but before I could pull its chain, I heard her tentative knock. She entered slowly, her head wrapped in a new, sky-colored scarf. She was gnawing on a splintered toothpick. Even before she sat on the bed, I knew what she was hefting in her hands.

"Your old scrapbook," I said.

We opened it together. For so many years she'd been keeping it safe. The cellophane tape had yellowed, and certain clippings had crumbled or torn, but there they were, all her children, women, and men, now spilling across the blanket. She pinched some from their pages: "Do you remember *her*? Or *her*? And what about *this* one?"

Yes, surprisingly, I remembered: some more effortlessly, more bitterly, than others. Jack Smith Jr. and Rachel Mickelson. Brenda Lee Kilbey, Monica Donnerstein. Photographs from various Kansas newspapers, from old *True Detective* magazines. Burke Wandruff. Lisa Henderson. I knew that only the rare among them had ever returned alive.

She browsed the pages until she found a picture of Evan. She held it toward the lamp; in my drowsiness I had to squint. "Strange how much he looks like Henry," I said.

"Henry, yes. But you know who he really looks like? Who they *both* look like?" She paused for effect. *"You."*

"That's not true."

"Really. He really does. Look at the eyes, the brow line. And the hair."

She wanted me to examine closer. But as she removed the picture from the light, her gaze lingered on the bedside table. She was staring at my travel bag, black vinyl with a picture of a grinning cartoon mouse. I remembered the last time I'd been home, when she'd caught me hiding the bag below the folds of clothes in my suitcase. Although she obviously knew what was inside, I tried sidetracking with a story about how Pen & Ink had received the bags as gifts from a children's book company. "Surely you know you can't keep secrets from your mother," she'd said. "I've *seen* you with that speedy stuff. I've *seen* your little glass pipe."

Presently I felt her stalking the subject again. She closed the scrapbook and caressed the underside of my arm. I didn't want to fight. I hated fighting with her; it always seemed as though my resistance, all my volume and huff, could crush her fragile health.

It seemed she wasn't certain where to start. When she finally spoke, she began at Dolores. "She was drunk tonight, right?"

"Seemed that way."

"You don't like her much, do you?"

"I guess I don't know her enough," I said. I'd always figured that Dolores resented my problems with drugs and the fact I rarely came home. Doubtless, she didn't want to retrieve me at the station; she would have preferred her evening at home with Ernest, with further glasses of bourbon. Yet I knew Dolores thrived on doing favors for my mother. For years she'd stayed supportive, especially since John's death.

Once again my mother looked at the travel bag. She removed the toothpick from her mouth and took a slow, steady breath. "You're still struggling with it."

"Can't get anything past you."

"It isn't hard to tell. What's it called again?"

"Crystal. Or meth. Crystal meth."

"That makes it sound pretty."

"It's not pretty."

She moved closer on the bed. I continued, my words diminished with fatigue. "It's made me paranoid and mean, and it's made me lose my friends." The pills were slurring my words. The leaden muscles and bones, the blankets pulling me partway into a dream. "At work the other day I was working on some kids' textbook, and my nose started bleeding. Little kids' books, all across the country, filled with stories written by some stupid drug addict."

"Oh, hon," she said. She placed her hand on my head, her fingers in my hair. I remembered certain childhood nights when she had scuffled into my room and run her hand along my younger forehead, my finer and redder hair.

"It's done everything except make me hallucinate. I don't think I've started doing that yet. So I haven't quite lost my mind; not yet."

She stood and smiled, pausing for the right moment. "See? Then maybe things aren't all *that* bad."

I tried to return the smile. The lamplight seemed to wobble and fade; it haloed my mother and moved with her, moving as she cocked her head and smiled, crooked and silly, the style she always used, back then, before bedtime. "Sleep now," she said. "Clear your head of all the bad stuff. We'll talk more tomorrow."

Tomorrow. I wanted to say that all I really needed was a solid rest, but I could no longer speak. My mother understood; she pulled the lamp's chain and stepped back toward the door. She was still speaking to me, but in the darkness her voice fell to a murmur, the consonants blurring with vowels. I thought I heard her singing softly; I thought I heard a whisper and a giggle. Perhaps she was explaining more about tomorrow. Perhaps she was repeating her good-nights and pleasant-dreams.

But something told me she was remembering now, those memories I'd been hoping she'd unveil, teasing me because she knew I was slipping away, teasing with the details of her disappearance.

The oncoming dream tugged harder and now the angles of the bed seemed awkward, wrong. With a shift, I recognized what was cramping me: she had left the scrapbook on the bed. I tried to move, but the pills had paralyzed my muscles, and I could only bump the book, carelessly kneeing its cover, scattering the random photographs and clippings.

My mother left the room. I fell asleep among the disappeared: the chipped newsprint paper, the tape and browning resin, all their lost and lovely faces.

THREE

HAD I BEEN alone, I could have walked to the Haven Café in minutes. But as her usher, I opted for the pickup, helping her off the porch, clasping hands like a stirrup to hoist her into the passenger seat. She wore my New York City sweatshirt, dirty gray and two sizes too large. She wanted to drive, but I objected. On the seat between us were her notepads, her cassette recorder held together with silver electrician's tape, and the pens she'd collected from Dr. Kaufman's, each advertising a different medication.

"He'll be impressed at how prepared we are," she said.

I wasn't so certain. With the new morning, I'd begun to feel a simmering distress over my mother's intentions: maybe she would seem overwrought or unruly; maybe Lacey Wyler's grandfather would expose her sham. "I hope you don't mind," I said, "but I'm going to let you do all the talking."

Main Street was red cobblestone flanked by dingy storefronts, all dust and broken bricks and milky windows. There was a library, a bank, and a filling station with a short-order grill featuring cheeseburgers for two and a quarter. "Their food's horrendous," she said. "Once John brought some home for us, and . . . just horrendous." She pointed out the overused town name, the stores and their unsurprising signs: Gas Haven, the maroon-roofed Pizza Haven. In my weariness, I wanted something stately or quaint, like chimneys heaving smoke, the green-white copper of monuments. Instead there was only the muted street, the sun half-hidden by clouds.

As we parked, I noticed an orange-jacketed woman staring from the nearby sidewalk. "That's the library lady," my mother whispered. "Always sticking her nose into everybody's business. Usually I just tell her lies. She'll be asking a load of questions after she sees you!"

"Don't say anything. I don't want anyone to know who I am. Pretend I'm not even here."

I shut the engine, took Lacey's button from my pocket, and pinned it to my shirt. With held breaths, we hesitated before the café. Starting today, she'd told me earlier that morning, we'd be doing important deeds. We'd be making something of ourselves.

Again I linked my hands to help her outside. I felt sleepy and sore, having woken dreamless in her bed. The power of the pills had dissipated after four hours. I'd also gotten a nosebleed, routine after crystal meth, droplets smudging the newspaper clippings. I'd pinched my nostril and canted my head against the pillow, the silence sharpening around me, daybreak bluing the windows to reveal her backyard garden with its doomed rosebushes and militant weeds. When the nosebleed finally stopped and I rose to leave the room, I'd found her posted on the couch, overanxious for our scheduled meeting.

During the night, her scarf had slipped; the patches of hair were damp and flattened on one side. Within the TV's varicolored test pattern, her face gleamed with slow trickles of sweat. "Are you feeling okay?" I asked. "Think maybe we should cancel?"

"Don't worry. Mornings make me look this way. Now hurry and get ready, so we can go."

Now it was nearly noon. The day had brightened her slightly. She took my arm, and we stepped toward the café, her weight straining my shoulder, my legs still cramped from endless hours on the bus. Surely we looked like a pair of crazies, but I didn't care, I was doing this all for her.

She pushed at the door, jostling its rusted cowbell with a loud, sunken clup. Immediately, we saw Mr. Wyler. He was waiting in a central cushioned booth, a stock-character farmer in his overalls, grinning in his blue button-down shirt and green John Deere cap. He'd already ordered from the grease-stained menu, a coffee mug steaming on the Formica table-top. As we approached, he stood and held a toughened hand toward us. "You're Donna, then? And you must be the son. The *writer.*"

"He writes books for a place in New York," said my mother. "But now he's focusing his energy on this."

I wondered what other lies or exaggerations she'd told; whether she'd fumbled through needlessly brazen explanations about the freelancing and temping, the disillusion and drugs. Times before, I'd heard her speak these things to people she barely knew. Perhaps she thought introducing her son as a New York writer could justify our "research," could convince these people of our legitimacy.

Mr. Wyler kept offering his hand until I shook it. "I've never met a writer," he said.

Only two neighboring booths were occupied; the customers gave us backward glances but continued eating. Mr. Wyler ordered another coffee, cream but no sugar, and my mother ordered two iced teas. His shirt was finely ironed and smelled slightly of popcorn. He seemed daunted by the notepads and the tape recorder. As he idly clicked the trigger of my mother's pen (PROCRIT, it read), I noticed the man's forearms and hands: old farmwork scars, puckered and jagged and pink.

For the opening five minutes, they chatted and smoked, both spicing the air with ardent small talk. Mr. Wyler sounded nervous and gruff; *if his voice were a drug,* I thought, *it would be crystal meth.* My mother's voice, in contrast, was muscular and thriving.

SCOTT HEIM

It seemed less tired and made me shrink in my seat. She thanked him for sending the buttons, for traveling all the way from Goodland. She asked him about the wife he'd mentioned in his letter. Was she enjoying her retirement? Were they planning any upcoming vacations? I felt her encouraging the man, nodding her head to nudge the pauses in his sentences. I wondered how she planned to ease the conversation toward Lacey.

The waitress arrived with the drinks, and Mr. Wyler ordered a slice of coconut-cream pie: his jagged teeth; the drawl of his vowels. "Coconut's my favorite," he told us.

"Scott likes peach," said my mother. "Or strawberry rhubarb." On the table below, she furtively pressed the tape recorder's button; its tiny looping circles now advanced the tape, advanced the tape.

"Lacey liked cherry pie," he said. "Plain and simple. But really, candy was what she liked best. All kinds."

My mother straightened: Lacey, at last. "Can't say no to candy," she said. "Please, tell us what happened."

He reached to his seat and produced a scrapbook fancier than my mother's. Printed on its black-leather cover were the photo-developer's name and, in fussy script, the words *Precious Memories*. My mother found her tortoiseshell glasses, rotated the scrapbook partway, and together they turned its weighted pages.

"Just so you get it right for your book," he said, "we don't agree with the police. Like I said on the phone, we don't think Lacey just *left*. Hannah and I think somebody *took* her."

With each new second I was feeling fidgety, progressively ashamed. From the street I heard tires grumbling along the cobblestone. A group of children running past; a single warbler, repeating its lonesome note. Mr. Wyler answered my mother's over-rehearsed questions, and they continued to scan the photographs, savoring Lacey's poses, the chronological flashes and fanfares of her life.

I saw the scrapbook as a way to escape, and excused myself for the bathroom. I locked the door and lingered in the cramped space, wanting meth, cupping my hands under the faucet to slap cold water on my face. Already I had registered the old man's hopelessness, his palpable dolor. But oddly, troublingly, it seemed my mother had not. This wasn't like her, and it frightened me. *Perhaps I should stop this before it really begins. Let her speak about Henry and all the others, but stop this business of interviews, of the book.* I leaned against the bathroom wall, examining each month's picture on the wall calendar. A covered bridge in winter. An abandoned railroad car; an oriole weaving its nest.

When I returned, I noticed instantly that something had changed. My mother was leaning away from the table, both hands dropped to her lap. "Like I said, she sure loved candy," the man was saying, but now she seemed abstracted, even angry. She wasn't replying or watching his face.

As I took my seat, Mr. Wyler continued: "There was this place back in Marysville, where she used to live. She only moved to Goodland with us when she was sixteen. This place used to make those big jawbreakers and those big chunks of taffy. You could get all kinds."

"Sixteen, then," said my mother.

"Peppermint taffy, sour lemon taffy, hot-fire flavor. Lacey sure loved that hot-fire flavor."

I thought of the girl pulling it, leaning her head, letting it curl into her mouth. But something in the man's words misconstrued this picture. *Sixteen.* In the button on my shirt—the same pinned, I saw, to the side of his John Deere cap—Lacey Wyler seemed much younger. Twelve, perhaps eleven, perhaps ten.

My mother had noted the discrepancy, too. Suddenly I realized that this was the reason for her swift spite. She turned the scrapbook completely around to face me—the cover bumped the tape recorder, but she didn't notice—and tapped a fingernail against a photo of Lacey. "Did you hear this, Scott? He said '*sixteen.*'"

"Almost eighteen when we saw her last. You should use the button picture, though. In case you're using pictures for your book."

My mother wasn't listening. "Just look at these," she said. Throughout the final series in the album, in snapshot after snapshot, the girl—or rather, the woman—looked nothing like the button. The Lacey of these photos dressed exclusively in black. Black stockings and boots; black sweater and pleated skirt. In some, she wore elbow-length black gloves with open fingers. Her hair had been cut, straightened, and dyed the same dark as her clothes. Her bangs were tipped purple, fringing her heavily mascaraed eyes. In nearly every picture, Lacey pouted at the camera, lipstick so thickly red it seemed she'd kissed ketchup. She reminded me of friends I'd had in high school or college, girls who'd worn patchouli oil and read science fiction and Sylvia Plath, the girls I'd dragged along to my first gay bars. Lacey was like those girls, but she bore no resemblance to the man at our table.

"We didn't care much for those," said Mr. Wyler, exhaling a breath of coffee and nicotine. "The way she looked, the things she said—that just wasn't her."

"Rebellious, then," my mother said. She found the pen and drew a star on her notepad, writing REBEL beside it, as though this held some special meaning.

"She was very young."

"But not as young as I'd imagined her. Not as young as the picture on the pin, or as young as you made me think when we talked on the phone."

He paused, blinking curiously at her. "After she moved with us," he said, "there was bad influence from kids at her new school. We think it's because of them that something happened to her."

He began a story about the terrible school, but my mother's absorption had faded. I couldn't look at either of them. Instead I advanced through Lacey's photographs, lingering on an extreme close-up—a different shade of lipstick, a phony mole speckling her cheek. In another, she posed beside someone else, their arms entwined. This time, however, the picture had been ripped in half. Lacey's companion was much taller and heavier, very likely a male. Only his arm and shoulder were visible. Like her, he was dressed in black. I couldn't see his face but noticed a change in Lacey's, something new, a glimmer like love.

"We believe she's out there somewhere," he was saying. "Probably being held against her will."

My mother put her hand on the sweating glass of iced tea, then dropped it again. The interview was a bust. She knew that Lacey had not disappeared at all, not in the way she'd wanted. Most likely Lacey was a quiet girl, a girl who loved music and autumn nights and long, maudlin poems, yet despised her new life, her small town. A girl who slumped in the back row during every spiritless, wounding class hour. A girl who finally escaped her grandparents—I could picture her speeding away in a car, her hand on his knee, this boy no longer torn from the photograph but here now, *hers*—for some city where her black would glitter instead of gloom. From the photos—likely taken by the boyfriend, then stashed secret-secret in her room—I felt I knew more about Lacey than her grandparents did.

From the kitchen came an earthy, peppery smell, like potato pancakes. The smell made me faintly nauseous, and I wanted to leave and head home. With a finger I traced the gold flecks on the Formica tabletop, still unable to look at Mr. Wyler. Yet he rambled on, huddling closer to the machine as though he wanted each word sunk, dead-target, into the pages of our book. "The last time we saw her she was chewing gum," he said. "Somebody must have given it to her. I don't recall giving her that gum, and neither does Hannah."

"What a sturdy memory you have," said my mother. Now she sounded scornful, almost mocking. "But she was eighteen when you saw her last."

"I don't think it was bubble gum, because it smelled like cinnamon, and they don't make cinnamon bubble gum, do they?"

"I've never heard of it if they do." Beneath the table, her foot found mine: cue that she, too, wanted to leave. The cassette tape, at some point, had finished its track; but neither she nor I had bothered replacing it.

"Funny how your mind works," he said, "when someone you love goes missing. Like that gum. Some nights I lie awake and think, what if someone done something awful to her, would they want that gum in her mouth? What if they put their dirty fingers in her mouth and took out that cinnamon gum before they did what they did. Maybe there was some sort of fingerprint left on that wad of our Lacey's gum somewhere. Why couldn't the police find that?

"Imagine what it's like to lie awake hours, and all you think about is prints on that piece of gum. Hours! That's the sort of hell you think about when you're put into this situation."

Mr. Wyler's final words were pierced by the ringing cowbell above the door. The town librarian entered, removed her jacket, and selected a booth. She sat and opened a hardbound book, her page marked with an orange fallen leaf. But she was clearly more interested in us. I could see why my mother disliked her: her scowl, her intrusive dark eyes, and her heavily hunched back, as though she'd spent her days crouched at tiny keyholes.

"It must be getting late," my mother said, and I could sense her using the librarian's interruption as our way out. She patted Mr. Wyler's hand and quickly improvised an excuse. We had to field a phone call between two thirty and three, she said; the call would mean more essential information for our book.

He seemed puzzled at our haste. "That book'll be such a help. Let us know if there's anything else we can do."

"Well, Scott and I are grateful for this. We should thank you for coming all this way to meet with us."

As we stood, once again Mr. Wyler extended his scarred hand. "God bless," he said.

We gathered the cassette recorder and notepads and pens, and I helped my mother from the booth. But before we could turn to walk toward the door, she paused. She put her materials back on the table, then took a single breath. "I'm not sure this disappearance will be right for us," she told him. "We were under the impression Lacey was a *younger* girl. We thought she was kidnapped from her home."

His expression changed: a sullen, set-adrift sort of look. "No. I'm sorry, but no."

They were speaking too loudly. The librarian was watching us, watching *me*, and now I noticed the rubbery droop to her face, aftereffects of a stroke. With a slight pull I tried to persuade my mother toward the door, but she only slid back slightly, her shoes scraping the floor.

The rest of her words rushed forth in a high, excited surge, emphatic so the whole room could hear. "When I was a little girl, something happened to me," she said. "I was kidnapped. Kidnapped and held in a basement with a boy, another kidnapped boy. A man and a woman did it. It was a very old man and an old woman, and they held us there."

Mr. Wyler put his hand to his mouth: his clenched jaw; his furrowed, questioning brow. "That's terrible," he said. "No. You didn't tell me this before. How terrible."

"But maybe it wasn't. I remember they paid so much attention to us! They gave us candy and told us stories and sang beautiful songs to us, sweet songs we'd remember our entire lives."

Stunned, he looked away, slipping backward into the booth. And I was equally dazed. "It's time to go," I said. I grasped my mother's wrist as though to tug her free: not from Mr. Wyler but from this impulsive, implausible story she'd left lingering in the air.

The morning's weather had shifted: the breeze now sharper, the clouds low and heavy, as though clogged with pearls. The overhead leaves rippled alternate brown and gold, and then the wind heaved stronger and colder, enough force, it seemed, to crumb the cement. *God bless*; my face burned with shame. Along the telephone lines, the town's crows trained their diseased eyes on us. Down the street, early Halloween candles glowed from the store windows: alone or in rows, fluttering within the crudely carved jack-o'-lantern eyes and wreck-toothed grins.

How badly I wanted to get high again. I kept my shameful head to the ground and opened the passenger's side door. When I got in beside her, she glanced at me as though our last hour had been harmless. "Cinnamon bubble gum," she said. *"Precious Memories."*

I put the key in the ignition but didn't start the truck. Waiting, I watched her; as the seconds passed, she only stared, peacefully amused, at the row of dashboard photographs. Finally I raised my voice. "When I said you should do all the talking, I certainly didn't mean *that*. Why would you say those things? Is this what you've remembered? What you were sup-posedly saving for me?"

"Oh, *shhh*. If you want, we can talk more when we get home."

"Of course we're going to talk more. You're going to tell me everything. You said you remembered what happened back then, and I want to know *now* before you go telling any-one else. Nothing like that will happen again until I know everything."

She slipped a hand into her sweatshirt, reaching into its cottony underbelly. "But take a look at this," she said. "I'm so bad! I'm nothing but a thief!"

She dropped something on the seat, beside the tape recorder, notepads, and pens. I raised it and saw that my mother had stolen a picture of Lacey. It was one of the little-girl images: the smocked rust-red dress, the buckled shoes, the shyly joyous curve to her mouth.

My mother's grin and gleaming eyes made me uneasy. It felt like the panic that had gripped both Alice and me, years ago, as we'd sat listening to her portentous warnings, to the tale of her own disappearance. I thought, too, of Dolores's worries from the previous night. I still wanted my mother to confess her memories, but this moment didn't seem right, not here in the truck. "You're horrible," I finally said.

"I know."

I started the pickup and shifted into reverse. Before I backed from the parking space, I braved one final look through the café's gauzy curtains. I could see the waitress in her paper tiara and yolk-yellow apron, shuffling from the librarian's table toward Mr. Wyler's. I saw her drop something beside his plate. And then I realized our mistake.

"We forgot to pay the check," I said.

I kept the truck idling and dashed back toward the café door, silently rehearsing my apology. A few bills remained in my wallet; I decided I would unfold them on the table and leave. Through the window, Mr. Wyler still sat at the padded booth, hunched over his coffee and untouched coconut cream, his scrapbook of pictures.

And then I stopped. Even through the tarnished glass, through the scrim of curtain, I saw every detail: the man now stranded and wearied, grandfather to the lost girl, old man so lost himself, at this table in this strange town. He was alone, and he was weeping. Our interview had ended; we had left him with the check, but still no Lacey. I couldn't yet see his tears, but I saw the twitch to his lower lip, the shuddering shoulders, the lewd thread of drool on his chin.

A noble man would have stepped inside to ask him more, would have paid the pale green check and somehow soothed his spokes of pain. But I was weak, not noble, and the weakness restricted me. I stood immobile at the door, unable to reenter the café, that space gone sour with his grief. I could feel my heart straining toward it, but my bones were too faint to follow.

At home she claimed she was tired again. This wasn't merely an excuse to avoid our discussion; I heard the fatigue in her breaths, and saw her body's awkward angle as she lazed beside the TV, her eyes half-closed, little movements making her wince. She asked for her robe and a "great big glass of iced tea." She unfolded the gold-and-green afghan, a gift from Dolores during a particularly long hospital stay, and spread it over her legs.

I stood above her, promising I'd let her rest if only she'd answer some questions. With a hand she shielded her face as though from sunshine. The words through her fingers were muffled: "Can't this wait until later?"

"Please stop playing games with me. I did *not* come all the way home, all the way on a smelly bus so cramped I could hardly move, with all those hideous people, just to have you play silly memory games with me."

"I'm not playing games."

"Just tell me one thing. Why would it matter that Lacey was so much younger? *Why?*"

My mother raised the remote and muted the afternoon news. "When Lacey was a little girl," she said, "she looked just the way I'd looked. But not when she grew up. She didn't resemble me at all."

I shook the snapshot in her face. "So that's why you stole this earlier Lacey, instead of one from now. Because she looked like you."

"Be careful not to tear that; it's going up on the kitchen wall."

"Why did you say those things?" I asked. "This stuff about your disappearance—we *have* to talk about this. Did you say those things to hurt him? Because if you did—and it's pretty awful if you did—well, I think it worked."

"I didn't say those things to hurt him."

"And this is really what you've remembered."

Again she guarded her eyes with her hand. After a sigh and a pause, she answered an exasperated "Yes," her attempt to decisively seal the conversation.

"I won't let you fall asleep," I said. "I'm going to stand here until I know more."

"Well, you'll be standing there a long time, then. Because I'm not quite ready to tell you the rest." She seemed momentarily agitated, but then her expression eased, as though she'd untangled an impossible knot. "You'll see what I mean," she told me. "The time has to be right . . . the *surprise*. But soon. The surprise will happen soon." Then she turned away, facing the sofa cushions, drawing the afghan over her chest.

Defeated, I went to her bedroom and sat on the bed. My face felt hot, as though it retained the scald of shame from our interview. I breathed the dried-apple air and dead flowers, shadowed by four walls of pictures in their cracked, flaked-paint frames. *None of it ever really happened,* I told myself. *She's making it up as she goes along.* Certainly Alice would agree with me; I wondered whether I should call to tell her I'd returned. Again I remembered Dolores's voice, almost taunting: *inventing these things to bring you home.*

From the window I could see, in a rare stripe of sunlight, her crowded backyard garden. There were so many things she'd taken from ramshackle houses, from roadside sunflower prairies, all the wrought-iron pieces, the chipped crockery and antique flowerpots. She'd dug holes among the dead roots; she'd tried growing zinnias inside a rusted spittoon. A tassel fern clung desperately to its spike, but instead of spearing the seed packet to the wood, she'd speared an old snapshot of John. I moved closer to the window. The picture of John should have been sad, but it was oddly comical. To fight the laugh, I remembered the chance abruptness of his death: the sleepless isolations of his trucking-company job; his four a.m. stroke on Interstate 70; the way she'd stayed strong at his funeral (*But I was supposed to go first,* she'd said. *Me, not him*).

I huddled at the window, the black travel bag only an arm's length away. I swore I could resist the urge; I could suffer the day without meth. My gaze wandered over the graveled driveway and garage, the broken earth and browning grass, and then, at the small porch that surrounded the back door, I paused.

The porch was littered with random red scraps, perhaps breeze-blown garbage from a neighboring house. I stared but couldn't figure it out. I left the room, moving quietly past the couch so she wouldn't wake, and when I opened the back door, I saw it wasn't trash at all. Lined neatly across the steps, along the floorboards and balusters and weathered handrails, were rows and rows of candy bars. Thirty, maybe forty or more: a hard-to-find brand called Cherry Mash, square-shaped chocolates in bright red-and-white wrappers. Cherry Mash: my mother's favorite.

Earlier, the porch had been empty; before we'd left that morning, I'd gone to lock the back door (*no need for that,* my mother had said: *nothing bad ever happens here*), and I'd seen nothing. Now, as I stepped out, I felt no stranger lurking in the garden; no glimmery eyes spying from across the adjoining fences or yards. I stood surrounded by the candy, my shoulders tense with a faint wave of fear. Above, the elms dropped their leaves; the darkening clouds tumbled dismally along. I bent to gather the chocolate bars, all that could fit in my pockets, in my outstretched shirtfront, and I went back inside.

In one of my mother's favorite stories, told intermittently to Alice and me during our childhood, she and her younger brother, Dan, were notorious adolescent thieves. They loved stealing candy, stalking the town drugstores, candy shops, and, best of all, the sparkling soda-fountain counter at Moynihan's Department Store. Cinnamon disks and jelly beans were simple; what they really wanted, the true treasure, was the chocolate bar called Cherry Mash.

Moynihan's was the only place that sold it. Made somewhere in Missouri, packaged in those vintage red-white wrappers, Cherry Mash was their little luxury. It was a miniature brown boulder of chocolate and pebbled peanut, filled with a maraschino goo that matched the color of, and quickly melted on, their two wet tongues.

And so, a stealing contest. They chose a morning in late August. They watched the revolving glass doors slowly turning, catching the summer sun, causing the rush of Moynihan's shoppers to appear, in that light, like astonished carousel horses. At the precise moment, my mother and Dan went slinking through. They waited to assure they wouldn't get caught, then began cramming their pockets with candy. Both equally desperate to win the contest; both eager for the sweet-cherry triumph.

My mother managed to steal nine, and then, with a final swipe, ten. She was sure she'd stolen more than her brother. She began striding toward the revolving doors—Dan thrilled and trembling behind her—when a man swooped to stop them.

The man was one of Moynihan's security guards. He forced them to return the Cherry Mashes; he left them waiting in a padlocked basement room. She would never forget his harelip or peeling sunburned skin, his silver badge or midnight-colored jacket. His fingernails ridging four red arcs on her arm.

Dan accurately predicted what would happen next. Ten minutes after the guard's telephone call, their father arrived at the store, grinning through gritted teeth, one fist drumming at his side. "Back we go," he said, almost singing, a voice he rarely used.

At home, as with previous punishments, their father stood above them, a silencing hand on each head. He ordered them outside, past the backyard, to the ivy-curtained woods beyond. From the lanes of gaunt trees, they were to choose a single "switch": the stick that would deliver their beatings.

By that point in their lives, they knew all about switches. The larger limbs, knobbed and bulky, left dull, brown bruises and a lingering ache in the bones. The smaller switches brought different pain entirely: a rabbit-shriek pain; a tiny, hot-pepper pain. My mother and Dan could never decide which pain was more bearable.

But that evening, they agreed they'd been punished enough. A silent, conspiratorial nod confirmed what they would do. Together they entered the woods, searching the clearings and bushes and trees for the perfect place to hide. They vowed to leave home and never return.

As they waited, the sun descended heavy in the west, bleeding at the horizon until it was gone. The wind grew cold. Eventually their stomachs were grumbling, and Dan tried making her laugh (*Know what would be real good right now? A Cherry Mash!*). They heard the scuffling of skunks; a single horned owl. Yet they stayed in the woods that entire night, sitting against opposite sides of an oak, hugging their knees against their chests.

By morning they had realized they couldn't simply disappear. Escape was never that easy. They waited until breakfast to sneak back home. Maybe their father had given up. Maybe he was ready to forgive.

As a boy, I always wished my mother's story had ended this way. Two children, a ten-hour night in the chilly woods, no water or dinner or blanketed beds. Why hadn't the father seen the damage? Why hadn't he only lectured them longer, or suggested simple notes of apology? *Dear Sirs at Moynihan's Department Store* . . . This is what I wished. Sometimes I wished further, devising scenarios with the cheeriest outcomes: perhaps he'd taken them back to the store and instead bought them clothes and marshmallow sundaes and school supplies; or perhaps they'd tromped through the woods, through the backyard, and into the house, only to find their bunk beds filled, pillow to baseboard, with mountains of Cherry Mash, their favorite, their forgiveness.

But their father had done none of these. That morning, the sister and brother stepped into their house, the curtains flaring with air, the hardwood floors bright with sun. They found him waiting sleeplessly in his rocking chair. He held a long, thick switch in his left hand. A narrow switch in his right. Dan went first, and Donna second. They kneeled before him as always, clenching jaws and holding breaths, taking both the dull lingering pain and then the sweet pinprick pain. The big switch across their arms and bottoms and legs, enduring it for him, then the small switch across their arms and bottoms and legs, again and again, enduring it for the father.

For the second consecutive night, the sleeping pills lasted half their promised length. I woke at three a.m. with her old story in my head. If my mother's account of her disappearance was true, then how could her father, with all his penances and commands, stay so callous? Why hadn't the loss of his little girl made him mellow or especially vigilant? My mother's stories just didn't connect. Gradually I'd come to doubt their dilemmas and skim, perfunctory resolutions. Perhaps not only her disappearance was false, but also the story of the theft and resulting punishment.

Yet I also understood how deeply it would pain my mother to lie to Alice or me. It wasn't typical of her to simply invent these stories, whether then or now. Were the stories indeed a result of her illness? Did she even grasp the actual truth in the stories she told? These questions sharpened in my head, and soon, in my worry, I carried the little black bag to the bathroom. To avoid the mirror, I opened the medicine cabinet:

John's Brut and Old Spice colognes; his toenail clippers and tweezers; his white and whittled styptic pencil. I crushed two lines of meth on the soapstone sink basin, sniffing to quell the headache, to ensure I'd be fully alert.

I went to check on my mother. Both of us had slept throughout the day, and we hadn't spoken since returning from our interview. In the living room I found her sleeping still, but there was evidence she'd woken earlier in the night. Surprisingly, she'd shut the television off. She'd lit the canvas tongue of a kerosene lamp, its white flame trembling shadows through the room. In a corner were the chocolate bars, neatly stacked into a white-and-red pyramid. Propped against them, conspicuous enough so I could see, was a single photograph.

I moved closer, squinting in the wobbly lamplight. It wasn't the stolen picture of Lacey, but instead a picture of myself at seventeen. I was wearing a stiff-necked shirt, my hair dyed from its usual strawberry blond to a preposterously bright red. I had silver hoops through my ears and, at the right temple, a dime-size dye stain. "How embarrassing," I whispered to the room.

It was my mother, I recalled, who had focused and snapped the picture. She'd been nothing like Grandfather Wyler. She hadn't objected to my daydreamy posing, to my earrings or rubber bracelets. She hadn't, years later, torn the picture in half or buried it secretly away.

I knelt and watched her sleep. The shadows darkened the creases in her face. She'd lost nearly all the lashes on her eyes, but the lids were beautiful, two violet petals. Around us, the air smelled of smoke and of her sickness: both the root and its result. I removed the crowning Cherry Mash bar from the little pyramid, and then I placed it beside her on the couch, its wrapper brushing the loose fabric of her robe.

In the kitchen, she'd been adding to her gallery of the missing. She'd stuck them to the refrigerator with vegetable magnets; she'd tacked them to the walls beside the cabinets and sink, next to her modern telephone that worked, and her antique Western Electric crank-handle that didn't. Ann-Elise Bridges. Catherine Custer. Vincent Grimes. Yesterday, she'd said she wanted me to learn their names. I'd promised I would.

I pinned my own photo among the gallery above the sink. I stepped back to regard it: the youthful face, the pale and skinny seventeen-year-old boy, now joined with the rest of the disappeared.

From somewhere outside, a noise broke the silence. A sudden, fleshy thump, not from the back porch but from the front of the house.

I leaned over the sink, straining to see through the window. A dark shape was moving across my mother's front porch. It was not Dolores or anyone familiar; from the height and broad shoulders, I could tell it was a man. His back was turned from the door, but I could see his busy motions, his arms in an orderly jerk as though playing invisible drums. I hurried for the door. The meth made me shaky but brave, and I twisted the knob, quiet so my mother wouldn't wake.

At the creak of the door, the man vaulted from the porch and went sprinting into the night. His footfalls were surprisingly fast, then faster, a violence of echoes along the street, the towering lamps and trees, the drab and slumbering homes. He sprinted and didn't look back. He moved like an animal, ghostlike and small and secretly fleeing. I stepped back against the door. In the dark distance I saw one last flash—the animal flail of his arm as he ran—and then his shadow dissolved into black.

Everything had happened so fast. I hadn't seen his face, hadn't pinpointed a brand of shoes or color of shirt. But when I looked down, I saw what he'd done. The porch was decorated with more candy bars, the red-and-white wrappers now ordered into shapes, stunted pyramids like the one my mother had made. One stack to the left of the door; another to the right. The shapes seemed to hold some concealed meaning, some secret I couldn't know.

This time I didn't collect the candy for her. Instead I toppled the pyramids with two bitter kicks. I opened the door and went back inside. The room's darkness stopped me, and I waited as the outlines steadily sharpened.

I heard her breathing before I could actually see. She had sat up on the couch, the afghan bunched in her lap. Although her eyes were locked on me, she didn't seem awake at all. I heard her laugh—an eerie, complicated glee that sounded nothing like my mother. The purple beads glittered darkly on her robe. She was eating the Cherry Mash, smearing chocolate on her lips and chin. As I watched, she took the final bite. She fell back on her pillow, returning to her deep, unknowable sleep.

FOUR

AFTER MR. WYLER and the stranger on our porch, I spent the first week waiting for some further event, staring from the windows at the vacant street, bolting upright in bed at any noise. But the days were ash-gray and routine. I began to wonder which parts were real, which had sprung from dreams or drugs. When I caught my mother stashing the candy bars in the basement storage room, she claimed she didn't know the stranger's identity. In fact, she said, she hardly remembered waking that night at all.

We settled awkwardly into autumn. We bought a pumpkin, carved it, but burned our attempt at a pie. We bought chocolate cats and witches for trick-or-treaters we hoped wouldn't come. Twice we debated informing Alice of my return home. "Let's wait and call next week," my mother offered. I knew she didn't want Alice to learn the depth of her sickness. I had more selfish reasons for keeping silent: this was *our* time, together, just my mother and me.

As expected, the meth made me restless. New York had provided ways to channel this energy, but the Kansas towns offered nothing. I'd lost touch with my few high-school friends. I'd forgotten to bring books or music, and I couldn't summon the patience for my mother's outdated computer. So I let her con me into afternoons with the faulty television—*Antiques Roadshow, Cold Case Files, Investigative Reports*. She'd take one end of the couch, and I'd take the other. Without speaking, she'd lift her feet into my lap, and I'd warm them with my hands.

Often she was frail and hardly moved at all. But sometimes she didn't seem so sick. Then I could almost forget her disease, almost forget *all* disease, and these days she insisted we drive.

She called the drives our "missions." We went to an abandoned Pratt County fairground where the body of a John Doe, or so she'd read, had once been found; to the newly renovated house where, once upon a tragic time, the Carnabys had lived.

Throughout the missions, I kept remembering our awkward argument: *I'm not quite ready to tell you the rest. The time has to be right . . . the surprise.*

Along the narrow avenues were houses with shattered windows, with gardens of car parts and sandburs and tumble-weeds. I watched her scribble street names on her notepads, names that might have once been functional but now were simply silly: Cowherder Street, Barley Boulevard, God's Green Way. We often ate in the Ford, taking the cheapest, quickest meals as we drove. We swung through random grocery aisles, post offices, Laundromats, and she'd casually ask whether anyone knew a missing person, a family member, a friend. She never had any luck. "There's always tomorrow" became her proverb.

On our missions, we acted like chummy children. Some-times she behaved as though a younger, healthier self was trembling inside her, just beyond the skin, incapable of pierc-ing through. We played road-sign and license-plate games. One cloud would be mine, and another hers; I'd see "a polar bear with a beard," and she "something exploding." One day we even invented nicknames. She wasn't feeling well, and once again I'd started that morning with a head full of meth. So she became "Tired." I was "Wired." I remember her think-ing these names equally cruel and hilarious, and I remember her laughing, a gorgeous, percussive laugh from the top of her heart. I wanted never to forget that laugh.

On our first mission, we saw a troupe of hunters carry-ing a freshly killed deer. On our second, we passed an empty school bus with a bright blue sign in its back window: THIS

VEHICLE WAS CHECKED FOR SLEEPING CHILDREN. "Oh, I like that," said my mother. "I think that's wonderful."

Fridays were reserved for Dr. Kaufman. The first two weeks I was high, and in my jumpy, meth-fueled paranoia I avoided meeting him, certain he'd sense it festering inside me. I vowed I'd wait until later that fall. I'd drive my mother to the office, help her to the doors, then walk back to the truck to read (her *Antique Homes* or *Country Collectibles* magazines; cartoon-illustrated addiction brochures from the lobby) until again I saw her, waving, through the glass.

Letters arrived, about a dozen per week. Most were addressed from Kansas; others came two or three times removed, families of Kansans who'd seen my mother's ads and wondered if she could offer some form of closure. Photographs fluttered from the pastel, finically folded stationeries, and my mother taped or tacked them to the kitchen walls. She got a letter from the wife of a missing Tulsa policeman. Another from the parents of a boy last seen near Kanopolis Lake, where I'd sometimes gone swimming when I was young. And another from a Montana mother, who'd included a videotape of her son's Christmas operetta; her scruff-haired wolverine of a boy barking the chorus of a song, *Shining star to lead us home, lead us home,* only days before he'd disappeared.

She even received a picture of a dead child. A parent from Topeka had sent it. The photo showed a blond-haired girl in her coffin, a satiny white dress, white roses at her chest. Her angel's face seemed frozen in pain, as though some horrible hand had bloodlessly plucked both wings from her back.

From the accompanying letter, my mother learned that the girl hadn't gone missing but had died in a playground accident. "We could *never* use this," she said. "Even if we *were* writing a book." Holding the photo, merely looking at it, left me dizzy with remorse. She hid it in a kitchen cupboard instead of pinning it to the wall, and we didn't speak of it again.

The nights got longer and blacker but I couldn't sleep through any of them. Sometimes I'd rise from the spring-creaking bed, ease my feet into her fuzzy pink slippers, and wander the dark rooms. On the couch, she remained sleeping with a calm courtliness. I'd check the drawers and closets and corners, an aimless zombie with my headache and itchy eyes, searching for no particular thing. Maybe I thought I'd discover some secret. Maybe, in my insomniac daze, these searches were all I could think to do.

One night I woke at the onset of a lightning storm. I could have swallowed another sleeping pill, but instead went for her slippers again, deciding this time to rummage around her basement. As I descended, I could see all the clutter she'd collected over the years. After John had died, my mother had taken up odd hobbies, and at the bottom of the stairs was the evidence: her arrangements of dried roses; her assembly of stuffed-stocking rabbits and milkmaid dolls with X-X eyes; three cracked, repainted carousel horses she'd found at an estate sale.

I pulled the string on a dangling lightbulb and moved farther into the room. In one corner were the washer and dryer, the piles of unwashed clothes. In another were networks of copper pipes and stacks of bricks, half-crumbled to powdery stains. The late October rains had leaked through the walls, leaving a wormy smell and puddles that oozed iodine-black on the bare cement floor.

Separate from the rest of the basement, along the south wall and below the stairs, was my mother's cramped storeroom. Inside, she kept shoeboxes filled with insurance papers and hospital bills; John's tackle boxes and hunting gear; the clumped green boughs and artificial needles of her dismantled yearly Christmas tree. Although she often locked the storeroom's narrow black door, tonight it had been left open slightly. I pushed the door with my foot and went inside.

In the center of the room, she'd assembled a small, rickety cot. Stacked on top were a freshly laundered blanket, a sheet and pillowcase, a fat feather pillow. The box of candy bars rested alongside; even without counting, I could tell she'd eaten nearly half of them.

Three warped pine shelves were mounted on the wall above the cot. On the middle shelf, beside the artificial tree, was another, larger box: oblong like a hatbox, with yellow and black stripes. *Moynihan's*, said the cursive imprint on the lid. The Hutchinson department store from my mother's girlhood story. The store I knew had closed nearly twenty years ago.

I lifted the box from the shelf, sitting on the cot to remove the lid. The storeroom had no windows, and its overhead light was weak, but I could still distinguish the contents. The box held a ragged foldout map of Kansas. Beneath the map were two leather binders, both unfamiliar to me, one in dusty brown, the other a faded tan. Both binders were covered with antique collectible decals, souvenirs from attractions my mother had never visited: Old Faithful; the Grand Canyon; the Alamo.

I brought the darker-colored binder into my lap and opened it. As I'd expected, inside was a small bundle of newspaper photographs with one-column clippings. MISSING. Each photo showed a different little girl.

The second binder held similar contents, but here, all the faces were boys. Although I didn't recognize most, I did find a photo of Evan Carnaby and, at the top of the stack, the recent Henry Barradale.

As I sat looking through the clippings—some of them yellowed and unmistakably old, even older than Evan's—I felt a disarranging panic begin to rise in my chest. For days I'd been worrying about my mother's health, about her possibly troubled *mental* health, and this discovery only heightened my fear. What was so special about this particular hoard of photographs? Why had she chosen to hide them away, and why hadn't I seen them before?

When my mother, on that first night I'd arrived home, had brought her relic scrapbook to my bedside, I'd easily recognized the smell of its pages. I'd remembered her drunken slump at the kitchen table, all those years ago . . . her daintily snapping scissors . . . her white fume of glue. But the leather books I now held in my lap were different. I could sense the significance in their orderliness, some restricted secret only my mother knew.

Then I considered the possibility that she'd actually intended to lead me downstairs, to her little storeroom, to the Moynihan's box. So many details from recent days—the pinup photographs and Cherry Mash; her improbable avowals and recollections—seemed part of some code she wanted me to unravel and solve. And because of her health, because it seemed the right thing to do, I was playing along. Perhaps she was upstairs now, anticipating my response, ready to reveal the details of her previously mentioned "surprise."

From outside came the drum of thunder; the swelling, enraged rain. I unfolded the Kansas map, flattening it against the pillow. Certain areas and towns had been circled with various inks; in the feeble light I noticed Hutchinson and Haven in blue, other towns in black, and the only one defined in red, Sterling.

Although I hadn't been there in years, I remembered Sterling from my childhood. The town lay along Highway 96, just northwest of Hutchinson, even closer to the Barradales' community of Partridge (which, as I looked closer at the map, had also been circled in blue). When Alice and I were young, our mother had often taken us there. She'd shopped for school clothes in their tiny secondhand store. Frequently she'd driven to the Sterling park and unleashed us on its playground, sitting at a picnic table or among the piles of toast-colored leaves while we alternated slippery slides and swing sets. Our family had no relatives in Sterling. Nothing about the town was especially striking or unique. Yet I remembered driving there, time after spontaneous time, on several boyhood afternoons.

As I folded the map and returned the photos to their decal-covered binders, I noticed another detail. Among the collection of little girls was an early picture of my mother. She stood in monochrome on a sunny lawn of clipped hedges, wearing Mary Janes and a circle skirt, a wide bow in her hair. First I saw how closely she resembled Alice. Then I saw how *all* the girls in the binder had similar hair, similar dresses and smiles. My mother fit distinctly with them, a member of this long-faded family.

I remembered what she'd said after meeting Mr. Wyler. *When Lacey was a little girl, she looked just the way I'd looked.*

Then I reopened the binder of little boys and studied the stack of pictures. As with the girls, I now could see the links, the resemblances. Henry and Evan. All the boys before and between.

And for the first time—perhaps due to the shadowy light, or my bleary restlessness—I saw what she'd meant when she said I looked like them. At that moment, I could have been holding pictures from my own childhood.

It was nearly four a.m. I returned the Moynihan's box to the center shelf, lay back on the cot, and threw the blanket over my legs. While I listened to the rain, I thought about the houses and streets and trees of tiny, red-circled Sterling; about Moynihan's and Old Faithful and the Alamo. I thought about my mother, Evan, and the freshly buried Henry. I wasn't sure what to believe, but maybe it didn't matter. This was home, after all—I had nowhere else to go—and I would indulge my mother through this crucial, confusing time that Dolores had called *that point.* Hers was a different world: a place of desperate inventions, of incongruous actions and reasons, separate from New York and its lonely, instant thrills. I would stay inside this world. I would keep her happy.

At noon I woke again and went upstairs to join her on the couch. She had opened a pull-top can of salted peanuts; I wasn't hungry but helped her pick at them. She didn't seem surprised that I'd slept in the basement. She stared unblinking at the TV, but instead of watching her regular shows, she'd switched to the local noonday news. From every acre of Kansas came all sorts of terrible things, larcenies and arsons and murders, delivered by newscasters with smiles like seared sugar. But already they had forgotten Henry. I sensed how this pained my mother: she still brooded about the day he'd gone missing, the day he'd been found. I knew she wanted to understand how it felt for those church-group girls, their stunned, tranquil circle of discovery. To understand the grief of Henry's parents. To understand his sisters, or the laughing friends he met for root beers after school. And I knew that sometimes—although she wouldn't admit it—my mother wished for the one who caused that disappearance, that glint of eyes in the shadows, that sinister grinning mouth.

I'd been rehearsing all the right sentences; I waited for the cheery opening melody of a commercial. "I found the things you left for me. I've decided to play along."

She didn't take her eyes from the TV. "Play along *how*?"

"I don't know how much of these things are true, and how much you're making up. But if this is what's keeping you happy right now, I'll play along with it. I've got nothing better to do, and God knows we could both use a little nonchemical excitement and happiness in our lives."

My breaths were timid and quick; I couldn't guess how she might respond. She looked at me—I could tell she sensed my discomfort—and gave an exaggeratedly puzzled grimace and shrug. "Okay," she said.

"So today we're going on another mission. I hope you're feeling up for it. Take a guess on our destination. *Sterling.*"

I waited for any reaction to show on her face. Finally, she smiled and said, "Give me a few minutes to call Dolores. We were supposed to do something today, but I'll cancel. Go clean up and change clothes, and I'll give her a quick call."

The afternoon was chilly, the roads still glistening from the morning rains. She wore her wig and the oversize New York sweatshirt, which she'd apparently now claimed as her own. She'd brought one of her maps, and the notepads, pens, and battered casette recorder. Sandwiched between the notepads—presumably to read aloud during the drive—were some of the newer mailed responses to her newspaper ads, as well as a yellowed, dog-eared copy of *True Detective* magazine. I remembered how she used to sneak new issues home from the prison, where it was forbidden to inmates; its pages detailed real American crime, lurid exposés on assassins, hijackers, rapists. She used to stand before Alice and me with *True Detective* in her hands, reading the biographies of vanished women and children, the sensational reports with frequent misspellings and off-focus pictures that smudged her fingers like moth dust.

To avoid one of these recitations now, I asked her advice on the best route to Sterling. "I thought I'd know it from memory," I said. "But I obviously don't."

"If you gave me the keys awhile, I could take you there."

"Absolutely not." After years in New York, my driving had its shortcomings—the truck's unexplainable noises confused me, and I faltered at traffic rotaries—but I knew, even after days of drugs, my hands were steadier than hers.

"Then let's take the prettier route." She gestured toward the windshield with the eraser end of a pencil. "Up here about a mile, then make a right."

Deserted roadside tractors . . . skies of waxwings and crows and the occasional red-tailed hawk . . . the sunlight in white shatters through the fast-passing trees. Two miles down the road she'd recommended, this scenery abruptly changed: along both sides of the truck, the ditches were charred black, evidence of recent brush fires. When we rolled the windows down, we caught the thick and scorchy smell. The truck moved between the burned lanes, axles humming, into this world of charcoal earth and clouded sky.

"Let's stop here a minute," she said.

"Don't you want to keep going? Not much longer before Sterling."

"But it's nice here—black instead of all the yellow and brown." She reached for her purse and brought out a wadded bloom of tissue. "Besides, I have to pee."

Ahead was an isolated oak, its trunk charred black, poised in its towering loneliness. Its leaves shone in glaring yellow-orange, as though the recent fires had settled in its limbs. I eased before it and parked. The black strip of ditch segregated us from long cords of barbed-wire fence, and beyond, a field scarred with cattle hoofprints. When I helped my mother out, she carried her purse, shuffled toward the brilliant tree, and crouched. "Just yell when you're done," I said, and turned away.

After two minutes she yelled, and I went to take her place. Dust and pollen had powdered her clothes. She'd tossed the tissues to the ditch and straightened the creases in her shirt. A yellow oak leaf, sawtoothed and dazzling, had fallen in her hair. With a wave of dread I realized no, it wasn't her actual *hair*, but the wig—and yet these phrases (*yellow leaf*; *my mother's hair*) seemed so lovely, I repeated them in my head.

She checked the skyline for cars. "Completely deserted. Like a place where somebody'd dump a body."

"And I suppose you want to go searching for one."

"I would, but I'm too tired."

It was my turn, so I stood beside the tree and unzipped. I heard her walking back to the truck, slamming the passenger door. At my feet was the snuffed-flame smell, and above, the acrid, dampened leaves. I tried and tried, but couldn't release: the unstable systems of my body, those days between binges. I zipped again and tightened my belt. *Soon I'll quit. It'll be good for me to quit.* But even thinking this, the craving surged bitter to my throat. I knew that unless I took a break, my supply would run out in a week, maybe two. I'd have to call Gavin for help.

I heard her start the Ford's rumbling ignition, and then I heard the radio, her country station's fiddle and pedal steel guitar now leaking from the seams of the truck. When I turned, she was speaking to me through the windshield. I tried to read her lips. "Look there," they slowly said. She lifted a hand and pointed.

Less than a mile ahead, a figure was walking the burned border of ditch. It took me a moment to realize the person moved not closer but farther from us; as I watched, my mother tapped the horn and jerked her head to hurry me.

I got in and lowered the music; she returned to the passenger seat so I could drive. "Let's creep up real slow and take a look," she whispered.

As we neared, I saw the figure was a boy. He was frowsy-haired and thin; he kept his gaze at his feet. He kicked at the stretches of rubble and fire-singed grass, then continued shuffling along, both hands pressed in his jacket pockets. We passed him cautiously. The boy didn't raise an arm or offer his thumb; he glanced up only after we'd eased by. Framed in the rearview I could see his pale skin. I could see the smirk on his mouth. I accelerated, slowed again, and at last braked so abruptly my mother caught the door's silver handle to keep from lurching forward.

She squinted at the road, searching for the spoil of another car. When none emerged, she turned to me. "Did you see his face? Did you see who he looks like?"

Her eyes and smile were huge. It was an expression I remembered from childhood, the savage face she'd sometimes worn while pinning me down, while tickling my stomach and ribs. She hadn't shown this face in years and it frightened me. "I'm not so sure he wants us to stop," I said.

Already in the rearview, the boy was marching toward us. "But I think he does," she said.

"We shouldn't stop."

"But we already have. We're waiting here, for him." With two quick motions of her head, she checked the reflection of the boy, then looked back to me. She tucked her bottom lip below the false white rim of teeth: a coy, flirting girl. Her wig was positioned wrong, but the leaf, still snagged at its side, was exquisite as gold.

"Let's *get* him," my mother said.

I began to nurse the truck backward, the boy's fierce face looming closer in the mirror. He seemed clumsy, bantam-weight, and, as he walked, he alternately cocked his head left side to right as though clowning for a camera. He had long, oily, gravy-colored hair and a bored, angular face. Beneath his open jacket, he wore an oversize sweatshirt, the kind with a bunched hood and kangaroo pockets and a gleaming median zipper, and he transferred his hands—or, rather, his fists concealed by overlong sleeves—from jacket pockets to jeans. I could see his pimples; his upturned nose. His miniature headphones, wire-tethered to a portable cassette player at his belt. And his eyes, lost dreamily in his music, reminding me briefly of my own youth: head in the heavens, feet on sturdy earth.

Before he could reach my door, I clamped my fingers on its handle. But my mother wouldn't let me protest again. She ordered me to lower the window, and I followed her instruction.

He stopped, looking inside to scrutinize the truck, my mother, and, finally, me. "Hey hey," he said loudly. I could hear his headphones, music like the tinny tongues of hornets.

"Hey hey, yourself," said my mother.

The boy leaned into the window, arms and shoulders and head, so brazen I shrank against the seat. Up close, I saw his eyes were damp brown. Above his lip was a tentative, whiskery fuzz. I guessed him fifteen, sixteen at most. He grinned with a crooked mouth, and with fascination I saw a crust of dried blood in one nostril. I risked my first breath of him: a muddy, stormy smell, a hint of unwashed hair and, oddly, of peppermint. Maybe he could smell us, too—our smoky, sweaty clothes, our individual drugs.

She smiled a broad, face-sweetening smile. "Are you *hitch*-hiking out here?"

He swiped the headphones from his ears, necklaced them, and thumbed his tape player off. "Not really," he said with a rasp. The peppermint smell, I saw, came from a clump of gray gum in his mouth. "But yeah, I could be hitchhiking. Are you stopping?"

"Surely you realize," she said, "that we've already stopped."

"I guess you're right."

She reached for the steering column, then shifted into park. With the same hand, she patted the space between us, daring him to get in.

"No," I said. "It's time for us to head home."

But my mother wasn't finished. "Don't you think this could be dangerous? Walking alone out here, down this deserted road?"

"Nothing dangerous about it."

"I saw the way you were walking. We both saw it. Don't you see you're just asking for trouble?" She clenched her fist, and this time pounded the seat. "Don't you know the sorts of people who drive these roads?"

The gum snapped in his mouth. "Aw, I'm out here all the time. I never see nobody."

"But we know those sorts of people. Kidnappers and killers! They don't operate in the cities anymore. These days they
patrol places like this!"

"Mom," I said. "Stop."

"Haven't you heard about that boy from Partridge? Just
about your age. You even look alike."

"Nope," he said.

"The killers wait until the right forbidden moment. Right
when your school lets out. When darkness isn't far away!"

Now I recognized this voice: ingratiating and girlish, like
an overzealous actress, with all the lilting, artificial volume
and tone she'd used while teasing Alice and me. Back then I'd
adored the mother of that voice. Now I didn't trust it, and I
wanted her to stop. "Shh," I said.

"Shh, yourself." And then, to the boy: "Get in."

"Only a couple miles 'til Sterling," he said. "I can walk
there myself."

"We'll drive you. Get in."

"He doesn't *want* to get in," I said.

She knew I wouldn't budge or offer my door to him. All
afternoon, like other afternoons, we'd been shielded from
the world. Together in the Ford, our pencils and pads and
recorder, our coded secrets and jokes. I couldn't allow our air
to escape; couldn't let him corrupt it with his skin and blood
and his knobby, graceless bones.

"We're going to stay parked right here until you get into
this truck," she said.

I tightened my grip on the wheel and wouldn't look at
either of them. But then, in a startling surge of energy, my

mother opened her door and stepped out. In that moment she didn't seem sleepy or sick. She reached back into the Ford and, with a lone sweep of her hand, cleared the seat: our map, our pencils and notepads, and Dolores's luckless lottery tickets, all spilling to the floor.

Still, her teasing voice: "Now come and scoot your scrawny butt between us."

Without hesitation, the boy made an arc around the face of the truck to the passenger side. He folded his shoulders and head inside, sliding next to me. She followed him in and slammed her door. Now we'd snared him like a fox. I could feel and smell his heat. I looked to the floor, where his feet began edgily tapping: two black high-top sneakers with the canvases frayed, shoelaces frayed, their rubber toe pads darkened with ballpoint-blue ink. He'd scribbled stars and zigzags of lightning; fat dollar signs; one smiling face, one frowning.

"I live up here a ways, just the edge of Sterling," the boy said.

"You shouldn't be out walking," she told him. "This could be one of those for*bid*den moments." I knew she'd memorized this phrase from one of her missing-persons stories, from *True Detective*, perhaps a perfumed letter from some abandoned family.

"Nobody's going to hurt me. I'm tough. I'm lucky."

"We don't believe in luck," she said.

The sun was falling in the west, and storm clouds had clustered in the sky. I began to coast along the burned road, moving slowly as though acceleration would spur the boy to violence. He sat only inches from me, our captive. Whatever scheme or pattern I'd wanted from the day, this certainly wasn't it. The boy raised his hand, touching the dashboard's photographs and newspaper clippings with two suspicious fingers. I saw his skinny wrist, its pale skin and single blue vein, its fake pen-ink tattoo of a five-pointed star. His hand was callused, the fingernails grimy, the cuticles ripped and gnawed raw. But the hand was powerful and young and for a moment I wanted to touch it, wanted to know how it felt to hold a hand like that, this busy, carelessly roughened teenager's hand.

And then I noticed his bracelet. Threads of purple and green, with tiny white beads. Exactly like Henry Barradale's: the bracelet he'd worn when he was murdered; bracelet on which we'd focused our elaborate stories.

I felt both fascination and fear. I looked at my mother, but she wouldn't catch my eye. I grew dimly aware of a small, rhythmic creaking sound, and I realized she'd started the tape recorder. Then she lifted her own hand to the dashboard, and quickly, like a striking snake, wrapped her fingers over his.

"You sure wear a lot of clothes," she told him. "The weather hasn't even gotten all that cold yet."

"It's my style."

"And you haven't even told us your name."

"You haven't told me *yours*."

"I asked you first."

The boy unfolded one side of his jacket to reveal an adhesive paper name tag stuck to his shirt. The tag had a blue border with the word OTIS stamped along the bottom. But nothing had been written inside the white square. "It says Otis because that's the town I was just at," the boy said. "A school music contest. We were supposed to write our names on these tags, but not me! Those music things are stupid anyway. Stand in a group and sing stupid songs, and there's some asshole judging you. And I can't sing worth a crap."

She was nodding eagerly. "I couldn't sing worth a crap when I was a kid, either."

"That's a lie," I said. Sharp in my memory was our morning radio, years ago: Alice and I listening as our mother's voice drifted from her six o'clock shower. "You've always had a wonderful voice."

She shook her head and interrupted me. "I kinda like Otis as a name," she told the boy. "What if we call you Otis?"

"Fine with me."

"Want to know our names? He calls me Tired. And I call him Wired." She paused, waiting for my conspiring smile. But I couldn't; it felt as though she'd broken a precise, sweet promise.

The boy seemed to consider her words. The dimming sunlight outlined his oily hair and the flecks of blood along his nose. He gave a choppy, counterfeit laugh; the sound seemed to pacify my mother.

"This pickup truck makes you guys look badass," he said in his corn-husk voice. "This pickup truck is pretty cool."

"This rattletrap?" She grinned, pleased with the word. "Oh, it's awful. I'd be lucky if somebody'd give me eight hundred bucks for it."

"Wish I had eight hundred bucks."

"Don't we all?"

It seemed they were rehearsing an intricate, classified routine. She had taken his hand again, interlacing the fingers. I wanted him gone. I kept my eyes on the road but could sense them nodding and smiling beside me. The pickup passed a faded deer-crossing sign and, beyond that, another, signifying the turnoff for Sterling. By now the ditches were no longer burned. Again the world turned yellow and brown. My mother was chattering and the boy was laughing, but I wouldn't buckle; I wouldn't be their audience.

She told the boy to look into her purse. He obeyed, perhaps hoping she would give him money. Instead he found more of her photographs, responses from our ads and pictures from newspapers, faces she hadn't yet pinned to the walls. Otis leafed through them, picking one out and holding it toward the light—a girl's school snapshot, her braces and polka-dot blouse—but my mother only shook her head.

"Oh, I didn't mean *those*. I meant for you to get my pills."

"What kind of pills?"

"Life or death pills." She waited for the words to penetrate. "If I don't take the right pills at the right times, I won't be around much longer."

He brought forth the pills and handed them to her. The headache darkened behind my eyes: it was the first time I'd heard her utter words like these. I had to protest, or I knew she'd continue, as she'd done that impetuous day with Mr. Wyler. "But that's not true at all," I said. "Now let's be quiet, and let's just take him home."

The road through Sterling ran parallel to a silty river; we passed streets lined with trimmed hedges and evergreens, the solemn Methodist church, the box-shaped houses white as butcher paper. The town was nearly identical to Haven—or Partridge, I thought, or so many other neighboring towns.

Perhaps, beyond one of those doors, the boy's parents sat waiting. *Soon we'll be free of him.* Yet even as I thought this, I knew he wouldn't reveal the correct house. I knew she didn't want to let him go.

"Living here's like living in hell," said Otis.

I saw this as my chance, and I tried to take control. "We feel bad for you. We really do. But you have to tell us which house is yours."

"Not yet," she said. "Let's drive around awhile."

Otis searched his coat pocket and found a stick of the peppermint gum; she cupped her hand, dainty as a soap dish, and he dropped it in her palm. "Yeah," he said, smirking at me. "Let's drive around."

"I will not 'drive around.' We really should head back home."

But Otis continued scrabbling through his pockets. Now I could see that one side of his neck was discolored, a purplish blue above the collarbone. I realized he'd been in a fight: the bruise, the rim of blood in his nose. A sudden fear surged high into my throat. I pictured him drawing a knife; turning on my mother and me.

Instead he pulled an apple from the pocket. He held it in his palm, astonishingly red; he brought it against his cheek, relishing its sleek chill. With a slow, comical blink, he swallowed his gum. Then he put the apple to his mouth and bit. When I didn't hear it crunch, I realized it wasn't an apple but a soft, ripe tomato. Otis kept it against his mouth, sucking its juice in a ruby rush, watching the road ahead as he ate.

My mother smiled and chewed the gum, waiting until his tomato was nearly gone. "I bet you stole that, didn't you?" she asked.

"They're my favorite vegetable. Two more in my pockets for later."

"That's funny," she said, "because what you're eating isn't a vegetable at all. The tomato is a fruit. Anyone will tell you that."

"What makes you think I stole them?" His *stole* came out *stold*, his voice cracking on the vowel, the alto boy lingering in the tenor man.

"We can see straight through you," she said.

The boy canted his head and let forth a laugh, muscles shuddering in his bruised throat. He seemed so vibrant and alive: the sort of vibrant that made me jealous; the sort I wanted, once again, to *be*. I knew Henry Barradale had been this way once. Maybe Henry, too, had scribbled shapes on his high-tops; maybe five-pointed stars on his wrists. My mother started laughing too, her ardor fusing with his, and, as I looked away, I pictured Henry at his funeral, the casket draped with roses and the football bouquet. Henry in the earth, the calluses bleaching on his hands, his heart drained and sealed, yet still fire-red as a boxing glove.

With a final bite Otis finished the tomato. Above us, the rows of lamps began flickering on. I turned onto another street, recognizing at once that we'd already driven the length of it. I had no patience left. "Tell me which house is yours," I said, even louder than before.

But neither the boy nor my mother was listening. He reexamined the photos with his grimy fingers. She put her hand there too, and said, "We know a lot about these people. These *missing* people. And I know what it's like to disappear."

Now I could sense where she was leading: once again, the old, misty story. "You're both acting stupid," I said.

"When I was a girl, someone scooped me up in their car and took me away. Took me right out of my everyday, little-girl life."

"Enough," I said. "Just stop."

"There was a boy close to your age. A boy who looked a lot like you."

I braked abruptly in the middle of the crumbling street. "This is nonsense," I said. "I won't let you tell these stories again."

"Sometimes you get lucky," she continued in her teasing voice, "and someone steals you away and treats you like their little princess or prince. But not everyone winds up like that. Others wind up like that boy Henry."

"Tell us where your house is," I yelled at Otis. *"Now."*

"Aw, I'll tell you when I'm good and ready."

"You'll tell us right now."

I was shouting, but my mother shouted louder. "You should be careful! You never know what might happen. Here one minute and gone the next!"

He had taken her hand; he could see what it did to me. The laughter, the sly affinity, the bracelet on his skinny wrist: it seemed I was the target of their elaborate, calculated trick. Frantically, I looked for a place to push him out of the truck.

Ahead on the horizon, along an arcade of sugar maples, was the entrance to a trailer court. I could see the torn shingles and dented siding; the three long rows of mailboxes.

Yet even as I sped toward our departure spot, I could sense them crafting their next sentences, following through with their act. "I'm too smart to disappear," he said. "Besides, you guys wouldn't hurt me. You don't have the guts."

Now she spoke directly to me. "It's like he's daring us to do it."

We'd nearly reached the trailer court, but I couldn't hear another word. I stomped on the brake, opened my door, and stepped out to the leaf-littered street. "We're leaving you here," I said. The boy's mouth twisted in mock fury and he defiantly crossed his arms. But I stopped the gesture, reaching in to grab his elbow, pulling him outside. My temper caught him off guard. The after-drug fatigue sent creases of pain along my chest, but as he started striking back, I only pulled him harder, fighting him farther from the truck. He scuffled and pawed like a cornered cat. I felt his fingernails slashing the length of my arm. "Stop it," I heard my mother say. "It's not supposed to happen like this." I shoved him away and turned to her, and as I turned, I saw his arm yank back and quickly forward. I tried to deflect, but his fist slammed the side of my head. "Stop it," my mother repeated. The boy wound his arm to strike me again, but this time seemed to falter or trip. I saw my chance and rushed back through the open door. I slammed it, locked it, and cranked the window.

"He *hit* me," I said, breathing hard. "He *hit* me."

"Don't let him go," she said. "This isn't the way we planned."

He righted himself, and in a convulsive rush came leaping toward the truck, thrusting his shoulders and chest against the door. In the baggy clothes his body was puny and wet with sweat, the bones and skin of a drowning boy. "Don't drop me here!" he screamed, his breath fogging the glass. "I don't really live here!"

"We're leaving," I said.

He drove his fist against the window. "You're supposed to take me with you!"

The twilight coiled around him but his face was shining through the glass. In the brake lights, his skin was tinted scarlet. I could see the rage flickering darkly in his eyes, flaring his defiant nostrils. And beneath the rage, his panic, so alarming and earnest and pure.

"You can't leave me here," he whined. "My father beats me. And my mother. I think he's going to kill us. I have scars all over my back and he's going to shoot me with one of his guns."

"All lies," I said.

Otis continued yelling, but I was done with him. I shifted into drive, and the truck surged forward. In the rearview, he drove his fist against his hipbone. He stamped his foot. Just then he seemed much younger than before; I recalled tantrums I'd once thrown, too, and knew that Otis was just a troubled, scab-elbowed boy who surely thrived on swindles and shattered glass, on playing hooky and telling lies.

As I watched his reflection, he jerked both hands from his jacket pockets. I expected to see some obscene adolescent gesture but instead saw the two tomatoes, his ammunition. He raised both arms above his head, bending the elbows as though hurling a heavy weight. Both tomatoes came whizzing toward the truck. His aim was sure as an all-star's; I heard the vacant *splutch*, the first and then the second, as they struck.

At the noise, I instantly braked. The boy turned and took off running. I saw his skinny, grinding legs and the flail of his arm, and in that moment I knew.

I waited to assure he wouldn't return. Then I glared across the seat at her. "That was *him*, wasn't it?"

She turned toward me, her face tensed with frustration. At first she refused to answer.

"The candy bars. That was him . . . the man on our porch."

"Yes," she finally said.

I could only stare, muted and confused. I watched her jaw slowly grind over the gum. Eventually I looked back to the road and drove, letting the quiet settle around us, between us, into the boy's absence. We left Sterling, its houses vanishing, its street lamps dimming in the violet distance. The fight had quickened my heartbeat; I could feel the rise of nausea, the migraine and constricted throat, all the splintery familiarities of an especially bad comedown. *Perhaps it's my mind, not hers,* I thought. *Perhaps it's mine that needs mending.*

Above the horizon, the sky was slashed with vapor trails from the early-evening planes. In the setting sun, they slowly changed from white to pink. My mother put the photographs back into her purse. Her lip was trembling; she blinked with a pained, unsteady stress. I knew that whatever I could say would be the wrong thing, the terrible thing. When I looked again, the sun was gone, and the slashes of pink had darkened to red, as though some angel, buried alive in the sky, had frantically scratched and bloodied its nails, wanting out.

At last I gave in, but I couldn't bridle my anger. "Mom, what is *wrong* with you? You're acting crazy." I could feel the debris of the meth, rising inside me, pushing forth the awful words. "I did *not* come all this way back home to play ridiculous games. I didn't come back to be embarrassed over and over by you."

"Please don't yell at me," she said. "Please don't be mad." Her voice was wounded and soft; the *please* made everything worse. In the shadows, she seemed younger, almost beautiful. *A yellow leaf had fallen in my mother's hair.*

"I don't know what you're doing," I said. "But you're scaring me."

"Let's wait and talk about this at home. First thing, after we get home and get comfortable. I was planning to tell you soon anyway."

The smell of him surrounded us. I thought of the candy on the porch; the piston of his arm as he sprinted away. I thought of the way he looked at her, and I thought of their linked hands. It seemed the boy knew secrets I didn't, and I swallowed hard: jealousy, its rotten olive taste. "He's a liar," I said. "He probably doesn't even *have* a father. He's a liar, and he'd been in a fight, and he probably would have stolen from us if we had anything to steal."

"But he looks so much like you when you were that age. Almost *exactly* like you."

We neared the final road toward Haven, lulled by the propulsive rumble of the Ford. Here and there the darkness was stung by firefly light. I rolled my window down and heard cicadas in the branches of trees, crankily chewing the air, signaling autumn's end. We passed a farmhouse with a partially collapsed barn; on its broken roof was a wind-bunched flag, unknotting its stripes and stars. Higher up, the blue had smudged to black, the stars blocked by clouds but still there, I knew, just beyond our sight.

"Mom, are you okay?" I asked, almost whispering. "Are *we* okay?"

She looked at me in silence. I turned the evening in my head, picking apart our shames and mistakes. I looked to the back window, the rectangle of glass where his tomatoes had struck. The red wounds stayed stunningly in place, two successful blasts of his target, and, as we drove the last miles, I thought of how I'd someday write about this, perhaps for Pen & Ink, perhaps for something else. I thought of silly, showy descriptions: the tomatoes like double-barreled bullets of blood, like ketchupy stars, like the twin gouged eyes of some irascible beast.

But then I realized the futility: they were only tomatoes, nothing less or more. All the images in my head, the possible ways I'd describe them, no longer mattered. The darkness softened our world, and I steered the pickup from the highway, toward the turnoff for home. Already I could sense the Haven streets, slate-gray as bars on a jailhouse cell. Already I could picture the mothers and fathers, safe with all their safe children, behind dusty windows, refueling fires, dimming lamps. The murmuring televisions, the clattering mismatched silverware, the shuffling chairs.

FIVE

I LED HER to the couch, gave her a glass of iced tea, and told her to wait. I washed my face and hands, the dried scratches of blood from my arms. I swallowed half a sleeping pill to calm the shock of all they'd said and done. In the basement room, as expected, I found her sewing kit; among the loops of embroidery floss were the colors she'd used for his bracelet, the precise shades of purple and green. I even found a few leftover egg-shaped beads.

When I brought the evidence back upstairs, she had switched off the lamp, sitting now within the television's glow. She'd replaced her wig with a blue-and-white scarf, and she'd taken his peppermint gum from her mouth. When she looked at me, she seemed both hungry and cold.

"Who is he?" I asked. "How do you know him?"

"He's just a boy I met."

"Right before we left today, you said you were calling Dolores. But you didn't, did you? You called that boy."

She put the glass to her lips, swallowed, and dabbed at her mouth with the sweatshirt sleeve. I waited for her to answer, but she kept silent.

"This time, we're going to talk." I took the seat beside her. "You're going to answer my questions and stop this nonsense."

"But are you still 'playing along' with me, or are you really going to believe what I tell you?"

"I don't know. Maybe I won't know until I hear it all."

"You think I'm making this up."

"I don't know what to think about the whole 'recovered memories' thing. It just isn't convincing, whether it's someone on TV or my own mother."

"Okay. But I'm not making it up. I remember."

Her voice sounded desperate again; I resisted the urge to take her hand. Beneath the Y on the New York sweatshirt was a pink tomato stain, and I reached to rub it with my thumb. "Oh, Mom. It's tough to believe that something could happen years and years ago, then come flooding back after all this time."

A deep, exaggerated sigh. "But it's *not* flooding back. I've remembered, little by little and piece by piece, all these years."

"Please tell me. Please?"

"I don't want to start with Otis."

"Start somewhere else. Go back to when you were a girl. How about the day you disappeared."

She closed her eyes, pausing to arrange the memories. The TV's light wavered sleepily over her face; from outside, the echo of a church bell, reminding me of the bell above the Haven Café door, and of Mr. Wyler, weeping soundlessly at his booth. I listened as the low tolling dissolved and the town went silent.

After nearly a minute, she opened her eyes. "I was playing in the playground," she began, "down the street from where we lived. I was there with Dan. He was on the swings with some other kids, but I just sat in the grass, coloring in my book. I'd colored bright blue for the stegosaurus, and red for the triceratops. I remember because they let me bring the coloring book along. I had it the entire time I was with them. It's one of my souvenirs. Why don't you go snoop some more through the basement—you'll find it down there."

"An old man and old woman."

"They were sweet. Very sweet and kind to me. When we got back to their house, there was another kid, a boy. They'd taken him, too, sometime earlier. Young, but a little older than me. The boy's name was Warren. They told us we looked like brother and sister. Warren and Donna. Doesn't that sound nice together? They said we could be their very own kids, even though they seemed too old to be our parents."

She took a noisier sip from her glass. "We never knew their names. They said to call them Mom and Pop, but it didn't feel right. Maybe if I'd been there longer than the week, I might have gotten used to it, but I didn't."

"Tell me more about them."

"The woman was big. Not fat, but fleshy. Fleshy, dimpled arms. She had liver spots on her hands and a ring with one purple stone and one blue. She had little wire-rim glasses, so thick they magnified her eyes. And gray hair, almost white. And she liked to sing to us. She sang church hymns I hadn't heard before. Not the usual ones you could hear every Sunday on the TV or radio, but strange songs, all God and Jesus and Holy Spirit, with strange, sad melodies. And she'd watch us like she was going to cry."

"You and this boy. This Warren."

"Yes."

"And what about the old man?"

"He was a farmer, I guess. He wore dirty boots with smears of manure on the sides. Sometimes he smelled a little like horses, like the hay or alfalfa. He didn't sing like the woman but he was just as nice. He's the one who gave us candy bars. And he sometimes gave us peaches, big fat fuzzy ones, with enough juice to spill out your mouth and down your shirt. Peaches fresh from trees he must have had somewhere on his farm.

"But the man only came down at night, not ever during the day like her. And it was strange, because he always wore something over his face, like a scarf or sometimes some kind of mask. Like he didn't want us to see his face. But even with the mask, he didn't scare us. He was so nice."

She kicked her shoes to the floor, lifting her feet to tuck them into the afghan. "Once I remember him wearing a dirty blue work shirt," she said. "There was a patch on the chest, but the patch didn't have a name—just STERLING REPAIR. We were taken to some small house, on a small farm, in a dark basement, but that's why I've always thought it was somewhere near Sterling—because of that patch on his shirt."

My hands were sweating and I'd tightened them into fists. In my left, I still held the purple and green floss, the tiny white beads. All my questions had doubled; I wasn't certain where to start. "They never let you outside? They didn't try to hurt you? You never tried to run?"

"I don't think we *wanted* to run. At least I didn't, not at first. I was a little bit scared—you know, of what could happen with my dad. Remember how horrible and mean he could be. I thought he'd punish me for disappearing."

"But surely he tried to find you. And your mother. Didn't she try to find you?"

"I don't know. Maybe they didn't try very hard. Looking back, I wonder if they almost enjoyed that I'd disappeared— Dan was so little at the time, but he told me later how our parents got a lot of attention for a few days, neighbors coming to visit, even a policeman showing up at our house. They got sympathy cards and gifts and big noodle casseroles as though I was already dead.

"So no, I didn't try and run. I didn't really want to go home. Maybe it's hard to understand, but I liked the old man and woman. They kept giving us candy. They let us play records and decorate the basement room. I was excited to see what would happen next. And I really liked Warren. He was closer to my age than Dan, and he understood me. He treated me nice, like a big brother. Nobody at school had ever treated me so nice. He talked to me, and he told funny jokes like nobody at school had ever done. And he made sure I wasn't afraid when the basement got dark.

"I remember they put some kids' games and an old record player down there for us. The games were difficult— board games designed for older kids maybe, a little too complicated for us—but we tried playing them anyway. We made up our own rules and shuffled the little cards and followed each other's game pieces around the game boards. And we played the scratchy, scratchy records. Sometimes a little too loud, but the man and woman never complained."

"What records? What were the songs?"

"Oh, fun things. Upbeat. Things you'd hear in an old movie, or in some old TV commercial." She cocked her head, remembering. "There was 'Jeepers, Creepers' and 'I've Got the World on a String.' And 'Don't Sit Under the Apple Tree.'"

My mother kept looking heavenward. Clearly and flaw- lessly, she started to sing.

Don't sit under the apple tree
With anyone else but me
Anyone else but me . . .
'Til I come marchin' home

"That's nice," I said.

"I loved singing along, but Warren said he hated singing, he had a terrible voice. I'd sing, but he wouldn't join in."

(Otis, once again, from the truck: *I can't sing worth a crap.*)

"Warren said he was an only child, his father wasn't home much. I could tell he didn't like it there. And he didn't care for school at all. We were so much alike. But I don't remember him saying anything about a last name, or where his home actually was. He just seemed happy to be away. Happy to be part of this—this adventure, I guess you could call it."

"Or *kidnapping.*"

"Yes, maybe. But not really. They took such good care of us! They treated us special."

"But they brought you back. They didn't keep you there forever."

Instantly, her expression changed; her gaze moved to the TV, then the window beyond. "And I've always wondered why," she said. "That was always the worst thing about the story, the part I always hated."

"Tell me."

"It was late at night. We'd been sleeping but they woke us up. The man was wearing the mask and it looked like she'd been crying. They left Warren in the basement room, and they told me to shut my eyes. They put a blindfold over my face. Put my coloring book in my hands. They said they had a surprise for me. 'We're going on a little trip.' And they led me upstairs and outside. Guided me into the back of a car. The man was wearing scratchy work gloves, and he was holding my hand. The night was warm—I remember it being so calm and warm. My eyes were blindfolded but it was the same car; I recognized the pipe-tobacco smell of it from the day they'd taken me from my street.

"And it was so late at night, and so warm, and I was sleepy. I didn't ask questions. I might have even fallen asleep. But at some point I woke because the woman was crying again. My blindfold had fallen off. Maybe they had taken it off. I could see we were back in Hutchinson, at the end of my parents' street. The car door opened. I heard the woman crying. Then I was outside the car, and they were driving away."

"And you never told," I said.

"I marched right back to my house because there was nothing else to do. I was afraid I'd be in loads of trouble. So I pretended I was sick. I acted confused and scared, and I coughed and even managed to make myself cry. But my parents didn't know what I was really crying about. For days they let me stay in bed while *they* got all the attention. There were more gifts from the neighbors; more food. And the policeman came back—stood right over the bed where I pretended to be sick. But I wasn't going to tell them anything. The woman had said they'd get into trouble if I told. Of course I believed this. The police would come and get them, and they'd be put away for years and years. The police could even come for Warren and me. We'd all be in terrible trouble."

She turned again to face me. "But all these years, I've always wondered—why me? Why'd they choose to take *me* back, but keep Warren? They'd told me again and again I could have been their daughter. What was so wrong to make them return me to my old life?"

As she spoke these final questions, my mother started to cry. I looked up, too stunned to answer or move. Her grief was muffled, but her eyes were full and wet; she blinked, and the tears broke in streaks on her face.

"I never got to tell my Warren good-bye," she said.

Delicately I took the empty glass from her hand. Comforting her should have been simple, but her story had made it immense, impossible. As I walked to the kitchen, the details solidified: bright peach juice in my mouth, the pipe smoke in my lungs, her apple-tree melody in my ears. It all seemed real now. So much information, so many secrets, after years and years. How had she guarded this story so carefully? Why hadn't she confessed, during some drunken or vulnerable moment, to John, to Dolores, to Alice or me?

I leaned against the sink. The faces of the missing stared from the surrounding walls. Out the window, I could see the corner of the porch where Otis had stacked the candy bars; and beyond, our parked truck, its windows spattered with juice.

I heard her composing herself, clearing her throat, taking deep breaths. Then she began again. "Sometimes at school, when I was feeling sad or wanted attention, I thought about telling other kids. I wasn't very popular; they made fun of my poor-girl clothes and the lispy way I talked. Maybe if I'd told them my story, I could make them scared of me. Maybe they'd gossip or put me in some place of fascination. But I never did. I never told a soul. I worried what might happen to the man and the woman, and especially to Warren."

"Secrets," I said.

"Oh, I can keep a good secret. Even when it's a lonely secret. Even when it's utterly my own."

After a pause, she began again. "I used to look for them everywhere. Whenever I got the chance—Lord, how I'd search and search. Playgrounds. Out the windows when I'd ride in my parents' car. In the hay fields or the pastures when we'd drive past farms. Maybe the department store in town, where maybe they'd be shopping, buying more candy.

"I just wanted to see them again," she said. "I just wanted my Warren."

I thought of Moynihan's; the girl stealing candy bars from the gleaming counter. The sweet-cherry flavor sending her back, transporting her from the father and his beatings to the warm, shrouded basement with the temporary brother, the new Mom and Pop.

And for the first time since returning home, I longed to call Alice, to tell her everything. The Cherry Mash, the missions, and Otis. The captives in the basement and their kind, vigilant captors. When we were kids, my sister and I could never guess our mother's thoughts as she hunched over the pictures at the table: her brown officer's uniform, the lost look in her eyes, her scissors and pushpins and cellophane tape. Now, at last, I thought I knew.

I took the pitcher of tea from the refrigerator, refilled the glass, and stood in the kitchen doorway. "This is nothing like your old story," I softly said. "The one you told to scare us."

"No. And I'm so sorry. I've kept it hidden from you, and I'm sorry."

I could feel her eyes on me, but wasn't yet prepared to stare back. On the inner rim of her glass, clumped along the crescents of ice, were soft brown granules of undissolved tea. For years, my mother had preferred instant tea, still buying it when no one else did. I'd always loved the tiny, inexplicable quirks like these, all the oddities that made my mother. I'd always thought I knew them so well.

Finally, I said, "You never stopped searching, did you? For years, you went back to Sterling to find them."

"Oh, I'd forget sometimes. Life would get crazy, with my job, and paying bills, and keeping up the house. Especially after your father died, when it was just me and you and Alice."

"But the memories would return."

"Yes. Out of the blue, something would happen. Every now and then I'd see a girl or boy on the sidewalk or in the grocery store . . . every now and then, in the newspapers or on TV, some kid would turn up missing. And I'd wonder. I'd feel that deep-down secret part of me slipping out. I'd step outside my usual life, and I'd get to drinking or acting crazy. I'd go through microfilm at the library, old papers from Wichita or Salina or Topeka, looking for faces, anything that resembled my story. I'm not even sure I knew what I wanted to find."

"And then there was Evan," I said.

"Yes. And he looked so much like Warren. A little ghost of him."

"Evan made you think the man and the woman might still be out there, taking kids, the way they'd taken you."

"Maybe. Or no, not really. I don't really know what I thought. By that time I must have known they'd gotten too old to keep that up, and probably they'd eventually—you know, *passed on*."

"But not him," said my mother. "I knew he had to be out there, somewhere. My Warren."

Her voice had gone raspy from fatigue, from the rough, disordered pain she'd poured forth with it. I realized we'd forgotten her meds. I opened the designated cabinet, gathering the prescription bottles—all week I'd been memorizing Dr. Kaufman's elaborate schedule—and then I went back to join her. It seemed the room's air had altered, each sound brittle and precise; stepping across the floor, simply returning to my space on the couch, felt like stepping on snakes. I handed her each pill from each bottle. Then the glass of instant tea. The television news had begun; although the sound was off and picture still wasn't fixed, I could see the familiar hawk-nosed evening anchor, the headlines hovering in boldface over his shoulder.

I waited until she'd finished the meds. "You've never told anyone, have you? At least not this much of it."

"Not until recently."

"You've told Dolores?"

"Some to Dolores, yes." She looked down at her hands, hesitating, considering her next words. Then she said, "And I told everything—all of it—to Otis."

And now, once again, the boy. *Her* boy. At some point during my mother's narrative—her overwhelming, zigzagging reverie—I'd almost forgotten the origin of our discussion.

"Otis?"

"Yes."

"But why tell your secrets to *him*?"

She spoke slowly, as though I were a child and couldn't understand. "Isn't it obvious? He might be the link."

She smiled, nodding. At that moment, I began to understand. *The link.* Once again I felt the sting of jealousy—a dark, lingering force inside me, its shadows clinging in the way nostalgia does, or love. But this was jealousy, not love, and it prevented me from hugging my mother or wrapping an arm around her slumped shoulders or her pale, warm neck. It prevented me from taking her hand, the skin rough and flaking, the side effects of so many meds.

"You barely know him," I said. "It doesn't make sense. You barely—"

"But it *does* make sense. Oh, Scott. I've been searching so long. All the other boys you found in that box downstairs—all little ghosts of Warren. And now I think I've found the right one."

The secret box, the secret scrapbooks. Little girls like my mother. Boys like Warren. *Tomorrow,* I thought, *I will finally call Alice.*

"Do you really think I only started this again when those girls found Henry's body? It's been weeks now. When the Barradale boy first disappeared, when his parents first reported him gone—oh Lord, his sweet, haunted face in the papers—

it all came back again. Another ghost, haunting me. And I started going out in the pickup. Long drives, searching. Sometimes just random roads. Sometimes back to Sterling again, after so much time away. And then, one morning after a long thunderstorm, I was driving down the foggy street, and there he was."

I stretched back against the cushions. I closed my eyes and remembered his smell: dirty hair and sweat-soiled clothes; tomatoes and hot, criminal breath. I could easily picture my mother, that day behind the steering wheel, grinning and slapping the seat, daring the boy to come along for a ride. From the way she'd behaved earlier, in the truck, I could guess everything she'd said and done, that day she'd found him.

"His raggedy shirt and his funny marked-up shoes. His little name tag. Poor thing. He told me about his rotten life. He hates his school. His stepfather is horrible to him. But he doesn't know his real father, doesn't know his grandfather.

"I started thinking, making the connections in my head. So much like Warren. Just think—maybe Warren grew up, had a little boy of his own. Maybe that boy was Otis's father. It was possible! And a few days later, I went back to Sterling and found him again. Pretty soon, little by little, I started telling him all the things that happened to me.

"Scott, don't you see? Maybe he's just another ghost, sent here to haunt me. But I think it's so much more than that. I believe—and I really do believe this—that he's the grandson of my Warren."

"And you've told him this."

"Yes. And he'll help us find out what really happened back then. Help us find that boy who started it all."

After this, we were silent for a long time. The sleeping pill had settled into my bones, but I was hungry and tried to fight it. Neither of us had eaten since lunch. I headed to the kitchen to cobble together another meal. I searched for anything remotely nutritious from her cupboards of dime-store foods, settling finally on our recent favorite, the cheese ravioli from cans, heated quickly on the stove then spooned into twin blue bowls.

When I returned, she was sitting before the TV. On screen was the nightly, post-newscast Missing Children report. The featured photo was a little black girl, thick glasses, her hair secured with barrettes. My mother took the spoon and bowl from me, then aimed the remote for volume. The girl was Barbara Wishman. She wore a purple sweater and a blouse with lace at the neck. Even through the TV's damaged picture, she already looked lost. A baritone voice said, "Have you seen . . . Barbara?" Under the photo scrolled her name, along with the date she had disappeared (July 14), the place (Springfield, Missouri), and a scatter of statistics. In fifteen seconds we learned her 4'8" height, her 90-pound weight, her age 12; we learned, too, other vitals that did nothing to describe the realness of her, the Barbara-ness of her, this child who no doubt had played hopscotch in her yard, had laughed at silly knock-knock jokes, had eaten canned cheese ravioli and ridden the morning bus to pencil her answers on math tests.

"Poor thing," my mother said.

Together, in the quiet darkness, we began to eat.

SIX

ACROSS TOWN, FRIDAY nights, the local high school hosted its autumn football games. My mother's house stood just five streets south of the ragged field—"the grid-iron," she called it—and at seven o'clock we opened the living-room window, pausing to listen in the dark. The hum and hiss of loudspeakers . . . the cheerleaders' rhyming screams . . . the flustered, bickering fans. The noise carried effortlessly through Haven. "One of these nights we're going to walk over there and watch the game," my mother said.

We both seemed to sense this would never happen. In the days after Otis, she'd fallen alarmingly sick, much weaker than before. Her migraines intensified; her lips were cracked and sore; she couldn't hold down food. She decided to postpone her appointment with Dr. Kaufman. Although she wanted to try another drive through Sterling and its surrounding towns, I suggested we wait until her health improved.

I wanted so badly to believe her story. And yet, so many inconsistencies; so many red flags. I asked her question after random question, longing for more particulars, and she answered as best she could. Did they ever let you outside? *(No.)* What food did they give you? *(Lots of meat, with mashed potatoes on the side. Lots of ice cream and candy.)* Didn't you miss Dan? *(Just a little bit.)* What kind of car did they drive? *(Not exactly sure—it was a sky-blue color, something like an old Imperial.)*

During these days she spent long hours on the couch, stone-hard naps with hardly any movement. Nearly every time she slept, I'd shut myself in her bedroom, sit on the bed, and pull the glass pipe from my travel bag. Lately the grains of meth, together with the dry air of the house, had given me nosebleeds, so I was using the pipe. Smoking had always felt dirtier than snorting, more criminal, but the dirty smoke in my lungs and brain seemed to effectively cap the recent events, her confusing flood of revelations.

And then the meth was gone. I'd smuggled so much onto the bus home, but my supply had swiftly diminished. By now

I'd spent all the cash I'd brought from New York. We could barely scrape by on her monthly social security and disability checks. Still, I told myself, I had to coerce Gavin into sending more, to support me a few more days.

Sometimes, before my mother fell asleep, she'd find a little money in her purse, and send me off to Hutchinson for errands. She wanted ginger ale or strawberry milkshakes; she wanted peculiar things like tube socks or hunting magazines. Driving back from the errands, I'd search the roads for repair shops; scan the horizon for peach orchards. I kept remembering her voice: "Let's *get* him." Remembering her eyes' discolored glint, warning of wrong in her head. Most of all, remembering their fingers, intertwined.

And so, that Friday night, I returned with her milkshake, her cigarettes, her chewable antacids and vitamins. I told her not to budge from the couch. I took the opposite end and lifted her feet into my lap.

The Haven football game had paused for its halftime show: a marching band, with its military snares, its brass trumpets and trombones. As we listened, my mother sipped noisily through her straw, her lips dotted pink with foam. Earlier I'd dampened a hand towel and pressed it to her forehead, but the towel had gone warm, and now, as the band finished its final Sousa march, she peeled it away and tossed it to the floor. I saw the pain each movement caused her. Eventually, she pulled the pillow from under her head and drew it over her face.

"Good night," I whispered. She whispered something back, but the pillow muffled her voice.

And then, a distant echo of whistles: the third quarter, set to begin. *V-I-C-T-O-R-Y, that's the Wildcats' battle cry.* I imagined the cheerleaders' gold boots; their ribbons and war-painted faces; their pom-pons, blue-and-gold shreds thrust at the spotlit sky. Yes, it would be good to take my mother to a game. It crushed me to see her so sick. Gently I put my hands on her feet and began to rub. From practice I'd learned the precise amount of pressure. Her heels were solid pink as school erasers; the prednisone gave her rashes and edema, but I was careful and slow.

Outside, the Wildcats chanted their battle cry, louder, then softer; then silent. My mother kept the pillow over her face. We remained this way, quietly listening, my hands kneading her feet until she fell asleep.

By now, the everyday aspects of the house were unnerving me. What I wanted most were bright colors: all the antiques and darkly varnished pieces of furniture, even the towels and oven mitts, were various shades of brown. More than anything I hated her refrigerator, a chugging, dented brown beast with a side compartment that yielded its own ice. It always seemed to wait until I neared to drop its interior tray; teasingly, the crescents would hit the bucket with a soft, crowded clunk.

That night, on opening the refrigerator to disable the ice maker, I saw what might have been the *real* reason for my mother's poor appetite. Just yesterday, on my Hutchinson errand, I'd bought two pints of ice cream—black walnut for her, rocky road for me—but now they were gone.

I stood in the cold light, thinking of possible jokes, ways to pester her about the missing ice cream, when I heard a noise on the porch. I went to the window, dreading another visit from Otis. Instead it was Dolores who stood before the front door. She'd restyled her hair; she wore an oversize yellow John Deere jacket that seemed too warm for the weather. Before she could knock and wake my mother, I rushed to let her inside.

At once I smelled the bourbon. I sensed the heat of her temper. For the past week, I'd been avoiding all contact with her, switching the telephone ringer off, even erasing her answering-machine messages. I hadn't informed my mother about her calls, and now I scrambled for an adequate excuse, a way to persuade Dolores to head back home. "She's fast asleep," I said.

Under the heavy jacket, she wore one of my mother's old sweatshirts. She wore tight jeans and her husband's polished cowboy boots. "You've been avoiding me," she said, "and I don't like it at all."

With a nudge, I moved her back to the porch, shutting the door behind us. "Let's go walk around for a while."

"But I miss your mom. We haven't talked in days."

"Really, she's very sick. We should let her sleep."

Dolores leaned against the porch rail, a post my mother had looted, years ago, from an abandoned roadside barn. She glared at me over her glasses and crossed her arms at the chest. The streetlamps revealed the clumps of mascara on her lashes; the mismatched hoops in her ears. She couldn't quite focus on my face, and I saw how drunk she truly was.

"You're ignoring my calls!" she said. "I *know* how sick she's gotten . . . you can't just swoop in from the city and expect to shut me out of your lives!"

All the volume and drama made me uneasy. Attempting to bridle her anger, I hooked a chivalrous arm in hers and began leading her down the block. Her grip was strong, her arm feverishly warm. The wind shuddered the trees with a suspicious hiss; dead leaves had collected along the sidewalk cracks. We walked down the shadowy streets toward the football field, its bleachers still brightened by the towering, humming lights. With each minute I felt her temper receding.

Halfway to the field, Dolores stopped and pointed. "There's the phantom house. That's what your mom and I call it." She was pointing to a yard with scrubby forsythia bushes; a gravel drive with a rusting Lincoln Continental. Behind the bushes stood a house with dark-curtained windows, the address 426 on its door.

"Some batty old lady lives inside. But we've never seen her—not once! We call her the phantom lady. She's got a fat son-in-law with a jacked-up truck and a triple gun rack in his back window. He comes once a week to deliver groceries and take the junk mail out of her mailbox. Your mom and I chatted with him once, and man, what a lunatic."

I stepped farther into the yard. The place was comparable to any other small-town spookhouse: its peeling paint, its broken shutters, its unassuming steel-gray mailbox beside the tiny luminous doorbell. When I saw the box, I knew what I had to do. Silently I repeated the *four two six*, memorizing it for later. Tonight, after sidetracking Dolores, I planned to dial Gavin's familiar number. I'd send as much money as I could, instructing him where to mail the package, and I'd watch the house until it arrived.

We reached the chain-link fence that surrounded the field. The game had just finished—disheveled players loaded into the buses, shiny blue helmets under their arms—but I couldn't gauge whether Haven had won or lost.

"I know something's wrong," Dolores said. "It's like I told you, isn't it? Something's wrong in her head."

The lights glittered on her glasses and exposed the blond dog hairs on her shirt. She turned to lean against the fence, away from the field, until her face was only a shadow. "I know you'll say it's none of my business," she said, "but I found your sister's work number and gave her a call. I couldn't wait any longer. Told her to come home as soon as she could."

"You didn't."

"And that's not all. I was so concerned, I called Kaufman, too. And you know what his secretary said? Your mom hasn't been showing up for her appointments."

"That's not true. I drove her there myself, just last week."

"Have you been keeping her from treatments?"

"What? Of course not." This had to be some miscommunication, some mistake. Where had my mother hidden, these recent Fridays, when I'd left her at Kaufman's office? Where, after entering the gleaming glass doors, as I'd waited in the truck? Had she ducked into a restroom, had she slipped out the side exit?

"You're making matters worse," Dolores said. Her face twisted into a sour, reproachful sneer. "You have no right to just *swoop in*—"

"I have every right to 'swoop in.' I'm the son, remember?"

"Away in New York for years doing God knows what, and all the while I've been right here."

I paused to stare at her. It was unclear what she meant by *God knows what*, but I didn't like it. Still, I tried to avoid arguing; from experience, I knew the unpredictable, wounding venom that the meth often injected into a fight, a venom that Dolores wasn't fit to see or hear. I looked beyond the bleachers and exiting cars, the edge of the field, past the houses and shifting silhouettes of trees. Finally, Dolores said, "Your mother's told me all about the drugs."

"Oh, please."

"I can tell you aren't sleeping. And how skinny you've gotten."

"You don't know anything."

"I know plenty. I warned Alice so she won't be shocked when she sees you. Your eyes've gone all crazy, and you're nothing but bones! You're an addict."

Finally I glared at her. "And you're a drunk. A drunk, nosy bitch."

She smiled, her face flushed with triumph. Immediately, I regretted my words. Her expression brought me back to a photograph I'd seen, the post-recovery card she'd sent, long ago, to her family and friends. That same self-satisfied smile. I CONQUERED IT, her card had read. I remembered my mother posting it to the refrigerator door. Dolores's card had stayed there for months until Alice, home for a visit and visibly disgusted, took it down.

"I didn't really mean that," I said.

"No, it's true," she said through the smile. "I'm a bitch, and I always have been. Your mom never would've wanted to know me if I wasn't. It's exactly because I'm such a bitch that your mom sticks with me, and it's why she's my best friend in this whole damn world. I'm the only bitch who's willing to help, and to stay right by her side. I wouldn't have it any other way."

As she spoke, I felt my resentment dissolve. She was right: she loved my mother fiercely. Proud, well-meaning, fustily tipsy Dolores. Where would my mother be without her help? All summer long, she alone had witnessed the evidence I'd only recently seen: my mother's aberrant gestures and manners and mistakes, each intimate clue across the house. Stacks of unfinished basement projects . . . the oily ooze of post-chemo vomit on the bathtub rim . . . new bruises on her arms and the backs of her calves. Perhaps, I thought now, after this day so unsettled by Otis and my mother's stories, what I needed was a confidant, an understanding ear. Until I could convince Alice to return home, Dolores was likely all I had.

"I'm sorry," I said again. "But you're wrong about the doctor. Honestly. I drove her there last Friday."

Dolores shook her head. In an oddly graceful motion, with her back still squared against the fence, she slid slowly down to the grass, the crisp brown scatter of leaves. She sat, hugged her knees with her arms, and said, "Then I'm sorry, too. What in the world's gotten into her? I've been worried sick."

By now, the last cars were steering from the football parking lot, and we watched the scarlet pairs of taillights diverge across the dimming streets. It was time to confess to Dolores. "Earlier tonight," I began, "she told me everything. All about the disappearance. A long flood of memories, back from when she was a girl."

"Oh, I can't bear to hear any more of that. I thought maybe she'd give that up once she got you home."

"At first I thought like you. I thought it was mostly for attention, or that this obsession with that Henry boy had made her—you know, like you'd told me before—that Henry made her pretend things had happened to her, too."

She reached for my hand, pulling me down to where she sat on the rough, rusting grass. "Don't tell me she's figured out some way to make you *believe*."

"After today, I think I've changed my mind. Her stories don't sound false anymore. She's been giving all these new specifics, things I don't think she'd make up. And I found her photographs. This coloring book she's been talking about. Everything, just the way she said. When I looked through it, there was a picture colored fancier than the others. At the bottom, it was signed 'Warren.'"

"You don't think she could've done that herself?"

"All these things about the basement and the farm . . . the sweet old man and woman. It all seems *real*."

I waited for her advice. Instead, Dolores seemed puzzled, her face pinched in an almost comic grimace. "You're confusing me. I know all about this Warren—she's told me about him. But what's this other mess you're talking about?"

"Their kidnappers. The people who took them, then treated them so nice. Like they were their own children."

"This isn't making sense. Tell me everything she told you."

Possibly, in relating her story to Dolores, my mother had condensed the events. I was concerned about breaking her fragile trust, and wondered whether I should continue. Yet I couldn't stop now. I recounted the parts I could remember. The dinosaurs and peaches; the scratchy, scratchy records; the ring with its blue and purple jewels. The woman and her hymns; the man in his gloves and mask. Board games and candy and Warren, Warren, Warren. Each time I'd pause to recall some feature or slant, Dolores would quietly urge me forward: a validating nod; a fluttery, sparrow's-wing motion with her hand.

When I'd finished, she said, "I think she's toying with us. Oh, your naughty, crazy mother!"

"I'm not so sure."

"Well, this certainly isn't the story she told me."

"It's not?"

"Far from it. Some things are similar, but mostly it's real different."

Dolores began relating the version she'd heard. I listened, filled with fluster and awe, nearly gasping at each discrepancy. Even her introduction differed from mine: instead of my mother and Dan in the local playground, her version starred only Donna, alone, in her parents' backyard. Instead of the sky-blue Imperial, the car in the version she'd told Dolores was a sinister, coal-black Cadillac with clouded windows and crumpled newspapers on the seats. And there was no old woman at all—just a terrible man, violent and mean, who'd kidnapped Donna and the boy named Warren.

"He locked them up somewhere," Dolores said. "Some kind of cellar under the earth, in the cold. I remember her saying they could hear animals above them, cattle or horses, clomping past. The light was weak in the cellar, but they could see shelves and shelves of Mason jars, all filled with peaches. And the awful man barely gave them food—just things like moldering bread and canned vegetables, still cold and in the can. And he was terrible to them. He'd scare them and kick them and punch them in the ribs. Your mom says she was certain the man would kill them both. He carried a long jump rope for tying them up, and a knife with a serrated edge and red tape on its handle. He'd sneak out from the cellar shadows at all the worst unexpected times to scare the life out of them. And she wasn't too specific on this, but sometimes he'd start touching them where he shouldn't be touching. If they'd cry, they'd get a beating with his rope."

"No," I said. "That's not the same story at all."

"Remember now, I don't believe a word of this nonsense. I mean, why would she keep this hidden 'til now?"

"I keep thinking that, too."

"But your mother—she insists it's the truth. She claims that she and this Warren boy eventually ran away. They escaped from the horrible man, but they got lost. Lost in some town they didn't know, and scared he'd find them again. They stole a bunch of those cherry candy bars from a department store, and then they went hiding in the woods until they were saved."

Shamefully, I turned my head to the emptied field. Across the yards of chalked and trampled grass, I saw random, fluttering shadows; and then, cocking my head toward the towering lights, saw a brood of autumn-night bats, ecstatically feeding, their bristly bodies plunging and circuiting through the lush insect fog.

Dolores squinted up at the bats, then back at me. "I don't know what to think anymore," I said. I tried focusing on the girl in her story, this fresh, distressing portrayal of my mother, but, like Dolores had warned, the story seemed more madness than truth.

"Your mom needs to pick one of those tales and stick herself to it," said Dolores. "She should know better than to tell crazy fibs to the both of us."

But which were fibs, I wanted to ask, and which weren't? My mother had been so specific when she'd confessed to me. Yet so much of this alternate tale—the jump rope and the spoiled bread, or the serrated knife, its red handle in the kidnapper's fist—seemed equally credible. What confused me were the coincidences in each story. *Peaches. Cherry candy bars.* Even something from her long-ago tale about her father's punishment: *Hiding in the woods.* Now I could sense my mother's threads of memory, intertwining and knotting, both the distant past and recent. All her uncertain truths and partial, changeable lies.

Initially, I'd planned to ask Dolores about Otis. She still hadn't mentioned him, and I wondered if my mother had chosen to keep the boy her thrilling secret. But I felt too exhausted to ask anything else. Soon I'd have to fix the missed appointments with Kaufman; I'd prepare the house for Alice. And soon I would confront my mother.

For now, I sat soundlessly with Dolores, our shoulders against the fence, heads still lifted toward the lights and the swirling, ravenous bats. When we stood to leave, we brushed the muddied bits of leaves from our jeans. "Back home," she said. Her boots thudded on the cobblestone, but my shoes made no sound at all. During the hour we'd been outside, the air had chilled considerably. Soon, the start of pheasant season; soon, Thanksgiving and the winter solstice.

After walking half a block, we turned to watch the bats a final time. Now, on the football field, we saw an even stranger sight: beneath the goal post's wide yellow Y, two children were playing tag. We couldn't see their faces; only their mittens and hooded jackets, their home-team blues and golds. They moved like tiny, unsupervised ghosts, raising their blue-wool hands, innocently touching, then fleeing, then circling back to touch again.

"Well, would you look at that," Dolores said.

I nodded, relieved that she could see them too. "But where are their parents?" I wondered aloud. "Don't they know how easily they could lose their kids?"

Dolores hooked her arm in mine, pulling me back toward home. "You sound just like your mother," she said.

In the deepest hour of night a noise roused me from sleep. It was a thick, reverberant thud, some unseen corner of the house. I sat up in bed, leaning forward to listen, knowing it wasn't a dream.

I waited for the noise again, but heard nothing. In the dark, I remembered those nights when Alice and I would wake to our mother stumbling drunkenly through the rooms. It was never the stubbing of toes or crashing of glass that woke us, but rather her subtle shuffling of feet: the right the left, the right the left. Wide-eyed, barely breathing, the two of us lay waiting for the moment when the shuffling stopped and we could sleep again.

Now there was no noise, but instead the worrisome absence of it, swelling. "Mom," I whispered to the half-open door. "You awake?"

Earlier, after Dolores had left, I'd arranged my mother's blankets and sat cross-legged in the rocking chair beside the couch. Her breathing had been ragged; she didn't seem to be dreaming. As I watched her sleep, I'd analyzed the stories she'd told, all their quirks and contradictions. I felt utterly powerless: it seemed nothing could prove or disprove her, and nothing could save her health.

Presently, there was only the purr of the heater, the swaying leaves against the window. As I moved, my socks slashed the carpeted floor, hurrying toward the sound.

When I saw the empty couch, I called to her again. And then, from the kitchen, came the smell: rich and sweet, like soaked cake.

Before I could hit the kitchen light, I saw her. My mother lay motionless on the floor. Within the clock's 4:27 glimmer, her arm bent awkwardly from her gown, white and bare like the neck of a swan. She had fallen beside the refrigerator. In the fall, she'd swiped a hand against the door, strewing the photographs and vegetable magnets. She'd toppled the garbage pail, scattering the trash. I rushed to sweep the pictures aside and shake her shoulder. Loudly I cleared my throat, hoping to rouse her—the cough edgy and alto from my mouth, like a child's—and I breathed the smell of blood.

She had struck her head on the fridge, the sharp corner of its handle. The door was slightly ajar, and when I tried to wake her, it opened wider, spilling light across her face. Radiant in its yellow was the back of her head, its queerly clumped hair. A wound had opened above her ear. The blood pulsed slowly along her forehead, across her brow, to the rug.

Her skin had gone pale. Her hand in mine was wet and soft, like a sponge. Carefully I jostled her, tapped her face with two fingers, repeating *Mom, Mom* until it billowed into one unbroken word. I stroked her hair, smoothing it from the blood, pressing my shirtsleeve against the wound.

At last she fluttered back to me. She turned her head, light fixing in her green eyes. The motion seemed to cause her pain, but she muttered, fraily, "Are you my pretty little pigeon?"

"Try and get up now," I said. "You have to get up. We need a doctor for this." The blood had smeared my sleeve and knuckles. I was striving to keep calm, but my panic was palpable, a current between us.

"Don't call the doctor. Did I only hit my head?"

"We are *going* to the *doctor*."

I helped her sit, helped her steady the dizziness, and then guided her to the living-room couch. She lifted her hand to her head, but I lowered it back to her lap. The blood was more conspicuous now, three streams glistening down her cheek in a red capital M.

She was cold. I ran to find her coat: my panicked ankles; my blurred, sleeping-pill vision. As I moved, I shouted to her: "This time, you've got to listen. That cut on your head is *big* and it's *deep* and what you need right now is a *doctor* and some *stitches*."

In a bathroom drawer, beside John's aftershave, I found a gauze bandage and a wrap for the wound. Briefly she protested again—*First just let me clean up that mess*—but she stopped when I touched the bandage to her head. To save the awkwardness of seeing her bare body, I left her nightgown on, and eased her into sweatpants and a shirt. I wrapped the gauze tighter, but the blood still beat from her scalp.

She put her arm around my shoulders, and we stepped into the night. Sometime during my sleep it had rained; the moon shone white through the sodden leaves, smearing her face like milk. Our movements were wobbly as we labored into the truck. On the late-night oldies radio, a chorus of guitars faded in, faded out; the female deejay tried to soothe us but failed, her voice more fire than air.

In my panic, I couldn't remember our favorite off-road route. I followed the signs that loomed in the Ford's headlights, each paved road gleaming its slick ribbon. "Hope you don't mind me driving so fast," I said, desperate to make her better. I hated myself for letting this happen, hated the way I'd yelled when she protested the hospital. As I sped toward Hutchinson, I silently swore I'd atone for the rot in my heart. I'd build an arsenal of good deeds, correcting all my stupid moves, my mistakes. I swore I would make her proud.

Somewhere on those roads, just once, she sleepily spoke. She remembered how she'd woken, feeling sick and knowing something wasn't right; she'd stumbled dizzy to the kitchen for a drink. I sighed and shook my head—*oh, Mom*—and asked if she remembered more.

But she fell quiet again. I thought she'd drifted back toward sleep. When I glanced across the seat, I saw her eyes had closed; the gauze around her head showed its dark grume of blood. Then suddenly, a corner of her mouth rose in an abstracted grin. In a weak, childish voice, she said, "What's wrong—you never saw a little girl bleed before?"

I stared, uncertain how to answer, and eventually gave a nervous laugh. Lately she'd uttered so many strange, unsolvable sentences. Some note in her voice wasn't right: a disharmony, as though she weren't addressing me but some other, invisible soul.

In fact, I told her, I *had* seen her bleed. I reminded her that many times, years ago, she'd been quite clumsy when washing dishes. Her butterfingers often slipped on knives, and the steam-hot water split her wineglasses, her bourbon glasses, into lethal shards. I remembered sobbing at the sight of her blood. I remembered trembling beside the sink as she bandaged herself, the suds foaming white to pink.

"And what's this 'pretty little pigeon'?" I asked. "Is that what you used to call me?"

No answer. In the hush, I moved my hand to calm her, reaching across the space where Otis had sat only hours before. But once again, she'd slipped into sleep. The wrap on her head had loosened. Her chest and arms were frigid, as though she'd been cradling a doll made of ice. I looked back to the road, the sky softening steadily to gray, and I drove.

A nurse wheeled my mother to a third-floor room, while I stayed in the eerily empty lobby, my pulse still thudding, to finish the hospital forms. It was just past seven a.m. Around me, the emergency room shone a bright, pervasive white, much worse than the brown tones at home. The white reception desk . . . white lamps and vacant armchairs . . . the white-bloused, perfumed intern.

From previous visits, I recognized floor #3 as the cancer ward. I'd illogically assumed that Kaufman would arrive, suave and savior-like, exuding his graces and recommendations. Instead there was a slouching, listless doctor with rolled-up sleeves and a loosened lime-green tie. He scratched a patch of flaking skin on his arm and asked if I would kindly sit and wait, reassuring me that she would be "in good hands." Someone would come for me soon. "I'll stay right here," I said.

I chose the largest waiting-room chair, its fabric rasping my skin like burlap, and scribbled more answers on the forms. My mother's insurance and disability benefits; a rough schedule of her trips to Dr. Kaufman; the dosages of Decadron and other pills I could only describe by colors or shapes. On the room's central table were one fake plant, one real, and a stack of outdated magazines: *Field and Stream*, *Highlights for Children*. The covers wore labels addressed to various names. Leland Armstrong, c/o Hutchinson Hospital; Laurie Hildebrand, HH 3rd Floor. I wondered where all these Lelands and Lauries were now. Whether they remained in Hutchinson or Haven or Sterling, healed at last; whether they lay cold in Rayl's Hill cemetery.

Twice I'd been to similar ERs for my own scares (the first time, for a fractured right wrist; and just last January, a misguided coronary fear after a five-day binge of crystal meth). I'd also visited my mother here, this same hospital, during various shifts of chemo. But tonight I had no Alice, Dolores, or John to accompany me. Tonight I sat alone in the rank and wrinkled shirt I'd worn to bed, the blood smears on my sleeves and jeans. I looked down and noticed, with wide, humiliated eyes, my mother's conspicuous pink slippers on my feet.

After completing the forms, I rode the elevator to the main lobby. The gift shop had opened for the morning: the stuffed monkeys and pandas and penguins; the dainty porcelain birds with secret keys to tinkle their melodies. In the adjoining aisles were fellow early-morning visitors, anonymous family and friends, all bleary and smelling of soap, all in varying degrees of shell shock. I felt their eyes on me. I stopped at the revolving racks of get-well cards, but couldn't decide which one she'd prefer. With the last six dollars in my pocket, I bought my favorite three: white horses congregating in a meadow; a trampoline with laughing children; an army of cartoon viruses, torpedoed by pill-shaped ships. WISHING YOU

WELL! HERE'S HOPING YOU BOUNCE BACK SOON. ZAP THOSE GERMS AND GET BACK TO WORK!

It was time to call Alice. At the lobby's bank of pay phones, I dialed with a queasy anxiety, but she didn't answer the early-morning ring. On the message, I told her nothing about Otis. I ignored the worsening details of my mother's illness, or Dolores's insistence that the cancer had spread to her brain. I told her only about the accident, and asked her to come as soon as she could.

When I returned to the third floor, the doctor explained I could go to her room. "Kaufman should arrive shortly." He checked his watch, and again scratched the spot on his arm. "Around noontime, I'd guess."

When I saw her asleep in the hospital bed, I looked to the floor to compose my breathing. The tiles were white and flecked with lemon-yellow. The room even smelled of lemons. When I looked back to the bed, I saw they'd dressed her in a baby-blue robe. An IV streamed slowly into the veins in her arm; another, into the surgical port in her chest. She no longer wore the gauze bandage (*Wish they would've let us keep it*, I imagined her saying, *it could've been our memento*), and the doctors had shaved a section from her hair. The cut on her head was purple, crossed with waxy black stitches.

I leaned closer to see the wound. Soon, I knew, she'd flaunt it proudly. She'd ask us to blow on it, to touch it with cold crescents of ice. I imagined myself doing just as she asked.

On a television bolted to the wall, a weatherman was pointing to a storm's splotched colors on his radar screen, but outside my mother's window, the sky was white and clear, its sun lifting bloated and red. I placed the get-well cards, unsigned, with no envelopes, on the bedside table, propping them against her untouched glass of water. Then I sat beside her in the white vinyl chair.

Eventually, she opened her eyes. The sedatives had slowed her movements, and her throat struggled to form the words. "Kaufman," she said.

"He'll be here later. Everything's okay."

She was trying to swallow. I dipped a straw into the glass of water, and lifted it to her lips so she could drink.

"You'll finally get to meet him," she said.

"Finally, yes."

"And they'll let me go home, right?"

I shook my head no, and instantly saw the panic in her eyes. "I think you'll have to stay a few days. A few more tests. They need to find out why—"

"Then listen." She was louder now, emphatic and fully awake. "You have to do something for me. Right away."

I sat closer on the bed. "An errand? Anything you want."

"Just please don't be mad at me."

"You're being silly."

"Promise you won't."

Yes, I promised, although I couldn't understand her distress. She shifted slightly to hold my hand, bumping the IV; through the gown's blue sleeve I saw the taped cotton where the needle had jabbed, a bruise already spreading beneath it.

"You have to go back home," she said. "Right away. Downstairs to the basement. Oh, please don't be mad."

"I'm not mad! I won't be mad! Just say what you want me to do."

"The basement. My little storage room. Please, take care of everything."

In my haste after the accident, I'd forgotten to lock the front door. When I stepped inside the house, I noticed the lingering odor, and thought once again of cake (red velvet cake, one of Alice's specialties, dark chocolate batter and blood-red food coloring).

I entered the sunlit kitchen, the scene of her fall. The floor was littered with garbage and random newspaper faces. The spray of blood formed an alarming arc, almost a complete circle, across the kitchen, as though someone had sliced the tip of their tongue and, openmouthed, spun a perfect pirouette.

A sob was rising damply in my throat, and, to fight it, I began to clean. She kept the paper towels above the sink on an antique red-maple rolling pin. I knelt and covered the blood with the towels. I dabbed the spattered newspaper clippings; the refrigerator magnets, tiny carrot and pepper and onion. Amid the trash was the straw from her earlier milkshake, and beside it, a silver key from a tin of sardines, one of many frivolous gifts I'd bought my mother on an errand. The sardines were her favorite, the kind soaked in mustard (on special, I remembered, at eighty-nine cents a tin), and when she'd briefly forgotten her sickness and ate them, the look on her face—dipping a saltine cracker, then lifting the flaked, coppery flesh to her mouth—had been sheer satisfaction.

But I could clean the mess later. For now, there was the basement; the dark, cobwebbed storage room. Gradually, with a rising dread, I'd begun to understand the reason for her errand.

I kicked the embarrassing pink slippers from my feet, then opened the basement door and descended. I pulled the chain of an overhead lamp to brighten more shadows. I pulled the lamp in the adjoining bathroom. I added some sun by drawing the miniature curtains that looked out, weed-level, to the garden.

A spoor of dried mud led to the little black door. The key was still in the lock. With a push, I opened the door on the room.

The boy was sitting on a foldout cot she had prepared for him. "Hey," he said, and put his hand to the scarf around his neck. "I know I'm supposed to keep this over my mouth, but she didn't make it tight enough."

"Oh, my God," I said.

He wore the tennis shoes from the day we'd found him on the road. He wore the sweatshirt with the overstretched sleeves. The shirt beneath was different—only a white T-shirt now, its neck frayed—but the name tag remained, the tiny OTIS at the bottom and the empty, nameless space above.

His eyelashes were damp, the lids heavy with recent sleep. His hair seemed curlier, messier. Above the ear was a spot where the barber had slipped. His face still showed the bored, bullying sneer; I wanted to push or punch him, to retaliate for our last contact. But I could only stand and breathe his smell. It was a humid, almost appealing smell, a sweet, adolescent sweat. With horror, I noticed his feet were tied with rope. His hands, dark with grime and balled in his lap, were secured with the silver KSIR prison handcuffs she'd always kept in the briefcase below her bed.

Beside the boy, at the foot of the cot, sat one of her quilted, bead-eyed rabbits. Scattered wrappers from the Cherry Mash bars, an empty carton of milk, and the missing pints of ice cream: black walnut, rocky road.

"She finally told you I was here," Otis said.

"How long?"

"Don't know. Two days, I guess. Just about three." He kicked his roped feet from the edge of the cot, bumping the empty rocky road to the corner of the room. "She'll get mad if you knock me around," he said.

A numbness began spreading along my knees and thighs; to keep from folding to the floor, I leaned against the doorframe. "She's in the hospital," I told him. "She fell. During the night, she fell and hit her head."

His eyes widened; his mouth opened like a trap. I could see the worry he felt was genuine. He asked would she be okay, and I told him no. I told him she was dying. She was incredibly sick, she was dying, and I didn't know how much longer she had. "That's the reason I left New York," I said. "I came back home to help her die."

I'd never said these words before. I spoke them with a detached, clinical quiet, and I knew the news hurt him. It thrilled me to see him hurt. I despised his sweating teenager's body, now thrust like a thorn into our house.

He said he needed the bathroom. I let him shuffle to the cramped sewing-room toilet. *Please don't be mad* kept repeating in my head as I waited outside the door.

When finished, he flushed, stood beside me, and let me lead him back to the room. He propped her homemade rabbit on his lap. He complained of hunger, but I told him that would have to wait. I had to think for a while. I had to return to her hospital bed.

"Aren't you going to make my rope any tighter?" he asked. "Aren't you going to put the gag back on?"

"No," I told him. "Not now."

But I found myself stepping closer to the cot. I found my hands moving over the ropes; over the knotted scarf, the paisley purple fabric she'd originally intended for one of the cancer newsletter's patients but had used for him, this boy disappeared from a trailer park in a lonely town, this boy she'd taken. With surprise, I saw the gag was not just fabric but a fully finished product: she'd withdrawn a completed scarf for this sole purpose. In my trembling hands, I saw the intricate stitches she'd used, stitches made special for another dying woman like herself, the scarf she'd now used for him. I pulled the gag tighter around his mouth. I knotted it twice behind his neck. I pushed him, gagged and bound, back to the sweat-salty cot.

He tried to speak again, but I couldn't understand. I shut the lights and left him in the dark. Before locking the store-room door, before racing back upstairs, I took one last look at him. The burn and bore of his eyes on me. The calculated whimper from the back of his throat.

SEVEN

SOMETIMES IT SEEMED that everything she'd recently done—all her fraudulence, the hoaxes on the mourning families and friends, and now, her capture of Otis—was shameful, monstrous, vile. And I felt equally guilty; I'd allowed it all to happen. For three cold days, as I drove from the hospital to home and back again, I searched for possible solutions and remedies. Nothing, it seemed, could lull the racket in my head. The only relief was dreaming of worse. Sins more wicked than ours. Somewhere, in some shadowy bedroom of a leaf-strewn town, a father bolts the door to a child's room, then steps closer to the bed. In a neighbor's garden lurks a weed with a fumy, blade-petaled flower, its poison choking the red roses. Somewhere a car is crashing; a phone is ringing in the center of night. The spider waits poised in the slipper. The bird swoops headlong into glass it thought was farther air. The strangler envisions a neighborhood of throats. The head finds the noose; the foot kicks the chair.

After discovering Otis, I began to feel the onset of withdrawal. The sudden rashes and nausea; the paranoia and delirious bouts of grief. Nearly two years had passed since I'd endured even a three-day stretch without meth, and I wasn't sure I could fight the symptoms. So, one evening, in desperation, I coasted through Hutchinson's Carey Park, hoping to find a dealer.

I'd learned the secrets of the park one summer during my teens (*close to Otis's age,* I told myself). Carey was more than just a duck pond and playground; more than a greenly sloping golf course. It was a park, I learned, where dealers sometimes sold acid and pot and cocaine. It was a park where men—older, fleshy men with downcast eyes and delusory wedding rings on their fingers—often cruised for sex. I never told my mother or my friends about these newfound secrets. Instead, I began driving there late at night. I'd linger in the gray moonlight, on the weed-snarled riverbank marred with desire lines and boot tracks, waiting for someone to approach or proposition me. Often, I stood alone in the woods that bordered the park, earphones in my ears and Walkman turned low as I watched the spangle and glide of the river, as I waited for anyone else to show. I'd feel feverish with the simple, primal fact of what could happen. Many times I'd chicken out. But there were other, rare nights when I accepted their offers, when I got high on whatever they gave me, when I fumbled through my first turns with anonymous sex. Those nights, in the shadows of the Carey Park trees, felt like waking from a lifetime of sleep.

But presently, it appeared that all the dealing had stopped. I saw three cars parked near the entrance to the woods, but my broken body wanted drugs, not sex, and I didn't stop to investigate.

My only hope was Gavin. Finally, I telephoned him and, during a prolonged, pleading exchange, tried persuading him to send half a gram to the mailbox down the block. I promised he'd receive a money order by the end of next week. Pitifully, I used my mother's accident to full advantage: recalling his squeamishness, I lingered on the blood, the stitches, the needles and curls of IV tubing.

Eventually, Gavin surrendered and agreed. Now all I could do was attend to my mother, to the boy in the basement, until the blessed package arrived.

During those first days, I brought Otis water, cookies, and sandwiches of dill pickles and processed cheese. I led him to the bathroom, then back to the cot. When I'd loosen the knots on the gag, he'd ask about my mother's condition; he'd want to know what events she'd planned for him next. "Please don't speak to me yet," I said, avoiding his dark eyes. As I secured the cuffs and retied the knots, I'd think of Henry or Evan; of my mother's stories of Warren; even of myself, back then, a thin and grimy boy.

I'd been watching the news reports, waiting for some bulletin about Otis. Surely someone was hunting for him. Parents, teachers, friends. Somewhere he had a bedroom; somewhere a bed, its pillows and sheets still tangled. In a solemn schoolroom, his vacant seat was waiting. The principal, the janitors, the surviving students; everyone peeked into the room as they passed, one last glimpse at that empty space, *the missing boy.*

In my mounting paranoia, I worried Otis would escape and run to the police. I feared they'd arrest my mother or discover my addiction. And I feared the boy himself, remembering his fists, the scrape of his nails.

I have to release him, I kept telling myself. And yet, for some remote reason, it seemed he didn't want to be free.

In the hospital room, I tried confronting my mother, but Dolores made this impossible. She became a loyal, ceaselessly chatting fixture, lounging in the chair beside the window. On the first morning, she'd brought a rowdy assortment of carnations, a tin of black licorice, and a silver Mylar balloon, now floating its cliché above the bed. She'd even snuck a pair of strawberry milkshakes past the nurses. When my mother couldn't finish, Dolores drank them both herself.

This same crisp, cloudless morning, I met Doctor Kaufman. He walked into my mother's hospital room as though he owned it, looking older and wiser than I'd expected.

"Ta da," my mother said when he appeared. He had wrinkled, impossibly long hands that protruded from his coat sleeves; rust-colored skin from too many tans; a frizz of white hair above each ear. His look was more professor than doctor. Only his eyes were lively, pale blue behind his glasses. He watched me warily, as though he knew, as Dolores already knew, the jittery escalation of my withdrawal.

"Well, ain't this a party," said Dolores. "All of us, here at last."

Kaufman gave a faint, fake chuckle. "Weather's starting to get wintry out there," he said; the inevitable, unnerving small talk. I wanted to push him away, push Dolores away, to confront my mother with all the questions in my head. *How did you muster the strength to steal him? Did someone see your crime? Won't his parents call the police? How can I sleep with that boy, below me, cuffed and tied in that room?*

For fifteen minutes, the three of them spoke more about the weather, about the doctor's children. I nodded and nodded, waiting to catch my mother's eye, but soon Dolores suggested it was time to let the patient sleep. Maybe the ladies could wait in the room, while the men (for once she called me *man*, not *boy*) could go to the lobby.

Dr. Kaufman led me to the receptionist's desk, now newly decorated for autumn. The cellophane butterscotch candies; the husks of Indian corn and striped, warted gourds; the scarecrows and pilgrim dolls. He planted his elbow beside the cheap tableaux and coughed into his fist. "So we should speak," he said. "I assume you haven't been apprised of the full situation here."

Behind the desk, the receptionist inched her chair toward the opposite wall, pretending not to listen. "If you'd just give me the specifics," I said.

"Around the beginning of July, I knew we couldn't do anything else. I told Donna this. She was supposed to let you know."

"I thought she was still going in for treatments. I've been driving to your office most Fridays."

He tilted his head, a deep, abstracted distance in his gaze. From down the hall, I heard the ping of an elevator's door; the rhythm of a wetly thrapping mop. Around us, the hospital was being cleaned, but the clean had a stagnant smell, as though the same water had been used for every mop, every sponge.

And then he began his over-rehearsed speech. It was the sort of speech I'd remember all my life: the one that every son, every daughter, waits to someday hear. He began by generalizing all the familiar facts. The non-Hodgkin's lymphoma or, specifically, the diffuse, large B-cell lymphoma. For years, her doctors had kept it localized; for years, different rounds of therapy had stopped it from spreading. There were the brief remissions, the shimmers and rallies. But afterward, unfailingly, the sudden returns.

"All this is familiar to me," I said. "Tell me the things I don't know."

The doctor nodded. He went back to the blistering days of July, when the tests showed no improvement from her most recent round of chemo. Kaufman tried injections with what he called "a biological agent." All this had further depleted her immune system. The bruises big as palm prints; the lumps and infections and sores. They agreed to stop the injections until her opportunistic infections ceased. In the meantime, her lymphoma spread. It no longer centralized in her nodes or the spot in her stomach. Now it moved through the blood, to the kidneys and liver. And maybe, after last night, he said, the spinal cord or brain.

"I remember she asked me how long she had," he said. "I suppose the time comes when you have to be frank."

"And what did you say?"

"Christmastime, if we were lucky."

I thought of Christmas, only weeks away. As always, my mother planned to center tiny electric candles in the windows, to spray flecks of aerosol snow on the glass. She would construct her artificial tree in the corner beside the couch. As I pictured this, I saw its clumped green pieces on the basement shelf, so close beside the pair of binders with the photos of missing children; just above the cot and the hungry, hand-cuffed boy.

Christmas. I tried imagining her face as he'd spoken the appointed date. Surely she wouldn't accept this conclusion. There were still so many things to do. Still Christmas dolls to make. Still, the rabbits and Santas and holiday elves; the handmade scarves to mail in carefully wrapped boxes. And soon afterward, the spring planting; her summer garden.

But I had heard Kaufman's words. I had listened well and absorbed his news. For a doctor—the lifesaving doctor she'd told me so much about—the man was unexpectedly imperfect; his breath was oniony and there were scalp flakes on his collar. I sensed the currents of power in him, yet I knew that in his imperfection, he could only save my mother so many times.

He posted his hand on my shoulder as though to steady me. "It's good of you to come back here. I know she doesn't want to worry you, or Alice."

"Alice checked out of this a long time ago," I said. "She got tired of hearing 'your mother's sick, she's going to die.' And then a remission. And then another, and another. For Alice, after the first few years, it was like crying wolf."

"Alice needs to know," he said, "that we're no longer crying wolf."

Kaufman sighed, and I could sense his impatience, his need to finish the discussion. Then he said, "We'll need to keep your mother here awhile. But after she goes home, would you like a hospice caregiver to start visiting? What about a pastor—would she appreciate that?"

I doubted I could endure a stranger in our house, some woman tarnished with countless previous deaths, bathing my mother with a sponge in the clawfoot tub. I certainly couldn't handle any starch-collared apostle, speaking in sentences peppered with angels and Christ. But "Yes" was what I told Kaufman. "Yes, those would be nice."

He reached across the desk and found a pen. "I forgot to bring my cards. But please—whenever you need me." He wrote his telephone number on the back of a medication pamphlet. On its cover were the words *If you're often tired and want to GET BACK INTO LIFE.* In the photograph, the powdered, genially grinning women looked nothing like my mother.

———

In the days before Alice arrived, I kept my reluctant promise and tended to Otis. Otherwise, I stayed away from home, from *him*, as much as possible. I patrolled the "phantom house" down the block, shuffling cautiously past to check for my package in its mailbox. But there was nothing; not yet. I tried calling Gavin for an update, but he wouldn't answer his phone.

Sometimes, driving to the hospital, I'd make impulsive detours to Sterling or Partridge or beyond. I discovered the Barradales had removed Henry's tire swing from its tree. I discovered that, indeed, among the list of names on my mother's rest-stop wall, was a single, looming WARREN.

But I heard nothing about a newly missing boy. Not in Sterling, not anywhere else. No alerts on the pickup's reedy radio; no thumbtacked posters with the boy's leering face.

Gradually, the withdrawal was getting worse, making me tremble and grind my teeth, making me pace the hospital floor like a cat in its cage. One evening in particular, Dolores visibly recoiled from me; I could see her concern in the creases around her forehead and eyes. Once again she refused to leave the bedside chair, even when I proposed relieving her by taking one of her nightly shifts.

"Absolutely not," she said. "Seems what you need is a good strong sleep."

Beside us, my mother looked peaceful in her blue robe, the blankets pulled to her chin. "Don't you need to tidy up at home?" I asked. "Go shopping, feed the dog?"

"This is what matters to me now."

"Then maybe just leave us alone a few minutes. Go out and smoke in the smoking lobby. Go get some coffee."

She waited with a suspicious frown, stood from the chair, and walked to the door. I listened until her footsteps stopped and I heard the hallway's pinging elevator. Then I sat on my mother's bed and said, "I know you're awake."

She opened one eye partway, then both of them together. "Thought I was fooling you."

"I can't go through with this Otis business."

"Please don't set him free."

"Alice will be here in two days. What the hell am I supposed to do then?"

"I'm just getting to know him." She was whispering now, as though one of the ceaselessly lurking nurses might hear. "And he likes me. I just *know* he's the connection to Warren."

"But you *don't* know that. How could you know that?"

"I told you—he looks so much like him. It all makes sense to me. I can just feel it."

"Wouldn't he tell you if his grandfather's name was Warren?"

"Oh, but the poor thing doesn't even know. He's never met his grandfather. Remember, his father abandoned him—"

"All of this is scaring me," I told her. "It seems like you're just believing what you want to believe, and you've let this go too far."

"Please," she repeated, and then fell silent. Somewhere from the room came the full, fat tick of a clock, a sound I hadn't noticed before. On the table, Dolores had left an empty can of Dr Pepper, its straw smudged dark red with lipstick; beside it, she'd started a crossword puzzle with ink an even darker red. I also saw my mother's pink-handled hairbrush;

tangled in its bristles, together with the real hairs, were the coarse, dark fibers from the wig.

"Just tell me why you're doing this."

"He can help me find that part of my past. Maybe we can help him find his father. Then, maybe, his grandfather."

This was all I managed to glean from her. Already we could hear Dolores's boots in the hall. "Hush," my mother said. Then, in a final whisper: "Please just take care of him 'til they let me out of this place." She truly believed, I saw now, that this was so: very soon she'd return home, get back to her life.

When Dolores entered, she helped me arrange the blankets and sheets. Once again, my mother feigned sleep, stirring slightly, lifting her head as we fluffed the pillow. Her movements were defenseless and weak, but at the last moment, so subtle only I could see, she winked.

Outside, the sky had gone dark. Dolores reached to turn down the lights. We stood together at the window, listening as, in the bed behind our shoulders, my mother fell back into sleep. Through the darkness, beyond the poplar trees, lay the distant, serrate neon of town. Above the skyline were so many stars. I had never seen these stars while living in New York. I wanted to question Dolores—*are there really so many? Is all this fatigue just tricking my eyes?*—but I kept silent. Perhaps if we watched long enough, just watched and mutely waited, we would see an actual falling star. We'd watch it rip across the night sky, and then, like hushing a secret, seal it shut again. Suddenly I had the feeling that we could reach through the window and jostle all those stars, sweep them crisply away, and some presence would be waiting, some solace within all that black. Not God, I thought, but something private, comforting, meant solely for us.

The black door with its chipped and buckled paint . . . the ancient key still shining in the lock . . . the dirty plate from which he'd eaten last night's dinner. I stepped to the door, a new tray of food in my hands, and held my breath.

Some mornings at the hospital, Dolores had been slipping me intermittent dollar bills; with the money, I found myself bringing Otis the things he requested. More pickles and lunchmeat and cheese; both mayonnaise and mustard; a thick, bland loaf of Wonder bread. Cans of grape soda. Chocolate-chip cookies, which I carried to the basement in my mother's pink piglet cookie jar.

As before, he sat waiting on the cot; it seemed he hadn't budged since I'd last left. "I wondered where you'd gone," he said when I clicked the light. "I'm starving to death down here." The room seemed smaller, cramped as a coffin, with his sour, suffocating smell in the air. He'd managed again to loosen the gag, but a rosy welt now stretched across his cheeks.

I presented the tray to him. "There's more upstairs if you want." I stood back against the door, careful not to distract him, and noticed how skilled he'd gotten at working his hands around the awkwardly clacking cuffs. He opened the jar of cookies and ate with a crude, doglike force. He guzzled one can of soda, then opened a second. Watching him was like deciphering some visual code: he'd devour a cookie, bite the sandwich, and swallow the grape soda, then start it all again.

I saw the odd, slightly misshapen arc of his skull; once again I thought of Henry.

Previously, I'd kept silent, simply standing back, the way a zookeeper stands back, until he finished. But today—after so many long hours in the truck, after so much frustration in the room with Dolores—I wanted to talk. I began with a story about the piglet cookie jar he'd placed beside the cot. I'd gone junk-store shopping with my mother, I told him, on the day she'd bought it. We'd found an old hay barn turned curio shop, some small town outside of Wichita. I remembered her opening the lid, seeing the price tag, and rolling her eyes. Soon she began bargaining with the dealer: she mentioned the preposterous prices of cancer drugs, and then uncovered her scarf, exposing her thinning hair. Like so many times before, this scheme had ultimately worked. She got the piglet for half its price.

"Then she's been sick for a long time," he said.

"Yes."

"She's been searching a long time, too. For my grandfather. Right?"

"But we don't really know it's your grandfather, do we?"

"She says it's true. So maybe it is."

His voice seemed more indifferent than convincing. It seemed he might be deceiving my mother: toying with her frailties, charming her with his strange teenage acquiescence. But I wasn't sure why. I watched him put down the sandwich, fingerprinting the slices of bread. He took another draw from the soda can. His hair had cowlicks from sleep; a pimple had swollen on his cheekbone; even his T-shirt showed handprints of grime.

"Aren't you going to take off that name tag?" I asked.

"She said I should keep wearing it. That I should stay Otis."

I could hear her singsong voice, commanding him with these words. How long had she sat with him, whispering and plotting, perhaps even while I slept upstairs? What rules had she imposed, what secrets and fictions had they discussed?

"It's about time we got rid of those silly cuffs and ropes and drove you back home," I said. "But first, you and I need to talk."

Otis sneered at the suggestion. Already he'd grown so accustomed to defying me, so skilled at his antagonism. Now, I saw, he was only refining the gestures. He finished the final chocolate-chip cookie; I watched his thin, veiny wrists and the muscles in his jaw. And then he spoke: in an effeminate, stereotyped lisp, he repeated my last sentence, mocking me.

It had been years, even decades, since I'd been taunted like this: high school, back when I was Otis's age, the stabbing shouts of *freak* and *queer* at my crazy thrift-store shirts and circus-colored hair. Now, part of me wanted to push him to the floor, to put my hands around his neck. A separate, weaker part wanted to pull him close, to examine the color of his eyes, his pimples, his unshaven scruff. I figured he was a failure at school. Very likely the punch line to jokes: a sneak-looker at others' tests; a shadow on the sidelines; a target during Bombardment or pin guard. Maybe he'd tried for the track team, not speedy enough, not strong, lasting four miserable practices before quitting. Or high-school marching band, rehearsing in his room on a borrowed trumpet, spit ricocheting in the valves, wrangling every broken note.

I decided to try again. "I don't want to be your enemy," I said.

"Fine. So you're not."

"But I want to know some things. She won't tell me, so I'm going to ask you. First I want to know how she got herself back to Sterling. How she managed to drag you all the way here."

"She didn't drag me. I came on my own."

"Why?"

"It's what she wanted. I guess it's what both of us wanted. It could make you believe her. And she thought it would help her remember things."

Now he was repeating my mother's words verbatim, his mouth careful on each grape-stained syllable. Again I pictured their joined hands, the alliance of their bodies in the truck. It seemed she'd known this boy for weeks, even months; as though I, not Otis, had become the impostor. "You act like you're in this together," I said. "Like you're playing a joke. But you're not fooling me."

He thumbed the tab on another soda can, tipped it to his head with his handcuffed hands, and drank. A satisfied, comical sigh. Oh yes, he seemed to say, we *are* fooling you. Maybe he wasn't a failure at school after all, I thought. Maybe he was smart, just as I had been smart. I could easily imagine him excelling at some sideline craft: maybe Woodshop, maybe Drawing 101. His hands furiously sketching, the charcoaled pages filling with faces of dead, decaying animals; red-chambered hearts dripping lovelorn blood.

"She's got it stuck in her head that she knows who you are," I said.

"What's wrong with that?"

"Don't you understand? If she's wrong—if you keep up this charade—it's going to devastate her. I won't let that happen, not now. I want her to be comfortable and happy. So we should end this before it begins."

I said these words slowly, forcefully, and as I spoke I could sense a shift in him, a softening. He put the empty plate on the floor, sliding it beneath the cot with his foot. Then he said in an uneasy voice, "But it's already begun."

I looked at his OTIS name tag. *The connection to Warren,* she'd said. Somehow he'd come back to her: some recent night she'd waited until the sleeping pills had numbed me, and then she'd heard his footsteps on the porch, struggling to the door to let him inside.

"Tell the truth," I said. "Tell me who you really are."

He wiped his mouth with his sleeve, pausing as he debated an answer. I smelled his sweat and the mustard on his breath and his rusty, oily hair. I listened closely to the world above us, but heard no owl or sparrow song, no passing tires on the street. Only the bustle of leaves; the inevitable sighs from the creases of the house. Otis brought his knees to his chest and hugged them. His breaths were finer, more stable than mine.

As he stared, I realized there were various possible answers, and he was reviewing them all, silently testing the consequences. My heart beat hard against my ribs. I feared he'd answer *Warren.* I feared he'd answer *Evan* or *Henry* or maybe, worst of all, *Scott.*

Instead, he spoke in an even softer voice: "I'm only Otis. Grandson of that kidnapped boy. I'm whoever she wants me to be."

We stared without speaking. His expression didn't change. Gradually, I began to comprehend his intention, his desperate sincerity. His voice and the look in his eyes reminded me of Dolores, that recent night at the football field, when she'd confessed her devotion and love. Perhaps, I thought, this boy wasn't trying to deceive my mother at all. Perhaps he'd seen the illness, the dementia, and now only wanted, as I wanted, to keep her happy. True, I hadn't yet learned his real name or age or history; I didn't know why he'd arrived here, why he'd accepted this ratty, rickety cot or offered his hands for the silver prison cuffs. But steadily, over the recent days, he'd revealed glimmers of compassion, some empathy that pushed for my mother's recovery or, if not that, at least her happiness. *Whoever she wants me to be.* I saw that it no longer mattered whether Otis believed my mother's theories and claims. For whatever inscrutable, delinquent reason, he simply wanted to provide that link, to be the descendant to her mystery.

He needed the bathroom, and I let him go on his own. Upon returning, he shifted to make room on the cot, indicating the space beside him with a hammer-like thump of his cuffed hands. I stepped away from the door and took the seat. With our bodies so close, Otis seemed edgy, fidgeting like someone newly famous. To cut the awkwardness, I said, "It gets so quiet down here, doesn't it?"

"Yeah. And you know what I've been thinking? If you add one letter to Haven, it becomes HAVEN'T. I guess that sorta sums this place up."

I looked at him, at his tilted, softly arrogant grin, aligned with the red welt from the gag. And I began to laugh. His joke had come randomly, perfectly timed; I wanted to keep composure but couldn't help myself.

When I stopped laughing, he reached for the can of soda and offered me its last swallow. Then he asked, "Is she going to get better? When's she coming back home?"

I told him I wasn't sure. The situation, I said, was much worse than we'd initially believed. But these were only the first of his questions, his surprisingly earnest worries. He asked further about her disease. He asked if there had been many visitors; if she had good books to read, or a decent TV. So I answered him as clearly as I could. I began a recent history of my mother, winnowing the basics from the details I held private and dear, but soon discovered she'd already revealed many things to him: the styles and demeanors of her doctors; her lymph nodes and the spot in her stomach; all the recurrences and remissions. She'd even told Otis the names of her pills. As we spoke, the concern grew increasingly evident in his eyes. I saw how much he'd warmed to her; somehow, with her dirty-mouthed jokes, her stuffed rabbits and pints of rocky road, she had won him.

"She wants me to keep you here. She wants me to promise you'll be here when they send her home."

"Then I should stay."

"But there's a problem. My sister will be here in a couple of days."

He couldn't offer a solution. I'd begun to sense his weariness, and when he yawned, I yawned in response: I needed sleep as well. When I stood from the cot, I expected him to ask to leave the basement room, to graduate to a more comfortable bed upstairs, but he stayed silent, as though obeying, still, my mother's orders.

"Just tell me one more thing," I said before I left. "One final thing."

"Okay."

"I know she's told you about Warren. This boy she thinks might be your grandfather."

"Yes."

"I want to know what else she told you. About the kidnapping, or the people who did it. Did she mention the sweet old couple? Or was it just one mean, horrible man? What exactly did she say?"

Otis paused to remember, one finger absently rattling the tiny chain between his cuffs. Then he shook his head. "She didn't talk much about any of that. Maybe she couldn't remember that part."

"That's strange. She said she'd told you everything, every little bit of her story."

"I don't think so. She only talked about Warren, and how much she liked him. How special he was to her."

I watched him closely for a wavering, some subtle flinch, but it seemed he was telling the truth. Eventually, I collected the remains of his dinner. Yes, it was time we both got some sleep. "She'll need me at the hospital early," I said. "I'll come back down before I leave." He didn't ask about the wrap around his mouth, and I didn't bother retying it. I shut the black door but left it unlocked. From my wristwatch, I discovered I'd been downstairs, this shadowy basement room with the boy, for over an hour. I felt strangely, pleasantly blue, as though I'd been visiting a ghost.

In a dream, I walked through an orchard with my mother and Otis. I took her left hand, and he took her right. Above us were the interlocking trees, their branches thick with perfect peaches. We pulled our shirtfronts forward, making baskets for the fruit. The sun was white with crackling gold spokes. The peaches were bursting at their seams. When we'd picked all we wanted, she selected one and began to eat. Otis ate, and I ate. Then the three of us stretched out against the grass, lying silent with our hands linked, reaching our fingers up, up, a thirty-petaled flower.

When I woke and saw her beside me, she wasn't the same healthy woman as in the dream. There were fresh bandages on her head, darker bruises on her arms. She opened her eyes and said, "I need to be home for Otis," as though she'd been dreaming him, too.

"Shh," I said, so Dolores couldn't hear. Then, in a whisper: "He misses you. You'll see him soon."

Under the blankets and tubes, she'd been turning increasingly stubborn. I'd brought the lower plate of teeth, two of her wigs, and her tortoiseshell glasses. She wouldn't bother with any of these. She picked at her scar and wouldn't listen to nurses. She begged them to please, please send her home.

Kaufman had confirmed a new tumor on her spine. When he told my mother this, her expression didn't change at all. It wasn't yet safe, he said, to restart another round of treatments; her body still held too many unhealed infections. He'd called the local hospice but hadn't decided on a date when she could leave. For the first time, he prescribed morphine: limited doses at first, which clouded the pain but let her speak and occasionally stay awake.

Dolores's flowers wilted and dropped their petals. No one brought replacements. The balloon placidly collapsed; its air escaped, allowing me to read its opposite face. BEE WELL, it said. What I'd thought were polka dots were actually bright bumblebees. The dead balloon didn't seem right for the room, and after helping my mother to the toilet, I snuck it to the trash.

The nurses provided a wheelchair; its right wheel sometimes stuck with a caustic squeak. At first, we used it only to wheel her to the restroom. She'd lean over the toilet while Dolores or I hugged her close for support. The shining porcelain burnished each detail: her stained blue gown; her stubbly head without scarf or wig; her mouth without its lower plate.

Eventually she saw the chair as her chance to smoke, to turn her face from all that blinding white. "Take me out to the fresh air," she told me.

The withdrawal made me sluggish and weak, but I helped her out of bed and into the seat. At last I could speak to her, separate from Dolores. "This strange man is kidnapping me," she told the receptionist as I wheeled her down the hall.

Once outside, I maneuvered through the parking lot, over the browned grass, between the parked cars. The day had turned windy. Ahead, at the lot's northeast edge, was a slope thick with sandburs, where we could watch the setting sun. Grunting, I pushed her to the top. I locked the wheels of the chair, sat on the ground beside her, and watched her fumble with the forbidden cigarette pack. The smoke that lifted from her mouth was blue, almost beautiful, and, for the first time in days, she tried to smile.

I'd waited so long to speak to her in private, but now that we were alone, I didn't know where to start. I wanted to admit discovering she hadn't actually kidnapped the boy; I knew they'd been toying with me, and now it was time to stop. But then I considered her fragility and Kaufman's warnings of dementia—I pictured her bleeding on the kitchen floor—and instead of arguing, I kept my voice calm. "I've been making peace with him," I said. "He told me he wants to stay where he is."

"Don't you think he might be the one?"

I rested my head against one of the slim rubber wheels. "Oh, Mom. What will happen if he's not? If ultimately this isn't what you're searching for?"

"But this has to be right—like I was destined to find the link. I've waited so long for Warren. Even if I never see him again, I just want to know what happened back then."

We looked to the west, where the sun, a wet and scalding red, had slipped beneath a ripple of clouds. I thought about the mother I'd dreamt in yesterday's dream: her strong legs marching through the orchard sand; her mouth against the dripping peach; her chin thrust forward to clear the juice from her blouse.

"I know you told a completely different story to Dolores," I said.

"But I haven't told her about Otis at all."

"I don't mean Otis. I'm talking about the old story. Your disappearance."

I expected her defiance, or even an admission of guilt. Yet she only sat and stared, the gown's edges fluttering in the breeze, distracted as though I'd accused her of some wicked, unsolvable crime. She blew another stream of smoke; I watched it float and dissipate. In the distance were the final reddened leaves, blurring against the bloodied horizon. When I looked back, she'd turned toward the hospital, watching it with composed but cheerless resignation.

At that moment I understood what I should do. Alice would arrive tomorrow. I would tell her to visit the hospital alone, without Dolores, without me. Alice would ask our mother what really happened when she disappeared. She would get her own version of the story.

My mother coughed and noisily sighed. "If I'm not going to make it," she said, "will you keep trying for me? Trying to find Warren?"

Not going to make it. A distinct tension had set into her muscles, and I reached to touch her arm. She relaxed a little, but the temperature and texture of her skin almost shocked me: so cold and pale and hard, like a plaster cast without signatures.

I wanted to see her laugh again, so I tried our little nicknames. "Tired," I said.

I hoped she would answer "Wired." Instead, she looked at me and simply nodded: yes, she was so, so tired.

"You know what I've been wanting?" she asked.

"Tell me."

"An old book about Hansel and Gretel. Really old, with lots of old pictures. If you have the time, I want you to try and find one of those books, and bring it back and read to me."

Lately, in her boredom, in the white cotton of her bed, she'd been dreaming such random, childlike dreams. Now I knew she'd been thinking of that little boy and girl, banished to the cold, crowded forest, yet another version of her Warren and her Donna. She wanted me to lead her there, to help her find the trail of crumbs so stale even the lice-laden birds wouldn't eat. We could call out to them together, Hansel, Gretel, two nimble voices threading through the green shadows, the obsidian trees.

"Will you find a book like that for me?" she asked.

"Of course I will. I'll look through the antique stores, and I'll find you one."

"It would mean a lot. Especially now."

She was still staring toward the hospital. I felt the breath catch in my throat, but I had to stay strong for her. For many minutes I could only watch the back of her head: the dry, peeling skin; the wide patch shaved in her thinning hair; the stitches fixed on her wound like the blue-black footprint of a bird.

Now I looked to the hospital, too. I lifted my arm and, with a finger, began counting off each third-floor window. "Five, six, and that one is seven. That one's your room."

"No, it's not," she said. "My room's back in Haven."

She had finished smoking, and she folded her hands in her lap. I still felt the disturbance from touching her arm, and, as I stood and looked down, even her hands seemed wrong. The skin around the nails, the knuckles, even the webs between the fingers had been rubbed raw, now flaked and peeling and rough.

It was almost time for the hospital's dinner rounds. Time to steer her back to the room. Gradually, above us, the parking lot's lights flickered on; higher up, the poplar leaves shivered in the wind. "Listen to that," she said. "What a sound. Like a tinkling sound."

Her voice had gone so quiet I could hardly hear it. "Tinkling like glass," I said.

"Like a thousand chandeliers."

We descended the slope, moving back to the pavement. Ahead were the sliding-glass entrance, the gift shop, and elevator, the long third-floor hall with its dialysis lab and solemnly shut doors. Soon I would pair with Dolores to once again hoist her onto the bed; soon I'd take my place in the chair.

We passed the final parked car in the lot, and I pushed her up the carpeted ramp. The automatic doors swept open to let us enter. Suddenly, once again before the doors could close, came the song of wind in the trees. "Stop," my mother said, so I stopped the chair. Held in place, both she and I, tricking the doors from trapping us inside. We listened. We heard the sound again. The wind like glass, the trees and leaves like glass: *a thousand chandeliers.*

EIGHT

ALICE DROVE HOME on the morning of the winter's first snowstorm. As planned, she called me from the hospital. She was standing at the telephones in the lobby, she said, steeling herself before entering our mother's room. She needed to ask once again what specific information I wanted her to gather. "Well, *anything*," I said. "Whatever she remembers about her disappearance. The kidnappers . . . the boy named Warren. Any details you can get."

I sat alone in the spindle-back rocker with a cup of hot tea, the blanket pulled to my chin, watching the snow through frosted windows. Wind rattled the gutters, the backyard trellis of withered ivy. The bare trees, black against the sky, were like veins of ink in ice. This was the storm that the weatherman, from the TV bolted above my mother's hospital bed, had so theatrically foretold. It was the storm she'd imagined falling over Rayl's Hill cemetery and Henry's grave, over all the discarded, undiscovered souls.

For the first time in days, I was high. Earlier that morning, I'd tromped through the drifts of white until I reached the phantom house. I'd opened the little gray mailbox and found, finally and blessedly, the package Gavin had promised. Then I'd sprinted home, the wind rouging my face, my footprints dusting at once with swirling snow. I'd run to the bedroom, and I'd fetched the straw and the glass pipe.

After the drug hit my blood, it was time to deliver Otis his breakfast: leftover pepperoni-and-mushroom from Pizza Haven, bought with yesterday's ten-dollar bill from Dolores. Although I suggested he come upstairs—a comfortable pillow and bed, maybe a nice hot bath in the clawfoot tub—he ultimately declined. He was worried about Alice's visit. Finally, we compromised: I unlocked the black door, insisting he roam the entire basement as he pleased. "But I'm not supposed to come upstairs, right?" he asked. "That's one of the rules, right?"

His voice had gone shrill with doubt or despair. It no longer mattered, I said; there were no more rules. He placed the half-eaten slice of pizza back in its white cardboard box, turned his face toward the dirty floor beneath the cot. I left him, returning to my mother's bedroom to smoke more meth.

Presently, I sat at the window, rocking. For days, I'd anticipated feeling livelier, more confident, on the drug. There was certainly the speediness—the grinding teeth, the familiar red surge in my pulse—yet the speed was insufficient, only superficial, and deep inside I felt no different than before.

When Alice arrived, I rose to greet her at the door. Her shoulders and hair were tufted with silver. She wore a fur-collared coat with glittering black buttons, yellow earmuffs, and matching wool mittens: items, I knew, from the little vintage store she owned, four hours away in Lawrence. She bent to shuck her snowy boots. "Those roads are nothing but ice! I almost skidded into the ditch." She went to the couch and, with a sigh, collapsed on its middle cushion.

I helped her with the rest of her things. Alice had brought Bones, her Siamese cat; when she lifted the hinged door of his carrier, he began his mute, slinking inspection of the room. She'd also brought two overnight cases, a small one for makeup and a large one for clothes, and a tin crammed with what she called "that great peanut brittle recipe." (In truth, I couldn't remember Alice ever making peanut brittle—that was our mother's holiday specialty, not hers—but when she spoke the words, *peanut brittle*, I imagined Otis stealing the tin, the crunches from his mouth like a complicated argument.)

I'd expected a brief, tense-shouldered embrace, but Alice seemed snug on the couch, and touching felt too awkward.

"You look different," she said. "And you're still biting your nails."

I looked down at them. "Habits."

She reported that the first drive from Lawrence, and then the second from the hospital to home, had been equally awful. Her car had a faulty heater. Her stereo stopped working, and "nothing but country bumpkins" polluted the radio. The snow had piled thick in the ditches, and yet she'd seen a surprising amount of roadkill. Skunk and possum, a young deer with stunted antlers, and even, oddly, an armadillo.

Less than three weeks ago, on one of our missions, my mother and I had seen an armadillo, too. I didn't tell Alice this. "Snowplows will be out by tonight," I said. "The roads should be fine before we head back to the hospital."

She removed the earmuffs and mittens and, as though only noticing now, said, "It's way too dark in here. Why were you sitting in the dark?" She looked to the TV: the power was on, but the screen showed only raspy gray static. "That screwy thing? Let's put on music instead."

She turned on the lamps, switched off the TV, and crossed to the stereo at the side of the room. I worried she'd discover one of the secret cassette tapes, perhaps our blundered interview with Mr. Wyler. But Alice merely pushed the play button, and through the speakers came the sounds of the most recent tape our mother had played: big-band music, antique trumpets and trombones, so saccharine and drowsy. The song had no lyrics, but instantly I recalled my mother's story, all the scratchy vinyl records, the basement melodies she'd shared with Warren.

The music relaxed us slightly. I breathed and recognized our mother's scent, as though she'd just breezed through the room. Alice sat again; with the earmuffs removed, I could tell she'd stopped reddening her hair (at John's funeral, it had been artificially darker than mine, but now was the same dull red, dulling with age). She seemed uneasy and unsure, and instead of starting the inevitable discussion, she again mentioned the weather, the troubles with her car; finally, she began a story about the regular customers at her shop.

I had to interrupt. "Tell me everything she told you," I said.

On the stereo, the orchestra played its final notes, leaving a silence between songs. We could hear the phone lines creaking outside, the ice snapping against the glass. The music began again; lured by the serenade of horns, Bones reentered the room and leaped into Alice's lap.

"Her story was preposterous," she said. "It's nothing like the ones she told you or Dolores. Honestly, I don't believe a word of it. It's like her brain's gone backwards. And the morphine can't be helping."

"Just tell me."

Alice leaned back on the couch and took a deep breath. "Okay. Here it is."

When our mother was very young, her parents were like strangers to her. They'd already raised older daughters and sons, guided them through elementary school and high school and beyond, and therefore could never afford enough energy, enough time, for Donna or Dan. So, one day the two children decided to run away. They packed a bundled cloth with clothes and a few days' worth of food. A scatter of green plastic army men for Dan; a coloring book, filled with pictures of dinosaurs, for Donna. At the last second, they added some cherry candy bars and a cake of pink soap. Then they knotted the top of the bundle and began walking down the block.

After half an hour, Dan grew anxious, concerned about their father's doubtless punishment. He decided to turn back. But our mother forged ahead, damp from the sweltering afternoon heat, determined to reach the highway at the city's easternmost edge. She marched along the ditches, the sack slung defiantly on her back. Two separate cars stopped for her, two friendly, concerned families asking if she needed a ride, but our mother turned both families down.

Then a third car eased to the roadside. A sky-blue Imperial: shabbier than the others, its front fenders dented and rusty, a splintery crack across its windshield. Inside, a woman was driving; in the backseat, a young boy. The woman was pretty, with long, auburn hair. She offered the girl a ride, and this time, our mother accepted.

The car radio played jaunty, outdated songs. (At this point, I almost interrupted Alice—songs like "Jeepers, Creepers," maybe, or "Don't Sit Under the Apple Tree"?—but I kept quiet.) Taped across the dashboard were newspaper photographs of strange-looking people: clowns, dwarfs and giants, ladies with misshapen bodies or shaggy black beards. One of the photos, the woman said, was her husband: she pointed to the man wearing a sinister rubber mask, his head tilted back, preparing to swallow a long, brilliantly blazing stick.

"He's the fire-eater," said the boy in the backseat.

The woman explained that she and Warren—the red-haired, bony boy, who, surprisingly, wasn't her son—were driving south to meet her husband. The man was integral to the operation of the traveling carnival. First of all, he trained all the horses. He also did repairs for all the trucks and the elaborate machines. And yes, he was the fire-eater in the side-show. The carnival had just finished its week at the Kansas State Fair, and was now headed to Oklahoma. "Wouldn't you like to meet my husband?" the woman asked our mother. "Wouldn't you like to see him perform?"

(At this point in her retelling, Alice paused to gauge my reaction. Her voice was nearly furious: "A *carnival*. Where'd she come up with *that*? Does she really think she's fooling us?" I begged her to please continue; we could discuss the details later.)

According to our mother, she was so enchanted by the prospect of the carnival that she didn't mind traveling far from home. And, oddly, as the woman pointed out, Donna so strongly resembled Warren they could easily pass as younger sister and older brother, the children in the traveling-carnival family. Right then, it seemed like destiny: perhaps our mother was meant to be walking down that edge-of-town road; the woman and Warren were fated to stop their car. Without much hesitation, our mother agreed to join them on the trip.

And the week at the Oklahoma fair was magical. She spent each day and night with Warren. They observed the fire-eater's performances from the intimate backstage shadows. They helped feed and groom the horses. Again and again, free of charge, they rode the Ferris wheel and red-armored Tilt-a-Whirl. They ate frivolous, sugary meals: my mother's Cherry Mash bars, plus the fair's cotton candy, its funnel cakes, its candied apples. They also had their nightly fill of peaches, preserved in Mason jars by the fire-eater's wife, kept cool in the trunk of the rattletrap Imperial.

But the carnival only lasted seven days. After Oklahoma came the Missouri State Fair, and the man and woman and Warren ultimately had to take the little girl home. They drove the Imperial back across the border, back to Kansas and our mother's town, and, finally, to the end of her block. *Oh, Donna, we've had such a wonderful time. Someday we'll surely see you again.* They handed her the clothes and pink soap and book of colored dinosaurs. They opened the door; they blew kisses good-bye.

Our mother understood that the kidnapping was wrong, even criminal. But she longed to someday see them all again. Therefore, she wouldn't betray them. She claimed not to remember those seven days, resolving never to tell her parents, or any other adult, about her disappearance. She'd never forget the man's funny mask, or the flames erupting in hot white spikes from his mouth. She'd never forget the woman's calm, compassionate voice; her silver ring with one sapphire stone, one amethyst; or her peaches, glistening gold inside their cool, mysterious jars. Most of all, she'd never forget her Warren.

After she finished the story, Alice left the room for a glass of water. I heard her exaggerated sigh and realized the kitchen was still a mess: the scattered photographs, the overturned garbage, and the paper towels, splotched brown with dried blood.

Our mother's stories were a series of knots, each so ornamented and individually complex, impossible to fully unravel. When Alice returned, her lips pinched in a frown, I tried translating my feelings into words. "There are still some coincidences," I said. "Things keep popping up, every version she tells."

"Surely you don't think any of that could be true."

"But the peaches. That ring with two gemstones. Candy bars. And of course *Warren*. Part of me still needs to know if anything, even the slightest possible piece, might be real."

"But how could we know? Her mind's changed so much. You've been here awhile now, seeing her every day, so you can't really tell how much it's changed. I haven't been home in months. It's terrifying how different she is."

Again Alice sat on the couch, watching me closely. I wanted to say she was mistaken; indeed, I *had* noticed the change. Both Dolores and I had witnessed so many escalations, these recent days: shifts of body temperature and skin tone; a gradual inability to sit in the wheelchair or even move from bed. We'd seen the constant tremble in her hands, up to her shoulders and chest, the tremble building to a labored shudder. The nurses had brought bedpans and shallow sickness pails. They'd followed Kaufman's instructions for morphine, adding and subtracting from the IV drips as though mixing intricate cocktails.

Could Alice, with all her months away from home, understand any of this? During daylight, our mother had been sleeping with her hands and jaw muscles clenched. At night she relaxed slightly, yet seemed possessed, speaking throughout her sleep. Disconnected murmurs; barely intelligible words and half-sentences that seemed directed to John, to her deceased brothers and sisters. "This behavior is normal at the end," Kaufman had told Dolores. On one of her yellow notepads, behind pages of notes from her interview with Sunny Barradale, I'd been writing the random things our mother said as she slept. *For John and me. Get the platelets up. Back there, deep in the forest.* Sometimes I couldn't link the words with any possible meaning. *The wheat fields. A sweet baby boy.* Other times, I understood whole sentences: *That feels so nice when you touch my face.*

Yet I still couldn't describe these scenes to Alice. I sat rocking and holding them secret, just as the boy, eight feet below us, on the shadowy cot, was still secret.

Gradually, I tired of her silence, her disparaging stare. "I hope you aren't mad at me," I said.

"Do I have a reason to be mad?"

"I took so long to tell you I'd come home. I shouldn't have waited until her accident."

"Well actually, it was Dolores who called, not you."

"Nosy, drunken Dolores."

Alice lifted the peanut-brittle tin from the floor and offered it, but I refused. "I used to think Dolores was nosy," she said. "And loud, too, and rude. But now, with all this Ernest drama, I feel sorry for her."

"Ernest? What drama?"

"Just a few weeks ago. She hasn't mentioned it? He went off with some younger woman. Totally vanished. On the phone she told me all about it—not that I'd asked. He even took their dog. And a huge chunk of her money."

"You're kidding. Really? I had no idea." Now my face felt newly hot with shame. All these recent days together with Dolores—the white afternoons beside my mother's bed as she slept, the trips across town to buy magazines or strawberry milkshakes or secret cigarettes—and she hadn't alerted me, hadn't mentioned Ernest or the dog? I thought of her cowboy boots, very likely his. Or her sweaters, still flecked with blond fur. Why had she confided in Alice instead of me? Had she even told my mother?

"When you asked if I was mad," said Alice, "I thought you meant something else."

Momentarily I wondered if she'd learned about Otis. Then I saw her looking me over, examining my forearms, stomach, and legs. I remembered all the arguments from the last time we'd come home, and knew precisely what was coming next.

"You've been sitting there, wide-eyed and shivering and grinding your teeth, the entire time I told her story. I knew you wouldn't want that peanut brittle. You're skinnier than ever. Is this what it's done to you?"

I let the question settle, then rolled my eyes and sighed. It was a gesture our mother, when confronted with a problem and unsure of its solution, often made. I wanted Alice to recognize this; when she didn't, I answered, "You know perfectly well that's what it's done to me."

Beside the rocking chair, in the blanked TV screen, I could see a miniature reflection of myself. Alice was right: the drugs had sallowed my skin, whittled at my bones. "I read somewhere that eventually you lose touch with reality," she said. "That you see things, or it makes you have psychotic episodes."

"That isn't always true."

She paused, smirking, and gave a soft laugh. "Maybe it could explain why you believe her silly stories."

She wanted me to laugh with her, but I couldn't. Slowly she leaned closer, searching for any evidence on my face. "You're on it right now, aren't you?"

Her question seemed more genuinely curious than accusatory. I moved toward her, too, further widening my eyes, and said a simple "Yes." Admitting this felt thrilling, a crack across a long glass window of lies. Now I could relax, settle back into the chair.

"What does it feel like?"

"It used to feel terrific. Now it's not so terrific anymore. But being high is better than not being high."

I'd explained all this to Alice before. Once she'd even sympathized, and claimed she understood. It was true that in that first year, the drugs *had* been terrific—the all-night parties with friends, the clubs, the anonymous one-night-stands—but at some stage the feelings had gone vacant. The highs got less exciting, yet I tried to maintain them, frantic attempts to avoid the lows. I remembered telling Alice about all the despair over Pen & Ink and other fleeting freelance jobs; the abandonment of so many articles I'd wanted to write; the series of failed relationships. "Eventually the meth obliterated everything," I'd said.

On the stereo, the orchestra finished its crowning song. We listened to the wind ripping branches from the trees and, from the kitchen, the thick drop of refrigerator ice. "I want to watch you do it," Alice suddenly said. "Go get your travel bag. Go get your little striped straw."

And so she'd remembered the travel bag and its cartoon mouse. She'd even remembered the straw. Earlier conversations, when she'd asked me to elaborate, my stories had been hazy—the losses of money and friends, the subtle withdrawals, the crying jags and sleeplessness and hospital scares. I'd always made these stories abstract, but Alice hated abstraction. It was so like her to remember the bag and straw: the tiny, the specific.

In the bedroom I found everything I needed. From the window, the snow was blanketing the backyard garden. The pouch of meth that Gavin had sent was iridescent black, and, as I held it to the window's light, I saw the crystals inside, faint occluded gleam within the black, mesmerizing as an elephant's eye. I was still so lost to it.

When I returned, I showed Alice the drug, my credit card, and the fast-food straw. "This better not be your attempt at intervention," I said. I sat on the floor and searched for something level, any surface where I could perform the pathetic scene she wanted. Beside the rocker was an old hickory trough, repainted in my mother's careful hand, now used for stacks of magazines. Stuck between the usual gardening and furniture titles was an outdated collection of crossword puzzles. Many were solved in others' faded-ink handwritings; our mother must have found the magazine at a junk store and, fascinated by what others hadn't finished, added the missing solutions. On one page, the borders of a puzzle were shaped like a valentine heart. She'd solved the hidden words inside (*Ta-da*, I could imagine her shouting, *There's another!*) and afterward used a crayon to redden the love of the heart.

This page seemed so appropriate, so obvious. I scattered the drug across the heart, crushed it, and sniffed twice.

"Happy now?" I asked.

"Don't know if 'happy' is the right word."

"How about 'satisfied'?"

"Maybe."

I cleared each nostril with my forefinger and thumb, then licked the residue. Alice wasn't fazed. Perhaps if I'd used the pipe; perhaps if I'd told reckless stories of Gavin and our other addict "friends." Perhaps if she knew I'd once tried injecting myself with a friend's borrowed needle; when the needle pricked my skin, I'd shuddered and swore my usual "I quit" lie.

She reached to squeeze my arm, as though proud of my performance. Her skin smelled faintly of patchouli soap; in the subdued gold light, I could see her strong resemblance to our mother. The pale green eyes; the slowly nodding head; the antique glimmer of her teardrop earrings. I thought of her cramped, curtained store, up north in Lawrence: the vintage veiled hats and lace-up boots, the rows of exquisite dresses. Alice had become obsessed with finding old valuables, then reselling them at her store. Although she'd never acknowledge it, it was clear she'd inherited this nostalgia, these bent aesthetics, from our mother.

From her strained smile, from her hand still touching mine, it seemed she expected gratitude at this, her acceptance of my actions. Instead, I felt the bitterness spread to my throat: another sudden, unstable emotion, so quickened by the drug. "*She* would never try to humiliate me like this," I said.

"Humiliate? This isn't about humiliation."

"You're trying to knock me down. It's because you feel guilty."

"What's that supposed to mean?"

"Because she's dying. She's dying, and you haven't been here for her. You're trying to gain power over me."

"That's ludicrous." She made a low, obstinate cough. "First, there's one good reason I haven't been here: because *I wasn't allowed*. You deliberately kept this from me. And second, I don't feel guilty. Years and years of near misses, doctors giving her this or that diagnosis, years of pretending things were worse than they truly were. How was I ever supposed to know what was real and what wasn't?"

"We didn't deliberately—"

"And get this through your head," she continued. "I am *not* our mother. She and I are not the same person. Not now, not ever."

"You're right. She would never ask me to do this in front of her."

"There are lots of things she'd never do. She'd never have the nerve to get the hell out of these horrible backward towns, like you and I did. And she'd never get addicted to some embarrassing, disgraceful drug, *like you did*.

"And what's more"—she paused, as though unsure how to go on—"I doubt that you or I would ever spend years and years pretending that a disease was ten times more serious than it probably actually was, milking it for everything we could, *like she did*. And I doubt that you or I would then someday realize that the disease had finally won the battle but not tell the people who were supposed to matter most to her, until it was way too late, *like she did*. And I highly doubt that I would do what the two of you have been doing—and don't think for a minute that Dolores's blabbing mouth didn't tell me about *this*—driving around the entire state of Kansas, telling people you're writing a book just to satisfy some screwed-up curiosity from years ago that I never understood in the first place."

Her voice had lifted to a shout; the cat had bolted from the room. Instinctively I'd coiled into the chair, rocking like a child. The meth was constricting my throat, but I had enough strength to speak. "Oh, Alice," I said. "We lost you long ago, didn't we?"

We both stared, unblinking, our breaths slowly steadying, the chair creaking as I rocked. Inside this house, the arguments were always whispery and shy. No voice had ever risen so powerfully. I wondered whether the boy downstairs had absorbed our furious words.

At last, Alice stood, reaching toward my face. "Your nose is bleeding," she said.

I wouldn't let her touch me. I hurried for the bedroom, closing the door, locking it behind me. Then I found the bottle of sleeping pills and swallowed three without water.

In the dark, I heard him moving through the house, the carpet hissing under his lazy shuffle. Somehow I knew it was Otis. I shut my eyes in an obstinate, counterfeit sleep, but he soon came slinking through the doorway. He stood near the bed, waiting for my reaction; then he reached beneath the blankets and scratched my foot. When I opened my eyes, I saw he'd removed the knotted scarf, and his jaw was busy with a wad of gum.

"Your sister left a note. She's staying with your mom tonight."

I reached to pull the chain on the lamp, squinting against its metallic light. On the nightstand were two sodas, both tabbed open, the smell leaving a synthetic grape smear across the room. I took one, sat up in bed, and drank. I was shocked to see the time was nearly nine o'clock; I'd been sleeping the entire day.

"Did she find you down there?" I asked.

"I waited until I heard her get in her car and leave. I was starving, so I came upstairs to eat. That peanut brittle. And that salami with the peppercorns in it."

"Sorry I was sleeping. I should've already been downstairs with dinner."

He shrugged; the look on his face convinced me that he'd snuck upstairs many times before. Yet after all this time, he hadn't escaped. "I've been watching TV and walking around," he said. "Your mom sure has some cool old stuff. And out back, too."

So he'd nosed around the rooms of the house, the back-yard garden and garage. Imagining this, I looked down to his wrists, then lower, to his ankles. The handcuffs and rope were gone. "You found the key," I said.

"Aw, come on. You know I've had it with me all along."

"Actually, I didn't know that."

Otis sat at the foot of the bed. He seemed peculiarly sol-emn, no longer smirking or averting his eyes; even the way he chewed his gum now seemed more man than boy. Yet I noticed his boyishly bad haircut, his wrecked complexion, and the unshaven fuzz above his lip, butter-colored and fine.

"I've been lying to you," he said.

"About the key?"

"No, about everything. This was all my idea."

His meaning still wasn't clear. Then he took a deep breath, and his confession streamed forth: "I'm nothing like I said. My name isn't Otis. It's Allen. I just turned eighteen, not fifteen like I told her. I'm not even in school anymore—dropped out, this past spring."

He watched me as though expecting astonishment or fury. In fact, I wasn't so surprised. For the past two days, he'd seemed distressed by my mother's prolonged absence, by my sobering reports about her feeble health, and I'd sensed a simmering of guilt in him. "And I bet you aren't related to her Warren, either," I said.

"Not at all. My real mom and dad are in Nevada. Same with my grandparents. I never go visit them; we don't even talk much. But I can tell you I've never known anybody named Warren."

"Your grandfather isn't the man she wants him to be."

He lowered his eyes in shame. "And *I'm* not, either."

He reached for the grape soda, mistakenly choosing my half-finished can instead of his own, and then finished it with three hard swallows. "I live with my uncle and aunt," he said. "But I'm hardly ever there. I take off in my car all the time. It's an '89 Mustang but it still runs pretty good. I parked it down the block, that night I drove here. I just checked, and it's still outside."

"Aren't they worried? Looking all over for you?"

"They probably haven't noticed I'm gone."

I drew my legs to my chest, freeing more space on the bed, and he relaxed slightly. "Okay, then no more secrets," I said. "Tell me how you first met my mother."

He took me back to that day—just weeks before I'd boarded my New York bus—that late-summer afternoon he'd first seen her. "I was stocking shelves at the store where I used to work," he said. "She'd been watching me a long time before I even noticed. I thought she was weird but there was something about her I liked.

"Later, when I was finishing up, she came back. She said I looked like someone from her past. She said she was very sick, and she needed to find this person before she died. I didn't think she was serious. I mean, I could see she wasn't so healthy—but I didn't think it was supposed to happen so *soon*.

"Then she wanted to know, did I have time to go driving and talk a little? And I thought, why not? We drove her pickup around Sterling. Around the whole county, out by the salt mines and then the old riding stable. We parked and just sat there, watching. The whole time she kept talking about this boy—this *Warren*. How they'd been kidnapped as kids, and she'd been searching for him her entire life."

I sat listening to Otis—*Allen*—continue his recollection of that day. He tried to remember all she'd initially told him, mentioning most of the now-familiar aspects: the peaches and candy bars; the old records and the board games they'd played. He recalled her painstaking descriptions of Warren's clothes and hair and eyes. But I couldn't quite decode, based on the boy's memory, which version of her disappearance she'd given that day she'd first spoken with him. Perhaps her memories hadn't quite solidified. Or perhaps—the more likely possibility—she hadn't yet concocted the elaborate stories she'd later tell Alice, Dolores, or me.

"We talked on the phone, every other day or so. I kept playing along, letting her think I might be connected to Warren. She really wanted it that way, you know? She'd been searching so long . . . so maybe I could be the one to make her happy."

"You felt sorry for her."

"At first it was kind of fun. Didn't think there was anything wrong with it. I memorized what I could from the things she'd told me. She said he didn't like to sing along to those records, so I pretended I couldn't sing. He loved that candy bar with the pink center, so I took some money from my aunt's purse and went and bought a load of those. And the peaches—she'd mentioned them eating peaches. I was going to get peaches that day you picked me up, but when I went to the store, all I could find was tomatoes. I don't even *like* tomatoes."

"You even lied about that."

"I guess so, yeah."

With the boy so close on the bed, crouched in the yellow lamplight and speaking his steadied, penitent words, I saw that indeed he was much older than his professed fifteen. *Allen.* He'd so easily fooled me, too. He still wore the ragged canvas shoes, my mother's beaded bracelet, and the sweatshirt, rumpled with the cozy remoteness of sleep. Only a single difference: he no longer wore the name tag with its blank white square.

Then I saw the marks on his neck, raw and faintly red. It was clear the marks were from a belt: the strangling leather, the red stain of the buckle. *Like Henry.* When I moved closer to examine, he flinched before I could touch his skin. "It didn't hurt," he said. "I just wanted to see how it felt."

Once again I leaned back against the headboard, staring into the boy's face until he looked away. He was still so frightening and foreign and strange. He'd finally left the basement room, removing his ropes and locks, to reveal his lies and gallant guilt. Yet still so many questions remained.

"So what made you come back here? Why have you stayed, all this time?"

"For *her*. I knew she really believed I was the connection. Now she had to figure a way to get you to believe it, too. Maybe I said it as a joke—you know, 'You guys should kidnap *me* and put me in *your* basement.' We planned it all out, and then she'd eventually tell you about Warren and all that time she'd gone missing. We decided you'd pick me up from the road. We'd pretend we didn't know each other. That she was kidnapping me.

"Then I took the joke a little further. I thought it would be good to get out of Sterling awhile. Not that anyone would notice. And your mom . . . she promised she would give me some money."

The boy spoke this last bit of information in a humiliated hush. I could picture my mother cashing her disability checks, tucking bills into a special envelope marked *Otis*. Yes, this explained so much. Clearly, the money had empowered the boy to lie, to maintain the charade.

"But I feel awful now," he said, hammering a fist against the bed. "I hate myself for lying. There's got to be some way I can make it up to her—maybe help find what she's looking for."

"It's too late for that." My voice sounded harsh; I softened it to try and ease his mind. "Remember, though: while you were lying, she was lying too. These stories she's been telling—she's gotten to the point where *she* believes they're true."

He stopped to consider these words. Then he said, "I think she stopped believing that I'm only related to Warren. Now I think she believes I really *am* Warren."

"You're probably right."

I was sticky from drugs and hours of sleep; soon I should try and eat, then drive to the hospital to join Alice. I was still filled with uncertainties and questions for the boy. I stared at him, again picturing his slow, slouching walk at the burned-black roadside, again striving to feel what my mother must have felt. It was easy to see how he'd fooled her.

As though he'd read my thoughts, the boy tentatively smiled, and for a moment I thought yearningly of myself at eighteen. "Allen," I said. "Is it Allen with two Ls, or one? With an E, or an A?"

"Two Ls. An E. Why?"

"Because that's my middle name. And that's how I spell it."

The boy swung his legs to the floor and began walking from the room, beckoning me to follow. I rose, shirtless and barefoot, from the bed, and went to join him on the living-room couch. Earlier, he'd been watching TV, its volume turned low as though he hadn't wanted to disturb my sleep. On screen was an old western movie, the distorted picture showing brown grass at the top, then the black stripe, then the sky's sky blue. And within that light, littering the floor, were my mother's scrapbooks and photographs. The clippings from *True Detective*; the letters dumped from her keepsake boxes; her cassette recorder and interview tapes.

"I've been looking through these things," he said. "Her picture albums, and her kitchen walls. And all these things here."

We sat on the floor, taking opposite sides of the mess. Reverently he dipped both hands into the pile. This was the first time someone, besides my mother or me, had examined the collection. It should have felt like theft or desecration, but, oddly, I didn't care, I wanted him to see it all. He began holding up individual photos, asking what I knew of each: the past missing children and adults, the notable details from letters she'd received. I surprised myself with how much I remembered. As the minutes passed, I told him the stories of Henry and Evan. Lacey Wyler. Even the recent Barbara Wishman (after the TV bulletin, I'd followed my mother's instructions and printed a picture from the library's Internet—Barbara's crooked grin and glasses, her skin as russet-smooth as the underside of a Hershey bar).

As I spoke, he stayed quiet, nodding and listening, examining each photograph or letter. It had been months, I realized, since I'd experienced this kind of intimacy with anyone besides my mother. As my addictions had deepened, all my friends had gradually dissolved from my life. I'd almost forgotten that essential need to speak with someone, to get this unexpectedly close. Granted, it was only this boy, this Allen or Otis, this stranger who'd deceived my mother and taken her money. But he was enough. During these moments with him, I felt a welcome solace, I felt less broken. I wanted to hook my arm around his shoulders with the verve of an older brother. Or, better still, to exist through him, to live as that boy again.

Then he unearthed the forbidden pictures: those that had scared me as a boy, the ones she'd kept tucked into manila envelopes. Most were pictures and articles from *True Detective*, grainy black-and-whites of bloodstained bodies, macerated bone. He unfolded a group of pages and handed them to me.

I looked at the photos and immediately remembered. Abigail Mercurio. "Tell me about her," he said.

I went back to my mother's early obsessions with the missing. One evening, I remembered, she'd returned from a long shift at the prison with another forbidden *True Detective*. On the cover, a girl lay bound on a pool table; at the frame's corner, one meaty hand visible, lurked her attacker. Back then I wanted so badly to understand my mother's offbeat fascination, and later that night I snuck the magazine to my room to read the lurid story. Abigail Mercurio, seventeen, had failed to return from a local bowling alley. Her mother, Josephine, waited an hour past curfew, then two. Then she called the police.

The *True Detective* told how her friends, in sworn testimonies, retraced Abigail's route. They'd dropped her at a convenience store, twelve blocks from home. They'd last seen her through the windows, gliding along the glowing aisles. In the succeeding days came anonymous telephone tips: near Route 17's bridge, a woman saw a man corralling a young girl, then pushing her into a black car. A sobbing teen with a blood-flecked blouse was spotted in the restroom of the city zoo. But these leads amounted to nothing. By spring, Abigail's purse surfaced, emptied and smeared with mud, in the city park. Inside were Abigail's driver's license; a lipstick and nail polish, both strawberry-red; wallet-sized pictures of friends, her pet cocker spaniel, and Abigail herself, grinning, arm-in-arm with her mother.

While the boy listened, I explained how much these photos had meant to me. I told him how, later in my teens, I'd even used these same pictures of Abigail to my advantage. When boys at school first attempted dating, bringing girls gifts of cheap candy and perfume, I disclosed my own secret: *my* girlfriend, gorgeous and shy, lived two states south, in Texas. Her name was Abigail. She wore long pigtails and had bright red lips. She pitched for her softball team, expert at hurling windmill, strike after strike. She collected stuffed monkeys; I'd even sent her one, a goofy, mutely grinning toy made from sweat socks and buttons for eyes.

I held up Abigail's school photo, taken weeks before her disappearance. "This was the picture I taped inside my locker. And everyone believed me."

"But I thought you didn't like girls," the boy said.

So my mother had divulged this, too; maybe he'd simply figured it out. Still, it was an honest question, free of judgment or scorn. So I told him he was right. I'd used the pictures as protection, the bulwark against my true desires.

"When I was a teenager," I said, "I used to go to Carey Park in Hutchinson. Out there, I could get drugs whenever I wanted, and I could even get anonymous sex. Those nights in that park, I knew there was no going back. My old self faded away . . . out there, I became someone new."

"But you didn't want anyone else to know. So you told them about this girl from the magazine instead."

"I was a liar. I wanted them to think I was someone else. Someone they'd talk about with pride instead of scorn . . . maybe I said these things so they'd always remember me."

Now he was eyeing me critically. I knew what he was thinking: these words, these admissions, could have been describing any of us. My mother, myself, and the boy: we'd all told these kinds of lies.

"That's the one thing I always shared with her," I finally said, "even when I couldn't understand her obsession. Both back then, and recently. I loved helping her make up the rest of their stories."

It seemed he didn't understand, so I explained. "We'd see these pictures on TV or in magazines. But it was always just the basics: the 'missing person' sign, with the smiling picture beneath it. We wanted more than that. So we got really good at inventing the rest. It made us feel like we knew these people. If we could give someone a little history, like a favorite food or a favorite song, some secrets no one else knew—*that's* what made them real."

He reached across the pile and took the *True Detective* pages from me. He looked through each photo, settling on the final frame: a model of Abigail's body, a recreation of the crime. The picture revealed no face—just a shoulder, an arm's inelegant curve, the rest obscured by shadows and weeds—but I could tell he imagined the skin as Abigail's. She lay beside a mud-stained mattress. Above her the trees, damp with recent rain, dropped leaves like kisses. The roots took tangle of her hair. Her legs were covered with earth, and the body's twist gave the appearance of struggle—as though she had strained, even in death, to free herself from the shallow grave.

The boy stretched out, lying back against the floor, his shaggy hair scribbling across the rug. "I wonder where her family lives now," he said. "Wonder where she's buried. Wonder how often they still think about her."

"I'm sure they think about her every single day."

He closed his eyes. The light in the room was dusky and frail, like the light in an old home movie. I got two pillows from the couch, sliding one beneath his neck for comfort, using the other for myself. And then, just as my mother and I had always done, the boy and I began to embellish and revise the story.

Perhaps, that night, Abigail Mercurio had trounced her friends at bowling, scoring 144 to their 120, 95, and 62. Perhaps she had used a blue marbled ball, and the next night, at the alley, another bowler found a red fingernail in the thumbhole, chipped on Abigail's attempt at a strike. We guessed that maybe, in that store, she had shoplifted a chocolate cupcake, waiting until the clerk glanced away from the ceiling's mirror to transfer it to her purse. Maybe she'd been softly singing as the car pulled into the lot; and maybe she was licking the cake's vanilla filling when she heard his voice, catching just then, in the lowered window, those asterisk eyes that already saw her death.

My mother would have been proud at our skill at reinventing the story. After we finished, we stayed motionless for a long, quiet minute. Then, in a whisper, Allen asked, "Was she always so cool?"

At first I thought he meant Abigail. Then I realized. "She was a great mom," I said. "Unlike anyone else's. She always wanted us to do things no one else got to do."

"What things?"

"She'd make up weird games. She'd find old cookbooks in junk stores, and she'd help us with the recipes. She'd take us places no one else had seen. I don't mean foreign countries or resorts or anything like that. I mean places like abandoned houses that were supposed to be haunted. Like rock quarries. Catfish ponds. Once, we found this field with wild blueberries growing everywhere. Places we weren't supposed to trespass."

By now it was very late. I'd told the boy so much about my mother; I'd revealed stories from my childhood, and admitted long-held teenage secrets of Carey Park. I could have revealed even more, but the fatigue and grief had altered my voice, forcing me to stop. Once again it was time to leave, to join Dolores and Alice and my mother. I headed to the bedroom for a clean shirt and jeans.

The boy pushed himself from the floor but went in the opposite direction, moving through the kitchen, toward the basement door. "Yes, she was a wonderful mom," I said as he walked away.

NINE

OUTSIDE THE HOSPITAL windows, the
storm became a sermon. Slow drifts were settling across the
parking lot; the deserted, frosted football fields; the edge-of-
town liquor stores and filling stations with their fractured
neon lights. One clear-sky afternoon last week, Dolores had
stared from the window and pointed out Hutchinson's dis-

tant city-limits sign, perpetually vandalized with spray paint and bullet holes; yet when she looked there this morning, she saw nothing but white. From the hall drifted a song from an intern's radio, the static crackling like shook tin, and when the music stopped, a female newscaster's voice—perhaps the same we'd heard in the truck, the night of the accident—reported the snow would continue all weekend.

The room, once smelling of lemons, was now only sour liniments and dripping medications. Alice sat at the foot of the bed; Dolores took the chair; I stood and occasionally paced. My mother was sleeping, and I could sense the comfort the morphine gave her: the richness, the smudging of tension. I realized this was supposed to relieve me, too.

Before noon, Alice decided to return to Haven. "I should feed the cat and catch a few hours of sleep." Later tonight, after one last visit to the hospital room, she would drive back to Lawrence, to her own home and little vintage shop. She had learned so much during her brief time with our mother: the padded bedside chair on which Dolores and I had frequently drifted to sleep; the wheelchair's faulty wheel; the nurses named Elva and Danny and Pearl. She'd learned all the bruises from the needles and the port in her chest. Alice had even gotten Kaufman's requisite briefing, the same he'd given me. And yesterday, during the short, single interval our mother had been awake and lucid, Alice had taken her outside to smoke, and therefore knew the scenes we could see from our hill in the hospital lot: the sunset over Hutchinson's trees, the long, white grain elevators, the desolate evening train with its echoing whistle.

Presently, Alice bent over the bed, kissed our mother's forehead just below the scar, and rubbed the kiss with two fingers. "Be back this evening," she told us. *The final time,* we all were thinking, *the final visit.* She still seemed upset with me, and I didn't try to stop her when she left the room. If the time had come for her to discover the boy, I could do nothing more to prevent it.

Dolores stood at the window, watching Alice exit the sliding doors and cross the icy parking lot. Then she said, "I have something you need to see."

On the bedside table, beside her deck of cards and gossipy tabloids, was the stack of my mother's mail. Almost daily, I'd been bringing it from home, but, since securing my own treasured package from Gavin, hadn't bothered opening the letters. And since Kaufman had prescribed the morphine, my mother no longer had the strength to read them, either.

As Dolores showed me now, the mail consisted of more than the usual bills. She'd received two belated responses to her missing-persons ads: one from Salina, another from Lyons. But Dolores wasn't interested in those. She held out a small white envelope: *"Here's* the one I want you to read."

My mother's name and address were written in a florid, fat-looped cursive on the front. In the upper corner, the return address was *The Triple Crown Riding Stable, Rural Route 2, Sterling, Kansas.*

As I unfolded the letter, Dolores stepped closer to look over my shoulder. "I didn't know if Alice should see this or not," she said. "I've been saving it for you. Go ahead—read it."

Dear Donna,

How nice it was to get the note you left for me. I'm very sorry I missed you when you were here. My brother in Goodland has been ill with leukemia, and my husband and I were away both times you came to the stables. (That is also why it has taken me so long to write this reply!) Perhaps we'll get to meet someday soon, though!

I'm sorry my assistant was unable to answer your questions. Unfortunately I'm afraid I won't be much help to you, either. But I'll try my best.

Before we bought the stables, they were owned by a family named Barton. They'd only been running things for a few years. I know they'd bought the place from a man named Robert Lockridge (hope I'm spelling that right!). Robert had inherited everything—land, house, horses, all of it—from his family, after his mother and father passed. But before the Lockridges, your guess is as good as mine!

I *do* know that the Triple Crown has been in operation for many, many years—probably more years than either you or I have been alive!

I'm wishing you the best of luck in finding out more information. *Please* do let me know if there's any way I can help with all the research for your book. It sounds like something I'd very much like to read when it's all done!

Sincerely,

Patricia ("Pat") Claussen

When I finished, Dolores took the letter from me, sliding it back into its envelope. "Right away I thought of her stories," she said. "Remember in my version, what she'd said? A sound like horses, clomping on the ground above that cellar? And then there was *your* version—how the man smelled like horses and hay, and how there was manure on his boots."

"Alice said the man from the carnival was a horse trainer."

(And in my head, kept secret from Dolores, were the boy's words from the previous night: *We drove her pickup around Sterling. Around the whole county, out by the salt mines and then the old riding stable. We parked and just sat there, watching.*)

Dolores thought of other connections, details I'd previously told her. "Sterling Repair," she said. "And that red circle on her little map." She turned toward the bed, directing a perplexed smile at my mother, and then looked back to me. "Do you know this Pat woman? Have you heard of these other folks mentioned in here?"

"That letter is all a big surprise."

"I suppose there's a chance it doesn't mean anything. Only a nice reply to some random note she left out there. Maybe we're grasping at straws. Could be this is just another part of her great big delusion."

"But I think we should drive out to the place. Don't you? We could take a little trip. Just the two of us."

The suggestion seemed to warm Dolores. I was reaching out; I was including her in the plan. She grinned like a child who'd made a first friend, and, with a sharp, sudden woe, I recalled Alice's story about Ernest.

"Have you been out there before?" she asked. "To the riding stable?"

"I remember driving past when we were kids. She'd take us out to Sterling sometimes, and yeah, there were days she'd take that route. Triple Crown—yes. I remember they'd sometimes braid the manes or tails of their horses. Mostly palominos, but they had some Shetland ponies, too, and one tall appaloosa that Alice loved."

"Did she ever stop so you could go inside and saddle up?"

"Never. I always thought maybe it cost too much, or she was worried we'd get hurt on the horses." I paused, trying to focus the vague memories. "To be honest, driving past the place was never anything out of the ordinary—I mean, no more important than any other part of driving to Sterling."

A slight draft shuddered the curtains. We turned toward the door just as Kaufman entered the room. I hadn't seen him in days. His skin seemed less tanned, and he'd started growing a thin moustache. He moved closer to the bed, beginning his usual small talk.

Dolores's distaste for him was immediately palpable, and she interrupted before he finished his sentence. "Any news to report?" she asked.

He nodded, still watching my mother. "We're going to let her have her wish." The doctor addressed me directly, as though unsure how to speak to Dolores; I felt a sting of privilege. "She was begging and begging to go home. So we've finalized things with the hospice, and I'd say two, three days, we'll be ready to go."

He unfolded some papers from his coat pocket and offered them to me. Dolores stepped closer and, just as she'd done with the letter from the stable, stretched to peek over my shoulder.

The papers were promotional brochures from Hutchinson Hospice. On one cover, an elderly woman sat at the transom of a small boat, two towheaded grandchildren rowing from the hull, gliding along a shimmering river. All seemed contented in their orange life jackets and wide, white smiles. *Just because she's dying . . . doesn't mean she shouldn't be living.*

"We all had a discussion yesterday when your sister was here," Kaufman said. "She had a little bit of energy . . . Alice took her outside, and when they came back, we all had our talk." He was enunciating carefully, as though addressing small, suspicious children. "We agreed it's time to let her loose."

"You agreed," I said.

"Time to go home. She doesn't have to fight anymore."

Let her loose. Even now, it was so difficult to picture my mother surrendering. There would be no more Friday appointments, I told myself. No self-administered Neupogen shots. No routine anxieties over her hair, her blood counts, or the rigid port in her chest.

No missions. No days for just the two of us, only son and mother, aimless drives across the plains on her urgent, ravenous search.

The hallway radio stopped with an audible click. In its place, a long, glacial silence. And then, for the first time all day, my mother opened her eyes.

We stood without moving. She seemed much thinner, tinier than before: her frail, exhausted body bent into the bed like a broken arm in its sling. Suddenly I wanted to leave with her, to wheel her outside and watch as she felt the fragrant, always startling chill on her face.

She opened her mouth and whispered a single word, meant for neither Dolores nor Kaufman, but solely for me. *Warren* was the word she said.

I stepped closer to the bedside. My mother had shut her eyes again but was straining, it seemed, to open them. I could tell she wanted to speak further, and worried she might begin the random, muddled speech that had recently accompanied her late-night dreams: the half-strings of sentences, the incoherent flares of memory.

But this time her meaning was clear. She repeated the words of her doctor: "I don't have to fight anymore."

"Take it easy. It's okay." I sounded artificial, like a character from some afternoon drama on her damaged TV. Once, I knew, she would have teased me about this. I wanted her to hear her teasing me.

"Bend down here," she said.

I took her hand and put my face close to hers. There were new bruises at her clavicle and throat; an arc of blood had dried on her bottom lip. Her familiar smell had diminished completely.

She lifted her chin, and I felt her breath against my ear. "Have there been any others?" she asked.

At first I couldn't grasp her meaning, and shook my head in confusion. She tried to swallow; the attempt caused her obvious pain.

"Has anyone disappeared?"

Still I couldn't give her an answer. I'd withdrawn from the game: no more tracking the news reports, no more library research or photographs pinned to the walls. So I moved even closer and started repeating all the false assurances, only faintly aware of my words. *Everything will be okay, soon we'll all be relaxing at home, you can slip into your nightgown and watch your own TV and I'll pour you a great big glass of iced tea.*

Her grip on my hand began to weaken, and, to compensate, I pressed hers tighter. Through the morphine she had flickered briefly: the glitter on the wave, inside the blank, black sea. But now she was sleeping again. She had turned her head, her delicate ear against the mattress. Dolores stepped beside me, and we stared down at my mother. With her fixed frown, her closed eyes, and her pinched, intent brow, she seemed to be listening for some imminent secret, her ear pressed close to the sheet. Her expression didn't change. She was patiently, trustfully waiting, as though someone or something, soon, might speak to her, a voice that would rise through the coils and cotton of the bed, through the ceiling of the second floor below, or the ceiling of the first. Even a voice, perhaps, from the earth itself. So none of us moved. My mother did not move, still mutely waiting, still listening for that grand, unreachable secret. How badly I longed to join her there. How badly I wanted to hear it, too.

When I got home, I couldn't find Alice or the boy. I went to the bedroom to smoke more meth, but, with a charge of panic, saw that Gavin's recent gift was nearly gone.

From some part of the house, I could hear a voice: small and wounded, like a cry, or the noise made to stop a cry. It was a pale sound, a ghost's sound, and I looked toward the pictures on the wall, where all the dead, my mother's parents and sisters and brothers, continued their quiet surveillance. I put down the pipe, but now could hear only the heater's electric chuff. A windowpane rattled; the wind combed snow from the roof. I cocked my head, believing the drug would sharpen my hearing: a precision, a squinting of the ear. Slow silence. And then, once again, the noise of someone crying.

I left the bed and moved through the house, passing the empty space on the couch, the mess on the kitchen floor. Reaching the basement door, I twisted the knob and descended.

The dirty cot had been dragged from the storage room to the middle of the basement. Beside it was the Christmas tree, now fully constructed, no ornaments or tinsel or spired star. Sitting beneath the tree, in the center of the cot, was Alice. She was alone, and she was crying. Upon seeing me, she tried to stop, hissing the breaths thinly through her teeth. Then she gave up and let the weeping unravel. I hadn't seen her cry in years—ever since our mother's first diagnosis, she'd stayed willful and defiant—and now the spectacle of it, the noise, was stabbingly brutal. I could only watch, unable to move, pinned in place by the thorns from her throat.

Behind Alice, behind the false evergreen shadows of the tree, the basement had been transformed. Sometime during the morning, while the boy was alone, he'd been stacking boxes and old clothes, shaping constructions from our mother's unused mementoes and antiques. He'd made totems of various heights, some orderly, others jumbled: I recognized old suitcases, maple-syrup sap buckets, and a revolving gemstone globe with a splintered stand. Rain gauges and egg scales. A dented gas can (OGILVIE OIL); a wooden pop-bottle crate (MOUNTAIN DEW FLINT MICHIGAN). The boy had tied objects together with wire, with

John's neckties, with scraps of my mother's scarves. I could see her stuffed cottontail rabbits, riding the backs of the carousel horses. The manual Remington typewriter on which she used to type letters, those days after I'd moved to New York, with their off-kilter K and L and comma keys.

By rearranging the room, he'd inadvertently brought back old images, focused so many blurred memories and moments. It was this renovated basement, I saw now, that had upset Alice: he'd exposed a history, the jumbled remnants of a life. I stepped closer and sat beside her on the cot. I noticed that to fight the chill, she wore her yellow earmuffs and mittens; beside her, with closed eyes and a loud, reverberant purr, was Bones the cat.

"Why did you do this?" she asked.

I started to explain, to reveal the true culprit. Then I saw that the door to the storage room had swung slightly open, and beyond it, the cramped space was empty.

I realized then that the boy was gone.

Alice still knew nothing of him. I knew if she heard the truth, the account of the kidnapped boy, she wouldn't believe a word of it. The events of the past days would seem preposterous, just as my mother's carnival story had seemed preposterous, and she would blame the drugs. So I confessed to building the towers behind us. I told her that yes, I'd assembled the Christmas tree.

Alice had lowered her head, bent as though crumpling from inside. I placed a hand on her shoulder, and softly, steadily, the trembling and weeping ceased. She wiped her nose with the left-hand mitten. "If you're going to stay here during the final days," she said, "then please, *please* try to stay away from the drugs. Please be yourself—not some nervous, hallucinating addict. Do it for her. Please just be Scott."

Unlike the previous day, her words carried no anger or tart, scolding tone. "I'll try," I said. Clearly, this promise wasn't enough for her, so I amended it: "Okay, I *will*."

We sat surveying the towers and stacks. Eventually, I remembered the letter. I took it from my coat pocket and dropped it on Alice's knee. In the dusky basement light, I watched her read the florid sentences. At first it seemed she'd cry again: her eyebrows trembling, her lower lip tucking between her teeth. But she remained calm. She finished the letter, read it a second time, then folded it back into the envelope and closed her eyes.

In her lap, the cat purred ceaselessly. Alice said, "Maybe you're right, after all. I think something really did happen back then. Something she's kept from us, all these years."

"What makes you say that now?"

"Because of this letter. The riding stable. You don't remember me telling you that story?"

"What story?"

"The one about the dolls," she said. "Years and years ago. *You* know—that time she drove me out to the horse stable in the middle of the night, and we buried the dolls."

"Really, I don't know what you're talking about."

I apologized for not remembering, then begged Alice to tell the story again. She took me back twenty, almost thirty years. As a girl, she said, she'd had an impressive collection of dolls. Remember? She kept them in a corner of her bedroom, their bodies assembled in a heavy hope chest, lined with crushed crimson velvet, secured with a gold escutcheon and its own set of keys. But when she was thirteen or fourteen, she decided she'd grown too old for dolls. She simply didn't want them anymore. Our mother said it was fine; if she wanted, they would take her collection to one of the downtown thrift shops and give them away, "so some other little girl could love them."

Alice paused. "But a few days later, she said she'd changed her mind. She had an even better idea." She lifted Bones from the cot, cradling him against her chest. "It was a winter night, probably not too different from tonight. When we lived in the old farmhouse on the hill, way out on Plum Street."

"Would this have been during the time she was drinking? Around the time of Evan Carnaby, when she first got so interested in missing people?"

Alice thought for a moment. "Yes, probably around that time."

"I had a feeling you'd say that. But keep telling the story."

"She said if we wanted, if it was true I'd grown too old for dolls, then she and I could 'lay them to rest.' I wasn't sure what she meant. But we put on our scarves and our hats, and she got two big shovels from the work shed. We crammed their little bodies in a laundry bag, and out we went. You must have been asleep in bed, but she didn't seem to care. We got into the car, and she started driving. After a while, the snow was falling fast and heavy. And I remember being scared—such a horrible feeling, a girl scared of her mother like that—scared because she drove so fast, and she wasn't saying a word, just staring at the road."

Alice spoke of the gathering snow, the slickly dangerous ice. She remembered their black coats and boots; the shovel blades clanging in the backseat. They'd arrived at the Triple Crown stable, parked at the end of the dark drive, and then gotten out of the car. "Follow me, as quiet as you can," our mother had said. They brushed plumes of snow from the fencerows before helping each other over. They moved with sly, tiptoed steps, hiking farther through the field with their shovels at their sides.

As I listened, I tried pursuing my sister and mother as they walked: the shelterbelt of juniper trees, frozen broom-weed tangling at their ankles, clouds creasing the high white moon. I could hear the croak of snow beneath their boots. I could see the palominos and the single appaloosa, snuffling neck-to-neck for warmth.

At last our mother stopped and leaned against her shovel. "Right here's a good enough spot," she said. She checked east toward the stables, then west toward the rows of white-tipped evergreens, assuring they couldn't be seen. "Let's hurry and finish." The ground was hard and obstinate, but she cut at it, Alice told me, digging just enough for a shallow mass grave. And together they unloaded the dolls. Alice lined them up, fussily tucking each body into the pockets of dirt. She smoothed their plastic faces with her mittens (I imagined their yellow, as her mittens now were yellow, the soil crumbling like gingerbread against the wool).

Finally, our mother refilled the hole to bury the dolls. Alice watched them disappear. Cold Kansas earth in their hair, in their plastic nostrils and nails, the sockets of their skulls.

I lay back on the cot. "I can't believe I have no memory of this," I said. "Really, you've told me before? Maybe it's the drugs. A story like that, and I didn't remember?"

"It doesn't matter now. What matters is that something happened to her, something connected to that place."

"You think she kept her memories buried, and only now they're floating back? I'm not so sure I buy that idea."

"Then maybe she *has* remembered. Maybe all this time, for years and years, there were only scattered pieces, a picture here or an impression there. And she's never been able to figure out the *truth* of it all. Maybe she's been going back, to Sterling and God knows where else, to find some kind of answer. Some way to make things clear again."

Alice gave the letter back to me. "Well, for some incomprehensible reason," I said, "she's always kept her search from us."

"Until now. It's like she's asking us, after all this time, for help."

Before returning the letter to my pocket, I reexamined its return address. "Dolores and I are going out there tomorrow. We're meeting at the hospital. We'll wait until the morphine makes her completely quiet and calm, and then we'll drive out to the Triple Crown."

"Please find out anything you can. If you learn any answers— anything—I want you to call me right away. Promise."

"I promise."

Alice placed the cat on the floor. She leaned back, resting her head next to mine, the cot's legs creaking under our weight. Only hours ago, the boy had been sleeping here. The canvas still reeked of his sweat and breath and ragged clothes; I wondered if Alice could smell him too. As she relaxed, auburn curls of her hair fanned across my face, but I didn't brush them away. We stared into the wired boughs of the tree, at the asymmetric angles of the boy's constructions, and higher above, the basement's black, cobwebbed ceiling. We could hear the storm, the snowflakes laced with rime, the wind swinging its gray rage against the windows.

"You're not going back to Lawrence tonight, are you? In this weather?"

"I have to. I'll go by the hospital for a bit, but then I've got to hit the road. Tomorrow morning I have to open the store."

"Just a while ago, when I was driving home in this mess, I was worried you'd already decided to leave. Then I came inside and didn't see you anywhere . . . so what made you come downstairs, anyway? Was there a reason you came down and found all this?"

"I'm not really sure," Alice said. "I was napping, but then something woke me up. It was strange—I thought I heard a noise down here. Like someone singing. It sounded a little like you. Like you were directly below, singing some old song. I didn't think you were back from the hospital yet, so I came down to investigate."

From the eastern edge of town came the remote rumble of snowplows, agilely clearing the streets. We waited, listening, but instead of moving nearer, the plows were driving farther away. Alice sighed; then, for a long while, neither of us spoke. In recent years, she and I had grown progressively deficient at articulating our emotions, and now, through the silence, I tried to convey how badly I wanted her to stay. I needed her here with us. *Alice checked out of this a long time ago,* I remembered telling Kaufman, that morning in the hospital lobby. But I'd been wrong about my sister. I could see that, all along, she'd truly wanted our mother to get well again, to be utterly healed of it. Her optimism wasn't as transparent or easily bruised as mine; and yet it was precisely this hope that had tugged Alice along, through all our visits home, through summer hospitalizations and autumn remissions, the past ten years of both good news and bad. Only now had she fully, finally grasped the irremediable loss. In the last two days, she'd experienced our mother's clenched fists during sleep, the garbled dream conversations, the wounds she'd reflexively bitten into her lips and tongue. The resignation in Kaufman's eyes; the drops of morphine from the amber bottle.

Around us, the room was shrinking and dimming. When Alice spoke again, she returned to that snowy field, that secret expedition to the riding stable, her memory of the shovels and dolls and fluttering snow. "You know what I've always remembered most about that night?"

"What?"

"After we'd buried them—after we'd shoveled the dirt over their little bodies and stamped it hard—she bent down and put her face against the ground. The side of her face . . . her *ear*. Like she was waiting for something. Listening and waiting. Not for the dolls, but for something else."

I thought of the way I'd left our mother in the hospital bed, only hours earlier: her obstinate ear pressed to the bed as the morphine rocked her back to sleep. I hadn't revealed that moment to Alice; by coincidence, she'd conjured the image on her own. Now, when I closed my eyes, I could almost feel the cold wind in my face. I could smell the horses' thick winter coats and hear their breathy apprehension. And yes, lying there on the ground: our mother, silent and smiling, her lashes sparkling with snow. Listening for that forbidden secret.

Together we turned our faces, daughter and son, aiming our ears against the rough canvas of the cot as though that secret lay below us, too. "Shh," I said. "Shh," Alice said. And we listened.

By morning, the snowstorms had subsided but the sky remained a greenish, cloud-crowded gray. As planned, Dolores met me in the hospital room. With equal parts sorrow and surprise, we noticed that Alice had left an uncharacteristic gift: before driving home, she'd bought a spray of red roses for the bedside table. Taped to the lip of the vase was a small pink envelope with Alice's handwritten note. "You should open it and read to her," Dolores suggested. But my mother was peacefully sleeping, and I couldn't muster the nerve.

We decided to take the pickup. On the dashboard, her photographs and clippings had yellowed and curled. I drove, while Dolores took the passenger seat: a reversal of that night I'd arrived from New York, a night that seemed so erstwhile now. We agreed to avoid the highway or direct city streets, to try and recall my mother's favorite route.

Dolores unfolded the map across her knees. For many miles, neither of us spoke. The muddied crests of roadside ice . . . the expressionless churches and houses . . . the flocks of coal-necked Canada geese. I kept expecting to see the scorched ditches or the lonesome oak from that day we'd encountered the boy—*wasn't this the road we took?*—but that scenery never appeared, as though it hadn't existed at all. I rolled my window down an inch, letting the wind rake my hair and clean the morning from my mouth. Dolores crossed her arms against the breeze but didn't complain. Eventually, she reached into her purse and produced a fifth of Jim Beam: "Sure, it's a little early for this. And yes, I really need a drink right now. And no, I don't give a damn what anybody thinks."

"I'm not exactly levelheaded either. Right before I left this morning, I did my very last bit of meth."

She looked across the seat, half-smiled, and took a noisy sip. "We're quite a pair, aren't we?"

"I guess so."

"But we'll stop when she needs us."

"Of course we'll stop. We don't really have a choice, do we?"

The truck rattled and knocked along the frozen dirt roads. The noise reminded me of the shovels in Alice's story, their incessant clang in that long-ago backseat. "Before she left last night," I said, "Alice told me something strange."

"About your mom?"

"I showed her the letter. As she was reading it, she remembered something. One night our mom brought her out to the riding stable, in the dark and in the snow, and they'd buried Alice's dolls. She dug a big hole in the dirt, somewhere out in the horse pasture. They put all the dolls in the hole, and then they covered it up."

"And you'd never heard that story before?"

"Alice says she told me about it, but really, I couldn't remember."

"Oh, Donna. All those secrets! Years and years of secrets!"

What thoughts had troubled my mother that night; whose faces had flared in her mind as she buried the dolls? Had she assigned them names, an Evan or an Abigail? Perhaps a Warren, a Donna?

"I know it sounds silly," I told Dolores, "but when we get to the stables, I want to walk around and start digging. I'd like to try and find those dolls they buried all those years ago."

"Hopefully the place stays open this time of year."

"Guess we should have thought of that before we started driving."

Dolores handed me the bottle. The alcohol would temper the speed of the meth, but I didn't care, I put it to my lips and drank. Ahead, the roadside snowdrifts were soapy and dense; the route grew narrower and snakier than the route from my memory. I still couldn't locate the sweep of land where we'd previously found Otis. Yet I knew I'd traveled these roads before. With my mother, on our missions; and with Alice, on past drives to small-town thrift stores and vintage shops.

On those road trips, Alice and I had always bonded in a smug insouciance: our giggles at the tumbledown mobile homes or outlandishly souped-up cars; our winces at the homespun billboards (REGEHR'S GUN SALES or NEW HARNESSES! COLLARS! REPAIRS!). Now, with Dolores, the mood had changed. It seemed our only bonds were the liquor and our numbing, mystifying stories of my mother. But I realized, as I took another drink from the bottle, that these bonds were sufficient.

She asked if I'd started making preparations for my inevitable return to New York. My initial answer was a quick, dismissive "No," but Dolores persisted, asking further questions as though the silence would wound us. So I said I hadn't thought too much about it. I wasn't certain how to persevere "after all this was over." I'd made so many plans when I left the city, I told her: I'd wanted these last days with my mother to be pure. The countless little thrills we could have shared, the spontaneous trips, the whims and lucky luxuries. I wanted to cook for her, nourishing breakfasts and suppers, extravagant twenty-ingredient recipes we'd always planned to try but hadn't. I wanted to take her to the circus, to rod-and-custom shows at the Hutchinson fairgrounds, maybe even a cookout at Kanopolis Lake. I wanted to pose for pictures, just my mother and I, at the downtown five-and-dime's photo booth, two-buck-fifty for a strip of four. I imagined us laughing in each shot, laughing to show we were tougher than drugs or disease.

Dolores was nodding, making appreciative murmurs at the stops of my sentences. "Sorry I've been talking so much," I said. "You only asked me about New York, and I've been chattering for the last five miles."

"Don't be sorry. I bet it feels good for you to say all that."

"Yes, it does." She offered the bourbon again; I eagerly took it. "You know what else I'm sorry about? I'm really sorry about Ernest."

She turned to watch the flat fields through her window: the emptied grain silos; the stripped and broken cornstalks; the circular hay bales swelling like blond loaves of bread from the snow. After a tense minute of silence, she said, "I just can't believe he took the dog. But I'm going to get a cat! One of those Manx cats—those ones without a tail. I want to name him Rascal. I think those cats are cute when they don't have their tails."

I could picture Dolores, jilted and reclusive, inside her house: drinking and smoking, watching the street from her window, her television droning and the tailless Rascal in her lap. Dolores without her husband Ernest, without her best friend Donna.

"I like those cats, too," I said.

"And so did your mom."

The narrow road began to straighten, and at last we saw the weathered Triple Crown sign. I turned into the driveway, pulled up to the office, and parked. The place was smaller, less significant, than the wobbly picture I'd always carried in my mind; it had all seemed so royal when I was a boy. We got out of the pickup and gingerly shut our doors. Once again, the snow was falling. To our left were the meager stables, the rickety gate and fence, and the barren trails that wound past the horse fields, along the roll of hills, through the distant windbreak of snow-tipped poplars and oaks. To our right stood a drab split-level house. And directly ahead was the office: a small white-pine log cabin, its gutters lined with pennants flapping blue and yellow and red. Lamps were glowing in the windows. Side by side, we stepped to the door and knocked.

The woman who opened the cabin door looked nothing like the pleasant Patricia Claussen I'd imagined from the letter. She was hunchbacked and thin, surprisingly masculine, with a long silver pigtail, blocky lumberjack boots, and a flannel shirt the color of crumbling bricks. She had scarred, puckered cheeks; her mouth was downturned and bitter, like she'd never said *I love you*. "Hope you aren't setting your sights on riding today," she said as she led us inside the cabin's single spacious room.

"You must be Mrs. Claussen," said Dolores, brushing snow from her sleeves.

"Everybody just calls me Pat. But we aren't scheduling rides right now. We just put the horses out to pasture."

After a moment's consideration, she thrust out her hand, and we shook. I heard the telltale creak of a rocking chair and looked to the opposite corner of the cabin, where a chubby teenage girl sat slouching beside a wood-burning stove, immersed in a geometry textbook, one hand busy in a family-size bag of cheese popcorn. The girl didn't bother glancing up at us.

"We know it's too cold and snowy to ride," I said. "We only drove out to ask some questions, if that's okay."

"You sound like those private detectives on those TV shows."

Dolores and I exchanged a quick glance, then laughed artificially. I took the letter from my pocket, held it toward the light, and explained who we were. At the mention of my mother's name, Pat Claussen brightened slightly. The girl in the chair glanced up from her homework to scrutinize us. The girl wore dark lipstick and thick, sky-blue shadow over her eyes; I remembered the photos of Lacey Wyler, that autumn morning in the Haven Café, the smells of coffee and coconut pie. I greeted the girl with a nod, but she turned back to her book.

"That's our assistant Cindy," Pat said. "She was here both times your mom visited. But didn't your mom come out here with you today?"

"She's in Hutchinson Hospital," said Dolores. "Lymphoma."

"Oh, dear. Oh, that's terrible. You just never know! I'm so sorry. The past few months I've been flying back and forth to Colorado to take care of my brother . . . cancer too. You just never know."

Dolores was nodding in tipsy agreement; soon she began sharing her own cancer story. *Nothing like a good disease for making a new friend,* I thought. I let them speak, stepping deeper inside to examine the room. Behind the file cabinets and the central registration desk were monochrome photographs of past and present horses, a display case filled with trophies, and hand-stenciled signs listing regulations and rates. But the dominant feature in the Triple Crown office was the collection of angel pictures. They covered the entire eastern wall, prints from old magazines and books, framed in huge baroque frames that seemed crafted from the same pine as the cabin. There were thirty, perhaps forty or more: solemn angels, rapturous angels, some with huge wings and others with small, angels with haloes of various diameters and heights. Weeks ago, my mother must have stood in this same spot, staring up at the pictures just as I stared now. *Which angel had been her favorite? Which most resembled her Warren?*

I turned back to Pat Claussen, interrupting Dolores's story. "Quite an impressive collection you've got here," I said.

"Oh, I had nothing to do with those. The angels were there when we moved in, so we didn't bother taking them down.

They're a bit of a trademark now . . . some of our regulars even call us the 'Angel Riding Stable.' You know, sometimes I think I like that name even better."

"Oh *that* would be a *terrific* name," Cindy sarcastically said.

Dolores took her hands from her coat pockets; she raised her voice so everyone could hear. "We want to learn more about things like that," she said. "*Past* things. I know that when Donna was here, she asked questions about Sterling, and the history of the stable, and the people who used to live around here. And I know you weren't able to answer. But there are lots of things we need to know! It's very important to us. Anything else you might be able to tell us about this place."

Pat Claussen paused to contemplate, clasping her hands at her chest. She tilted her head toward the ceiling, its high exposed rafters and transverse beams. Ultimately, however, she could only provide a slight, one-shouldered shrug. "Honestly, I'm not the one you should ask. I think you should find a lady in town by the name of Pamela Sporn. She usually goes by Pammy. Works at the Sterling post office; she's been there years and years." She put one hand to the side of her mouth as though confessing a secret. Then she whispered, "Pammy's what some people call the 'town gossip.'"

"Could we go see her today?" I asked Dolores.

"It's Sunday," Cindy said through a mouthful of popcorn. "Post office is closed."

"I've lost all track of the time," Dolores said weakly. "Hours, days, weeks . . . things have been so difficult lately." As she spoke, she seemed close to tears; I moved to stand beside her, placing a soothing hand on her back.

Pat went to the desk, found a Triple Crown business card, and scribbled Pamela Sporn's name on its reverse. "Don't know her number, but you'll certainly find her at the post office. Oh, I just *know* she'll have stories about Sterling and about this place. She'll know all about the Bartons, and probably about the Lockridge family. Maybe she'll know about anyone before them, too."

"That hideous old busybody," Cindy said. "No doubt she'll also tell you every name of every single horse we've ever had out here. She'll know about the original house and the cabins and that time they had the tornado and that time they had the fire—"

"Now, *Cindy*," Pat Claussen said. "That poor woman is *not* a hideous old busybody."

I walked across the room, toward the wood-burning stove and the softly creaking chair, to stare down at the girl. "Wait. This is the first we've heard of a tornado or a fire. Why didn't you mention those to my mother?"

Cindy scowled, dunking her hand into the popcorn; when she pulled it out again, her fingertips were orange with powdery cheese. "Because she didn't ask," she said.

"Those things happened a long, long time ago," said Pat. "Possibly even before the Lockridges were here. All we know is the land was severely damaged in the tornado, and then just the following year was the fire. Must have been terrible! The way I heard it, the fire destroyed all the papers for the horses, all their progeny records, almost everything. Destroyed the main house, and the farmhands' cabins that used to be connected. Apparently a few people were killed, even, and nearly all the horses."

In Dolores's face, I could see a flustered tension; she was striving, just as I was striving, to make some connection, some link between these newly conjured images from the past and the impenetrable stories my mother had told. "Then that's what we have to do," I told Pat Claussen. "We'll go find this Sporn woman. Hopefully we can get more information from her."

After a long, uncomfortable minute, Dolores regained the strength to speak. I could hear the impatience in her thank-yous and good-byes. She zipped her coat, tightened the scarf around her throat, and began inching toward the door.

But I wasn't satisfied yet. I knelt beside the chair, clamped my hand over Cindy's fleshy wrist, and squeezed. "Just one last question," I told her, so softly only she could hear. "And don't lie to me. I want to know this: when my mother was here, either of the times you spoke to her, was she with someone else? Or was she completely alone?"

She didn't try to pull away. "I don't remember," she said. "Alone, I think."

"Think harder. Was there anyone at all? Maybe a boy who looked a lot like me?"

With our faces so close, surely Cindy could see the desperation in my eyes, my nose raw and runny from the meth. But she didn't look away. She shut her geometry book; a log crackled inside the black stove. Then she blinked twice and said, "No. She was by herself."

Across the room, Dolores had opened the door to leave. I loosened my grip from the girl's wrist, stood again, and hurried away, following Dolores outside, back to the fluttering snow. Pat saw us to the entryway; I heard the squeak of her boots, the rustle of her red flannel shirt. She stood at the door, murmuring the standard well wishes: hopefully we'd get to enjoy the holidays with Donna; hopefully she could find peace. "And maybe you'll still have enough time for researching that book of yours," she said. I turned to look at Pat again, but it was too late, she was closing the door. Yet in that half-second before it slammed shut, I glimpsed the cabin wall with its multitude of angels: their haloes and deathless shine; their radiant gowns and lushly feathered wings.

Dolores marched to the truck, returning to her warm passenger seat, her remaining sips of Jim Beam. But I didn't follow. Instead I moved toward the stables, the wooden fence crusted with snow. I was thinking of my mother. Thinking of the tornado and fire; thinking of Pammy Sporn. I placed both hands on the fence's upper rail, and, with a surge of strength, pushed myself over and into the field.

Now I was alone. I surveyed the ground as if to see the battered, ancient heads of Alice's dolls, emerging from their mass grave to greet me. But there was only the hoof-tracked snow. When I looked toward the windy western horizon, beside the trails and trees, I could see the crush of horses: austere and riderless, with their winter coats of sorrel and gold and steel-gray; their muscular haunches; their slowly heaved breaths. I wanted to run to them, but the snow was falling harder, hard and heavy and fast, so fast that soon I couldn't see the horses at all.

TEN

KAUFMAN WAS BUSY all day, and assigned
two interns the task of moving her home. The interns were
boys from Hutchinson Community College. Both had a
clumsy, apologetic charm; they'd attempted a polite formal-
ity with their khakis and button-down shirts. Yet I noticed
they wore tennis shoes, they carried tins of snuff in their

back pockets, and their haircuts showed impressions from their baseball caps. As we left the hospital, the boys waited as I thanked the nurses. They transferred my mother to a stretcher, then wheeled her down the halls. We passed the aisles of other patients' rooms, both closed and open doors; we passed the disorganized gift shop where I'd bought cards that first hospital morning. *Wishing you well. Here's hoping you bounce back soon.*

It was still snowing, and the roads were icy and frail. What Kaufman and the interns had called an "ambulance" was actually a Chevy van the same gray shade as the snow. Its antiseptic-scented carriage was roomy enough for the stretcher and the portable hospice bed. The interns sat in front, hardly speaking during the drive. I took the seat beside my mother and watched her sleep. Now and then her scabbed lips trembled soundlessly. I held her hands and spoke as though to an impatient child: *We're almost there, just a few miles more. Soon you'll be home, all snug and warm.*

I bent lower to whisper stories of New York in her ear. Just down the street from my apartment, I said, is a cramped antique store with the most amazing things. There's a crotchety old lady who hardly hears a word you say. I bet you could get a good bargain out of her. When you finally come to visit, I'll take you, and we can buy whatever you want.

At Pen & Ink, I told her, the textbook writers are required to follow certain guidelines. We can't write stories that might upset our young readership or rile their parents. No stories about illness; no addiction or alcohol or drugs. Nothing about disappearances or kidnappings. So I guess that means I'll have nothing to write about! I suppose I can't go back! I'll have to stay with you forever!

A few miles from home, my mother made a wet, clotted cough: leaking from the corners of her mouth was a rusty grit, like the undissolved grains of instant tea that often floated in her glass. I dabbed her mouth with my shirtsleeve. The nurse named Pearl had told me she'd done this twice before, and Kaufman had said it was normal toward the end.

Even as she coughed, I couldn't stop whispering in her ear. I'll find the answers for you, I said. I'll learn about Warren. I'll learn what happened when you disappeared.

When we reached the house, the nurse from Hutchinson Hospice was waiting on the snowy front porch. Her station wagon, with an identifying HH sticker on the door, had replaced Alice's car beside the garage. In the nurse's hands were clipboards and two overstuffed medical bags. *So here she is,* I thought, *the one assigned to join us at the end.* Her clothes were plain and seemed a size too small; although her skin smelled piney with soap, I saw faint stains on her blouse. There were flesh-colored hearing aids in her ears. When she smiled, she regarded me pityingly over the rims of her glasses, as though she knew I hadn't slept in days.

Upon seeing the hospice nurse, the interns bowed their heads and waited for instructions. As a girl, she'd doubtlessly endured constant teasing from boys like these. Now she was their sergeant, coaching as they retrieved the stretcher and bed from the van. Lastly, they moved my mother: tentative and painstaking, as though moving a sculpture. Above their heads, the power lines and branches were creaking in the wind.

When we got inside the house, they all stopped to look at me. "For days and days she's been waiting to come home," I said. "If only she'd wake up to enjoy it."

"It does get lonely in the hospital," said the nurse. "Without all your things around you."

It was time for proper introductions, and the boys offered their dampened hands. The nurse's name was Mary McVickers. The interns were Wesley and Doug.

"And this is Donna's son," Mary said, as though they were seeing me for the first time. "He's the primary caregiver."

The title was daunting, unnecessarily official. But Mary had used my mother's name, where so many others had said *her* son or *the* son. I straightened and shook the boys' sturdy hands. Then the three of us helped Mary unfold the starched hospice linens: one red blanket, one yellow, and a heavy sheet of blue plaid. Thankfully, nothing was white. As we arranged the bed, I watched ruffs of snow melting from the boys' coats, flakes fading gently from their commanding shoulders, from the napes of their necks. Strangely, the snow wouldn't melt from my mother. I couldn't take my eyes from it, the bits of snow clinging to her earlobes and lashes and hair.

It was clear the interns hadn't noticed these particulars, the tiny sounds and sights I knew I'd carry forever. Their job was finished now; they prepared to leave, shuffling their feet, murmuring like hypnotists. "Good-bye," said Wesley. "Our prayers are with you," said Doug.

Suddenly, my mother coughed. We all looked down at her. She was still sleeping but had spat up again, the grainy fluid tarring her lips.

"That's common at this stage," Mary said. She bent to the floor for her medical bag, but by the time she could unzip it, I'd already cleaned the mess with my sleeve.

When Dolores arrived, she couldn't keep still. She sifted through the mail, watered the browning plants, sprayed paper towels with furniture polish and ran them over the room's dust. She organized the magazines, then set a bowl of oyster crackers on the coffee table, as though preparing for a party. She helped me tote Mary's things from the station wagon: the aluminum oxygen tank, the packages of bathroom supplies, and a new wheelchair, which we folded sacredly into a corner. Neither of us spoke about the chair; we seemed to sense she wouldn't need it again.

"I'm willing to mosey on over here whenever you need me," Dolores told Mary. "I can stay as long as you want."

"Whatever's best for Scott."

"Dolores is welcome anytime," I said. "They're best friends. They've been through a lot together."

Dolores lifted her chin, lightly blushing with pride. We were colleagues now. In the lamplight, I noticed the lenses of her pink-framed glasses had been smudged with fingerprints, as though she'd been holding her face in her hands. She wore the same jacket and boots from yesterday's trip to the stable. She stepped to the bedside, smoothed the blankets, and bent close to my mother's face. "Are you really sleeping," she asked, "or are you fooling us all?"

"I think she's fooling us all," I said.

Mary showed us a sheet of paper on her clipboard, where she'd written the various dosages and instructions in impressively ornate calligraphy. "Since today's the first day, I'll go through everything with you. After this, you can both take over the duties."

"So that means you won't be staying here?" I asked.

"Oh, no. Is that what you thought?" She patted my arm, like an aunt. "I have too many others to oversee. You're the caregiver now. But I'll be back every day. You know, to help things along."

Hearing this, I recoiled from her touch with abrupt resentment. I'd mistakenly assumed she'd give us her full attention; I hadn't realized her obligations, her further doomed and bedridden patients. Dolores saw this change in me, and I sensed her scrambling to avert any possible scene. She tried to ease the tension by relating stories of my mother, telling Mary about the antiques, the carousel horses, the handcrafted scarves. "Now, why don't you run and get some of those to show Mary," Dolores said. As I left the room, I thought of the legion of women to whom my mother had mailed her scarves, trading stories of doctor reports and diagnoses, communicating in their exclusive, reckless lexicon. I wondered how many of these women were still living; how many would outlast my mother.

When I came back, Mary was standing by the antique high chair, running her hand along the finials, staring at me with an awkward pity. "Here's what I want to know," I told her. "Will she be able to talk some more? Or will she just be sleeping now, until the end?"

"I'm not entirely sure," said Mary. "We need to keep the morphine very strong."

"I just want to talk to her."

"Oh, you should always talk to her. You should talk all you want." Mary moved closer; I briefly feared she would take my hand or hook her arm through mine. "One of the best things is to keep talking. Use as pleasant a voice as you can. At the end, they might lose the ability to speak, and they might not be able to see well. But their hearing stays. Their hearing's still good. It's their last connection to the world."

Behind us, Dolores cleared her throat. "I bet you need to eat something," she said. "Maybe go to the bedroom for some rest. Or how about a bath? Bet you could use a nice hot bath."

Of course: my sloppy appearance, my sour smell. This explained the suspicion in Mary's eyes; surely the interns, returning to Hutchinson in the van, were ridiculing me now. And so, shamefully, I took Dolores's suggestion. I locked the bathroom door, stripped, and twisted the bathtub faucet as hot as I could stand. In the tarnished mirror above the sink, my eyes were bloodshot and swollen. I felt too tired to shave, and the toothbrush proved too severe for my bleeding, meth-softened gums. As the steam filled the room, I tried thinking of ways to describe my appearance, words that my companion freelancers at Pen & Ink might use: *gaunt . . . repellent . . . pallid.* Yet I knew they couldn't write a story about me. And no one, certainly no acquaintance from that old life, needed to see me now.

After the bath, I returned to help Dolores. She had removed her boots and pulled the rocking chair closer to the bed. The room was darker and smelled of evergreen, as though my mother had been dreaming of trees.

"It was getting drafty, so I adjusted the thermostat." She saw my dampened hair and smiled. "Now you're sparkling clean."

"Where's Mary?"

"She had to see another patient. She'll be back around noon tomorrow."

"I can tell she doesn't trust me."

"She was only worried, that's all. She said to make sure you were careful with the morphine and the pills."

I leaned against the mattress, the space beside my mother's feet. Without my help, Mary and Dolores had propped the bed forward, and they'd replaced the hospital gown with her favorite lavender robe. On the floor was a round rotating fan, its base stamped with the Hutchinson Hospice logo, its flurry on the air. I realized that the evergreen was artificial, from Mary's aerosol can; beneath it were the alkaline smells of urine and sweat she'd tried to cover or breeze away. I closed my eyes, and eventually Dolores stopped rocking the chair. For a long interval, neither of us spoke; I knew that both of us wanted my mother's voice. Anything to hear it again, a sentence, even further bits of her dream-speak, that unintelligible wander of words. But the moments passed in stillness. We grew acutely aware of her breathing, the ragged, sand-scrape pulls of air. These breaths had started only yesterday. They were sharp and percussive, and I tried to focus instead on the noisy heater, or the empty and fill of the refrigerator's ice. I listened to the sounds outside the walls: the limbs snapping from the trees, the occasional sparrow or arguing dog or distant horn. The noise of the living world, with all its persistent, unhesitant cadences.

Eventually, Dolores broke the quiet. "Did you call that Sporn woman?" she asked.

"Not yet. With all this ruckus of bringing Mom home . . . I'll do it first thing tomorrow."

"And I think you really should eat something."

"I know. I look terrible."

"You'll look better if you put some food in your stomach."

Nearly two weeks had passed since I'd last made a trip to the Haven grocery. I went to the kitchen cupboards but found only a can of soup, split pea with ham, a flavor I knew my mother had hated. The can was coated with dust; she'd surely bought it long ago for John. I stood at the stove, watching it simmer in its battered, red-handled pan. I thought of winter afternoons when I was a boy, cold days when she often surprised Alice and me with our favorite cream-of-tomato soup. But the split pea was nothing like her cream of tomato. It smelled faintly rotten, its color the same sullen green as the pickup's seats.

In the chair beside the bed, Dolores was rocking again, humming softly to herself or maybe my mother. "Going down to the basement for a while," I told her. She nodded without looking up. I stuck a spoon in the thickened pool of soup, then carried the pan downstairs to eat alone.

The basement remained as Alice and I had left it just two nights ago: the smells of laundry and loam, the dust and cobwebs and diffracted gray-white light, and, farther in, the Christmas tree and the boy's tall, intricate constructions. I saw that it would take hours, even days, to dismantle the towers. I put the pan of soup on the floor, and then lifted a corner of the cot, dragging it back to the storage room. Beside the space where he'd once slept, the boy had loosed the contents of his pockets: a silver rat-tail comb; six pennies, two keys, and a lint-crusted quarter; a single wadded wrapper from a Cherry Mash bar.

Beside these items were the pictures she'd once kept in the secret binders, the children who resembled Donna and Warren. The boy had also unfolded the map, displaying the ink-circled towns of Haven, Hutchinson, Sterling. Lastly, bunched on the floor, was the pillow where he'd rested and dreamed.

He'd centered the name tag, facedown, on the pillow. Its paper was rimpled and smudged with fingerprints, but it was the same he'd worn on that day we'd found him on the road. I touched a finger to its adhesive and turned it over.

(My mother's voice, on that overcast day in the truck: *Did you see his face? Did you see who he looks like?*)

For the first time, a name had been written in the white space. But the name wasn't ALLEN. It wasn't EVAN, HENRY, or even WARREN. The name on the tag was my own.

I stuck the name tag to my shirt and went back upstairs. In the rocking chair, Dolores had drifted to sleep, her fists clenched. Her face seemed troubled and tense, while, nearby, my mother's was utterly calm. Morphine was the opposite of crystal meth, but seeing its effect made me want something equally precious and potent. I knew I had to call Gavin again.

I wasn't certain how to wheedle him into sending a second package to the phantom house, but I couldn't risk the impending days of withdrawal.

First, I checked the messages on the bedroom answering machine. Kaufman had called to ask if things had gone well with Mary. Next, a message from Alice, saying the roads back to Lawrence had been fine, that she and the cat had arrived without harm. "I'm thinking of you," Alice said. "Please tell Mom I'm thinking of her, too."

Surprisingly, I still remembered the number for Gavin's apartment. After five dismaying rings, someone finally answered. But instead of Gavin, it was his brother Sam. Instantly, I could picture their luridly painted apartment walls, could smell the incense and the scorch of the pipe.

At first, Sam didn't remember who I was. When I reminded him, he said, "Oh, right. Back in Kansas."

"Yes. That's where I am now. And I really need to talk to him."

"So you haven't heard." His vowels were short and raspy, like a continuous cough; he was obviously high. "Gavin hasn't been here for days."

"Please. It's very important."

"I'm not sure what to tell you," Sam said. "I think he might've skipped town. Don't know if he's in trouble, or if he's playing some kind of joke. But Gavin's gone. Here one day, then gone the next. It's like he disappeared."

Just before midnight, she began randomly murmuring again. The sounds lured me from the bedroom and woke Dolores from her chair. We found a yellow notepad and one of Mary's ballpoint pens, its HH logo on the side, its plastic cap grooved with teeth marks. But we couldn't decipher my mother's words. Her voice had gone thinner, curiously distant, as though she spoke through water: the neurons firing, all the secrets and thoughts, all the fading, unfinished intentions.

"She's talking to someone who isn't there," Dolores said.

After a time, the noises stopped, and then, suddenly, her eyes opened. We hadn't seen her awake in days, and she seemed confused, trying to turn her head on the pillow. Dolores dropped the notepad and pen to the floor. "It's okay, Mom," I said. We could see that her awakening was nothing like we'd hoped. "We're right here." I soothed a hand against her heart, the way I figured she'd done when I was a boy, back when something outside, some thunderstorm or nocturnal noise, had frightened me.

It seemed she didn't realize we'd brought her home. Gradually, her breaths began to change. In sleep, they were ragged, yet came at steady intervals; after she woke, however, they quickened to sharp, panicky coughs. She was still fighting it. I could sense the flutter of her thoughts, could feel her straining to unscramble them. "She needs water," Dolores said, hurrying to the kitchen for a cup and the box of hospital straws.

I sat at the bed's edge and vainly tried to ease the trembling. Her gaze moved across my face, but I could tell she didn't recognize me. Her struggle brought forth bitter memories of New York: the three separate times I'd seen friends overdose, those fights against the speed of too much crystal meth or cocaine, the helplessly rigor-mortis holds of ketamine. The seizures, the darting eyes, the curled, clawing hands. How I hated myself for thinking of them, those fellow addicts from that ancient life.

Dolores placed the cup against my mother's chin, and I bent the straw to her mouth. The new hospital straws were clear, corrugated with bendable necks, nothing like the ones I'd snipped in half and used for meth. My mother tried to drink. The muscles were twitching in her face; it was taking all her strength. Finally, a little water flowed through the straw. We watched her trying to swallow, her tongue moving dully across her broken lips. The blood was black where it had dried, warm red where the skin had newly split. We found the tube of ointment, thumbing it onto the sores as Mary had instructed.

"She seems cold," Dolores said, so I went to the bedroom, opened the old steamer trunk, and unfolded one of my mother's favorite quilts. The quilt was ragged, with many pieces missing or loose; she had bought it at an estate sale after a neighbor had died. Its meandering red and white pattern, she'd told me once, was called "drunkard's path." I remembered thinking how maudlin that sounded, how sad.

When I came back to the room, the trembling had doubled. I'd never seen her so scared. In Kaufman's hospice pamphlets I'd read stories of the submitters, the obeyers, the bedridden women and men who'd inevitably asked their doctor or God to "set them free." But I'd also read the stories of those who wouldn't relent. My mother had always been one of the latter: she'd remained stubborn, convinced of another eventual rally. And Dolores and I had always encouraged her.

Part of me wanted to try this encouragement now, to remind my mother of the unfinished projects in the basement and garage, to extricate the passion from her dread and fear. But another part, the pragmatic part I'd so often erased through meth, knew I could no longer embolden her. *Palliative care* was the term explained in the pamphlets, and we understood that our job was to ease the symptoms, to abate the pain, to surround the bed and hold her hand.

"Maybe it's time for more medicine," said Dolores.

"According to Mary's schedule, we should wait a little longer."

"I don't care about that schedule. She's in pain, and she needs it."

Dolores caressed her face, trying to calm her movements. I unscrewed the bottle of concentrated morphine, pointed the dropper between her lips, and squeezed, a brown *plat, plat,* two drops more than the recommended dosage. We watched as she struggled with it. The eyes squeezing shut, the involuntary swallow. I realized the irony of Mary leaving the morphine with us, the bleary-eyed alcoholic and the meth addict, the pair she called the "primary caregivers." It was all so comically compliant, so Midwest. A New York nurse would never trust the bottle in our hands. My mother would have laughed about this; she would have devised a joke with a fractious punch line, and we would have laughed with her.

Now we could only wait, keeping her calm until the drug took effect. We gave her more water, and Dolores spoke soothingly in her ear. She seemed to know instinctively how to perform, to understand what my mother needed, and watching this skill made me sharply jealous. But I reached across the bed and touched Dolores's hand, trying to convey my gratitude. I still hadn't broken down, not yet. I'd seen my mother's tears, and I'd seen the nurses at the hospital struggling. I'd even seen Dolores, even Alice. But something had stalled in me: I could feel the hovering weight, the compression.

Dolores described the snowfall, the latest soap-opera episodes, the women who'd asked "How's Donna doing?" at last week's Bingo. But nothing she said would steady the tremors. Sometimes it seemed my mother wanted to respond; she even made low, wheezing huffs from the back of her throat. We tried to understand, but the responses came too quickly, jaggedly, and when she stopped to swallow or breathe, the effect was like an enormous book snapping shut, shutting off the incomprehensible words.

"When I was sick," Dolores said, "you know what I really liked? I liked when someone would read to me."

Although I wasn't certain, I could guess that this *someone* was Ernest. I could feel her straining to not mention his name. "Then let's find something," I said.

Dolores leafed through the magazine rack, while I went to the shelf of antique children's books against the wall. Nothing seemed quite right. I remembered my mother's request for *Hansel and Gretel*—she'd begged me, that evening in the hospital parking lot, to search the bookshops and antique stores—and now I longed to read that familiar story, escorting her through that dappled forest with the little boy and girl, following their footprints down the tapering path. But I hadn't found *Hansel and Gretel* for her; I'd even failed at this.

Then I remembered the letters she'd received. The responses to her classified ads; all the articles she'd clipped from papers and magazines. I knew she'd saved a bundle in the kitchen cupboard, and I left the room to find them. When I returned to her bedside, Dolores leaned back in the chair to listen; I put the stack on my lap, unfolded the first article, and began reading to my mother.

In early May of 1998, Sharon Stevens, 36, of Lansing, Michigan, disappeared. She was last seen by a group of schoolchildren, walking along Main Street near the downtown area. Sharon was tall and had shoulder-length brown hair. She was wearing a gray Minnie Mouse sweatshirt. She had two tattoos: the letters ATN on one shoulder, a bright bluebird on the other.

Christopher Godlewski was twenty-five when he went missing from his parents' home. A known abuser of heroin and other drugs, Christopher was last seen in downtown Kansas City. He was unemployed, although he used to serve in the marines. Since that cold January day in 2005 when Christopher disappeared, his younger sister has given birth to twins. His family has never given up hope, and they wait patiently for the day when he will return to meet his nephews.

I looked up from my lapful of envelopes and clippings. My mother seemed peaceful now. Dolores held out a hand; I surrendered part of the stack to her. Previously, she'd frowned on my mother's collection of the missing—on what she'd called "her morbid obsession"—but now she submerged herself, reading the articles with dramatic inflection and finesse. Nadine Schroeder . . . Jane McCandless . . . Richard Rose. We alternated reading them, more ages and dates, their distinguishing shirts and hats and coats, the desolate cities and streets where they were last seen.

After fifteen minutes, her muscles relaxed and her breathing steadied. She was sleeping at last. We could hear the insistent wind; the sleet-sharp branches against the gutters and eaves. Dolores found the clipboard and pen to chart the morphine dosage, the precise time. Then we gathered my mother's collection and walked to the kitchen.

Dolores poured two glasses of tea. We drank through the bendable hospice straws. The tea was cold and lemony, and it roused me slightly. "It's really happening, isn't it?" I asked.

"I think so. Are you afraid?"

"I don't know."

"When you were in the tub, I asked Mary how long she thought it would be. Her guess was sometime this week."

"But I want to solve this—this *mystery*. We still need to connect with this Sporn woman. I feel like we're getting so close now."

"We can't leave your mother alone like this. You'll have to drive to Sterling on your own."

In my pocket was the business card with Pamela's name, and the number I'd found for Sterling's post office. "Maybe she's free tomorrow. I'll call first thing in the morning."

Dolores leaned against the fridge, hesitantly sipping through the straw. She turned to watch my mother, and, after a long pause, looked back to me. "When I walked in today," she said, "I could hardly stand it. Seeing her lying there, looking nothing like her old self. Even her smell was gone—her soap and shampoo and perfume."

"I know. I know."

"I wanted things to be the same for her here. I guess I thought that once she came back home, we'd get to have her again. The same Donna as before."

She slid her arms around my shoulders and pulled me toward her. It was a clumsy hug, like the hug of two aging men. The tea splashed from my glass, onto our shoes and the floor.

Then Dolores pulled away. She was staring over my shoulder, at the gallery of the missing on the kitchen wall. "Well, look at that," she said. "Another picture of that boy. His aunt must have sent more . . . Henry Barradale, right?"

Shadows had darkened the room. We moved closer to examine, and she tapped a fingernail on the specific photo. But the face she'd noticed wasn't Henry at all. It was my own face, the picture I'd pinned there as a joke. The snapshot my mother had taken when I was seventeen: the pimples and brooding scowl, the earrings and coal-black clothes.

I removed the picture from the wall and folded it into my pocket. "Yes," I told Dolores. "It's the dead boy."

ELEVEN

AS IT HAPPENED, Pamela Sporn was expecting our call: Cindy, the miserable, popcorn-crunching girl from the stable, had dropped by the post office to forewarn her of our visit. On the phone, she expressed her sympathy over my mother's health. "Please, call me Pammy," she said. She couldn't wait to meet me, but was "swamped with work" until Friday. She gave the address for a Sterling bar and grill, which I copied onto the Triple Crown business card. "I've never been interviewed for a real-life *book*," she said before hanging up.

In the three days before Friday, the withdrawal symptoms grew sharper, more wounding, than before. I tried staying vigilant at the bedside with Dolores; tried assisting Mary with her daily two-hour duties. I helped them with the sponge baths and morphine and meds. Even helped with the Foley catheter, which Mary said would decompress the bladder and relieve unnecessary pressure. They lifted the nightgown and swabbed her with a gleaming yellow jelly. I saw her stomach and Cesarean scar; I saw the dense, surprisingly blond patch of hair. "You don't have to watch this," Dolores whispered. When the catheter entered, my mother's eyes fluttered open, but she still couldn't speak, couldn't truly recognize my face.

Nights, I'd stand for hours in the dark room, watching. Sometimes I'd touch her neck for a pulse, the delicate way a blind boy touches a face to determine rage or joy. Sometimes I'd simply listen to the rise and fall and breath.

By Friday, the snow had stopped but the cold was bitter, soundless, permanent. Dolores arrived at sunrise, and, minutes later, we heard Mary's station wagon turning onto our street. I walked outside to help her with the medical bags. On her car seat were two cans of the evergreen spray, a stack of hospice pamphlets, and empty prescription bottles. Hanging from her rearview mirror was a tiny, sun-faded teddy bear, clutching a valentine with the words I LOVE MOMMY.

"We've scheduled the pastor's visit for later today," Mary said. "I hope that's okay with you."

"That's fine. Anything—fine."

Back inside, I saw Dolores checking her watch, and knew it was time to drive to Sterling. I found one of John's old jackets and a pair of his gloves; I gathered the notebooks and pencils and tape recorder. "Lying about this supposed book still doesn't feel right," I told Dolores. "But if it means getting some answers, I'm going to do it."

"Too bad I can't come along."

"I'll be back as soon as I can."

"Maybe you should make a day of it. Don't you need a little time outside the house? After you talk to that woman, go drive somewhere! Go clear your head for a while."

"There's nothing else for me to do."

"Drive around Hutchinson. Get your mom a strawberry milkshake. Hell, get us *all* strawberry milkshakes. I'll give you some money."

Mary looked up from her clipboard. The lamplight glinted on her crucifix, the pink plastic of her hearing aid. "They opened some new stores at the mall," she said. "There's one of those outlet shoe stores, and a Mexican restaurant."

"Ooh, *Mexican*," said Dolores. She turned to Mary and, as though I were a child, said, "He really likes Mexican."

"No, I'd rather just come right home," I said. In truth, I was achingly hungry, but knew I couldn't hold it down; all the years of crystal meth had corroded my stomach lining, and the spicy food would make me sick for days. But Mary and Dolores couldn't quite comprehend this, just as they couldn't comprehend how difficult it was for me to leave here. This house—our immediate, encompassing world—was all I had left. This room and blanketed bed; these final glimmers and movements that composed my mother. I couldn't extend myself beyond these last days, and I hadn't planned for anything else.

Dolores saw me to the door. Before I could protest, she stuffed a grimy wad of bills into the pocket of John's jacket. "Now go find out any answers that woman might have," she said. "But honestly, I bet your mom would want nothing more than for you to take a break. So do the things you did when you were young. Go out and be a kid again."

Pammy Sporn was waiting at a green vinyl booth, the lone customer before the lunchtime rush. She'd already ordered a plate of French fries and a pint of pale beer. The sight of the food brought the nausea back to my throat, but I swallowed and deeply breathed, I took the opposite seat and placed the recorder between us. When Pammy smiled, I instantly liked her better than the women from the Triple Crown. She was tall, with a wise, wrinkled face, yellow teeth, and tarnished yellow hair. She even wore a yellow shirt. *Like an ear of corn,* I thought, and wished my mother were here to note the weird resemblance, too.

The walls of the bar and grill were covered in vintage Kansas license plates. The air smelled of sawdust and beer. Above the bar, a television was softly playing, but its picture, like the TV at home, was a formless snarl of colors. I saw that each table had been fitted with a dainty chrome jukebox, chiefly country-western standards. On ours, Pammy had chosen incessant Elvis: "Don't Be Cruel" was ending, and "Heartbreak Hotel" came next.

The waitress emerged from the kitchen to take my order. I asked for a glass of water, no ice. Pammy ordered another Old Milwaukee. As I shrugged free from John's bulky jacket, I realized I'd been wearing the same soiled shirt for days; the SCOTT name tag remained stuck to its front.

"I'm so excited to talk with you," Pammy said. "People at work are always saying I should tell my stories to somebody writing a book." She lowered her fork to touch the tape machine—two tines on play, and two on record—and our interview began.

For many minutes, I let her dominate the conversation. I breathed slowly, trying to will my sickness away. Eventually, I knew, I'd find some strategy for steering her toward the town's history, the riding stable. I wanted any possible knowledge of a peach orchard, an Imperial, a Warren. But for now I let Pammy talk about her job at the Sterling Post Office ("Twenty-two years and counting!"); I listened as she confessed she'd never wanted children or a husband ("Believe me, I suffer enough headaches sorting mail every day!")

Then, although we were alone, Pammy lowered her voice and raised a hand to her mouth. "But that doesn't mean I can't submit a good story for your research," she said.

She wanted to tell about a boy she'd known in high school, back in the fifties. His name was Bill McCoy. Pammy had developed a crush while watching him sink free throws during basketball practice. Her junior year, she'd sat behind Bill in concert band: he was first-seat alto sax, and she a red-faced, reed-squeaking beginner. She wanted him to notice her, she said. Only that. All the gossipy oaths, the secret pursuings. She'd even been paired with Bill, one lucky afternoon, at the local hospital's First Aid fair. She still remembered his clipped, manicured nails. Still saw the crown whorl on his scalp when he hunched to resuscitate the airless mannequin: tilt head; clear mouth of debris; breathe, rest, breathe.

I found it hard to pierce questions through her reverie. I let her ramble for five more minutes, then ten. Bill had been so sweet, his eyes were the prettiest blue, and my, was he ever a gentleman. "He was like our town's movie star," she said. "He could've *been* someone."

But Bill McCoy, I knew, had no link to the information I needed from her. Finally, I interrupted with a nod. "That's quite a story," I said. "Any theories on what happened to him?"

"Nobody knows. Not long after graduation, he just left town. Didn't tell a soul. Just took off . . . *gone*."

The waitress returned to set our drinks on the table. No further customers had entered the bar and grill, and the TV's images hadn't aligned. With a silver flood of quarters, Pammy re-fed the miniature jukebox: Elvis, ceaseless Elvis. She finished her first beer and began the second. She'd stopped eating her lunch, but now used the table's squeezable ketchup bottle to trace a lacy mess of stars across the fries. With her head lowered, I could see that the blonde was artificial. I could easily picture her in bed, the faded dye stains on her pillow, each soap-opera heartache washing her with its television wave. The peeling red-rose wallpaper, the framed Bill McCoy photograph on the nightstand.

"Do you think Bill's story might be something you'd follow for your book?" she asked.

"Maybe later. Right now, I need to ask you some important questions. They might seem strange, and they might not make much sense. But I've heard you're the one who knows the most about this town, and I hope you might supply some answers."

The one who knows the most. Pammy grinned and nodded at the acknowledgment. On the table surface, my hand was shaking: a combination, I knew, of the meth withdrawal and the worry over the things she might reveal. Or worse, the things she might *not* reveal. Pammy had noticed my shaking, too; it was strong enough to shudder her beer. Beside her glass, the tape machine's wheels made their wee, rhythmic creak.

"We're looking for a person named Warren," I said. "He would have been five, maybe ten years younger than you. Do you remember anyone by that name?"

"Warren as a first name, or a last?"

"A first. Anyone here in Sterling, or somewhere near here."

"I know a family with that *last* name. They live just south of town. Wheat farmers. They moved from Saskatchewan . . . they've only lived here a couple years." She closed her eyes, thinking. "Can't say I know anybody with Warren as a first name, though."

"Then what about this: do you know any family who might travel around with the state fair? Either now or in the past? Town-to-town carnivals, that sort of thing?"

"Carnivals? No, not carnivals. But quite a few people moonlight at the state fair for a couple of weeks every fall. Don't know anyone who travels with it, though."

"What about a business called Sterling Repair? Surely there's a Sterling Repair in town."

"Used to be. Earl Borders ran a shop called Sterling Maintenance and Repair—radios and televisions and whatnot—but he closed it down a few years ago. People were going to the new computer repair places in Hutchinson, and his business went belly-up."

"Do you know how long he'd been running the shop?"

"Oh, a good ten years at least. I'd say ten, eleven, maybe twelve."

I took a drink of the water and watched Pammy drink her beer. Her answers were coming eagerly, abruptly, and yet nothing was cohering, none of the crucial questions had been solved. On the jukebox, another song ended, and rising in its place were the opening strains of "Are You Lonesome Tonight." Pammy leaned back, savoring the sound.

"All right," I said. "Now I want to know all you can tell me about the history of the riding stable."

She sighed, frowning slightly. "Yes, Cindy *said* you'd be asking that."

"My mother went out there, and then I went out there, but those ladies couldn't help us much."

"I like to call it the Angel Riding Stable. Have you seen their collection? So *darling*. I sure would love to have all those pretty angels hanging on *my* walls."

"I want to know about the Lockridges. Or even better, if you have any facts from the years before that." I looked closely at the tape machine to confirm it was indeed recording, and then I turned the notebook to an empty page. "Can you talk about the late forties, maybe the fifties?"

She gave a fast, hair-loosening shake of her head, as though dispelling unwanted memories. "For years, that place had nothing but terrible luck. Everybody used to think it was cursed! First there was the tornado. I was just ten or eleven, but I remember. Touched down southwest of here, then drew a long line right across Sterling and up through Little River and all the way to Marquette. Knocked the steeple off the Congregational church and demolished half the grade school. Some people lost all their crops or their livestock. I think twenty people were killed, maybe more."

"Pat Claussen said the land out there was badly damaged."

"The main house was sturdy and withheld the winds, but the stables were nearly destroyed. They used to sit farther away from the house, and unfortunately, in the direct path of the storm. Those poor horses. There'd been a handsome chestnut Morgan they called Whirlaway—they'd named him after the famous Triple Crown winner—and the tornado damn near broke that poor horse in half. Supposedly the wind ripped all the hide off one side of him."

She paused to see if I was taking notes, so I quickly scribbled on the pad. "In the weeks after the storm," she said, "the town picked itself up and started to rebuild. They had the funerals. They had a fund-raiser for the church, and then one for the school, and then a special one just for the stable. People were very upset, because that place had always brought a load of business to town, so of course they wanted to get it up and running again."

"You said twenty people . . . were any of those killed out at the stable?"

"I don't think so. No, not then. Not until the next year, in the fire."

"Yes, Pat mentioned that a few people died then."

"I believe there were four."

"And this fire—it happened just a year later?"

"September 1951. Nobody ever found out how it started. But it was bad. Burned down the owners' house—they were called the Huntleys, and they were there before the Lockridges—and it burned down the cabins where the hired hands were living. And all the stables where they kept the horses. New stables, rebuilt just after the storm the year before.

"I remember how pretty the place had been before the fire," she said. "The old Huntley mansion, with the white pillars and the balcony, and forsythia bushes and a tall weeping-willow tree. That house was like a museum. Inside they had expensive antique furniture, expensive sculptures, and paintings and whatnot. And then the pair of smaller cabins behind the house, like quaint little boxes, and behind the cabins, the rows of new stables. Folks in town would drive out there, just to see how pretty everything looked. But then, on that one horrible night, it all burned to the ground."

"So it was the Huntleys who died in the fire?"

"Not all of them. Only the missus was killed. She and her husband were some of the richest folks in Sterling at the time, practically millionaires. If you go and search through the newspapers, you'll find that's pretty much all the stories talk about—the death of the wealthy Huntley woman. I imagine she and her husband gave a lot of money to churches and schools, both here and in Hutchinson. And they'd been a big help in rebuilding things after the storm the year before. People thought quite highly of the Huntleys."

I couldn't let her stop now; I nodded to urge the story forward. "Please. Anything else you can remember."

"Well, the fire happened late at night, with everybody asleep in bed. It woke the people in the cottages first—the hired men—but by then it was too late. Because of the way the buildings were connected, the fire just—what's that word?—*engulfed*. It engulfed everything. Fire on all sides, everywhere. They couldn't get to the horses. But one of the hired men tried his darnedest to save the Huntleys. There was a teenage girl, named Rebecca—she was the Huntleys' only child—and the hired man wound up rescuing the girl and the father. But he couldn't save the missus."

"Do you know anything else about the Huntley girl?"

"I didn't know her very well at the time. She was older than me, and they'd sent her to a private school in Hutchinson. I know she'd been a champion show rider. But I saw her only three, maybe four times, dressed all fancy and nice, out with her parents on the street or in church. And then, after the fire, I never saw her at all. Mr. Huntley packed up what little they had left, and he and his daughter took their memories and their grief and moved somewhere up East. By the time the Lockridges bought the land to restart the business, Mr. Huntley and the girl were long gone."

Pammy stared at me, waiting to hear what questions were next. But her stories still weren't connecting, weren't providing the solutions I needed to bring home to Dolores and my mother. I reviewed the notes on the pad, barely legible words from my jittery hand, and then I tried again. "You said three others died in the fire," I said. "Any chance you remember who they were?"

"Yes, of course. One of the hired hands was killed. He was young, just out of high school, I think. The other man— the older hired hand—was burned very badly, but lived. And here's the saddest thing—this older man was the one who wound up saving Mr. Huntley and the daughter. But in doing so, he couldn't save his own family, and the two children died inside their cabin."

"Do you remember their names?"

Pammy turned her face to the wall, as though some answer might be hidden among the Kansas license plates. I looked there too, but saw only meaningless numbers, letters, flaking paint. The room was silent, and I realized the jukebox had stopped playing many minutes earlier. Between us, the tape recorder's wheels were slowly spinning, preserving our words.

Finally, she looked back to me and said, "I can't recall. You might be able to find out more if you go through newspapers from that time. Library records, something like that. But like I said, most of the stories focused all their attention on the

Huntleys. They talked a lot about the loss of the art and the antiques, and the loss of all those thoroughbreds. But they never said much about that young hired hand or those two little children. It's sad. It's like they died in the fire, and then the world forgot them. It's like they just faded away."

I put the pencil down. Pammy looked at me suspiciously, at my face and the name tag on my shirt, and then she raised the glass of beer and drank. As she finished, to her surprise, I reached across the table and touched her hand. "Two children," I said.

"Again, I can't remember much. You'll get better information from newspapers. But I know that the older man— the older hired hand—was living in one of the adjoining cabins with his wife and their two little grandkids. The man was burned from saving the folks in the mansion, but he made it out alive. And somehow his wife escaped unharmed. But the two children—it was a brother and sister, I remember, just an innocent little boy and girl—wound up dying in the fire."

As she spoke, the room began to blur, the walls soft and wobbly, each license plate loosening its numbers and letters. I suddenly felt very ill, and tried to stand from the table. *Warren,* I was thinking. *Donna.* My hand bumped my glass, spilling water across the booth, the knees of my jeans. I stumbled over the sawdust-scattered floor, hurrying to the back-corner restroom. *Just an innocent little boy and girl.* I didn't bother with the light; didn't look in the mirror. I bent double and vomited loudly into the sink, not caring that Pammy or the waitress could hear.

As I was walking back, my vision was dark, and I briefly lost my balance. For a moment, the woman at the table wasn't Pammy at all, but Pat Claussen—then she briefly changed to Dolores—and then once again she was Pammy Sporn. "I'm sorry," I tried to tell her. I'd never before had hallucinations like this. I'd never felt so sick. Echoing in my head was something I'd said to my mother, weeks earlier, that first night I'd arrived from New York: *I haven't quite lost my mind; not yet.* And my mother had smiled and replied, *Then maybe things aren't all that bad.*

Then Pammy was standing, waiting for me to rejoin her at the booth. She had hastily mopped the spill, leaving wet lumps of napkin across the table, and I thought of the bloodied paper towels on my mother's kitchen floor. "I can see you aren't feeling well," she said. "I hope I didn't say something wrong."

"No, everything's fine. Everything's going to be fine now." I was still struggling to focus on the room, on the vinyl booths and sparkling jukebox. I managed to lean down, gathering the gloves and jacket, the pencils and notepads and recorder. "Really, you've been a lot of help. You've provided the link— the information about the stable and the fire. This is exactly what my mother needs."

She shook her head. "I'm not quite sure what you mean."

"I'll take your advice about the newspapers, and I'll find out more. If only I had more time."

She followed me to the door of the bar and grill. She moved with a weak, sluggish limp, as though our hour of answers and revelations had been one long and arduous race. When we stepped out into the bracing air, Pammy leaned against the wall, under the faint blue shade from the overhead awning, and watched as I stepped toward the truck. I opened the passenger door and slid the interview materials onto the seat. Then I turned to tell her good-bye.

"Don't go yet," she said. "Isn't there something else you need to know? You were supposed to ask me about the boy."

"The boy? What boy?"

"Cindy—from the stable—told me you'd asked her about a boy. Someone who looked like you. She said you'd surely ask me, too, that it seemed especially important. She said you almost—well, *scared* her when you asked about this boy."

I shut the passenger door and returned to Pammy's side. In her hand was the empty beer glass, laced with white webs of foam. Now I could see she wasn't quite as tall as I'd initially thought; her blouse wasn't nearly as yellow. Above her head, along the canvas of the awning, hung an unbroken row of icicles; higher in the sky were the gathering, graying clouds.

"He's just a boy named Allen," I said. "Dropped out of high school last spring. I think he lives around here with his uncle and aunt."

"Allen," she repeated. Tightly she shut her eyes, her brow tensing as she pondered the name. "I'm not sure. You say he looks like you?"

"He used to work at a grocery store. Can't you think of anyone? Seventeen or eighteen? Sort of pale and skinny, auburn-reddish hair, living here in Sterling?"

"I'm sorry. No, I can't think of any person like that. Certainly no one named Allen."

I unfolded the photograph from my pocket, the picture of myself I'd removed from the kitchen wall. "Then I guess it doesn't matter anymore," I said. I placed it in Pammy Sporn's hand.

She looked at me with apprehension, then brought the photo closer to examine the face. "Is this him?" she asked. "Is this the boy?"

I couldn't form the true answer. I could only stare at her, smiling. And then, in a sudden rush, I wrapped my arms around her in a stiff but sturdy hug. A gesture of thanksgiving and surrender: an embrace not only from me but also from my mother. For a moment, I felt Pammy recoiling; she floundered, trying to lift her arms. Then she relaxed and let me hold her. Neither of us spoke. Pammy Sporn and I remained like this, under the clouds and the awning's blue shadows, until at last I let her pull away, until I turned and headed back to the truck.

The roads were slick, but I reached the Hutchinson Public Library four hours before their special collections department closed. Throughout the drive, I'd been reprising Pammy's stories in my head, her secrets and suggestions, pairing them with everything my mother had confessed to Dolores and Alice and me. Already I felt I knew what I'd find in the *Hutchinson News* microfilm reels. I believed I understood how my mother had disappeared, and believed I understood why.

Four hours was just enough time. I worked fiercely, in spite of the sickness, taking notes, feeding Dolores's loaned dollar bills into the vast, thunderous copy machine. My search began with the tornado of 1950, the victims and photographs and aftereffects. I worked through to the spring of 1951 and the fire. I persevered until the end of that year, and by then I'd learned enough for my mother, by then it was time to piece together my knowledge and go back home.

In the rearview mirror, I looked alarmingly ill; the fatigue was numbing my legs and arms. But I kept my hands on the wheel, steering south across town. While I drove, I planned the words I would say to her. I thought about Mary's advice: *One of the best things is to keep talking. At the end, they might lose the ability to speak, and they might not be able to see well. But their hearing stays . . . it's their last connection to the world.*

The rocky, frost-crusted roads . . . the spent fields of wheat . . . the distant grain elevators, towering like ivory monuments from the snow. The radio played only static, as though the cold had frozen the frequencies. I passed a ditch littered with tires and upended grocery carts. Then a split-level farmhouse, where once, years before, my mother had purchased a used lawn mower. I remembered her leaving Alice and me in the pickup as she went inside to finalize the deal. The sun piercing the windshield; the white hens circling the gravel drive as we waited and waited.

Back then, she'd tried so often to succeed: her repeated attempts to impress Alice and me, which had consistently, dismally, failed. I remembered the clothes she bought us, the shirts and sneakers and jeans she'd believed to be the emblems of adolescent popularity, which only proved awkward or gaudy. Or the comet she said we'd see if we hiked to the top of Quarry Hill: we expected spills of gilded seeds, light suspended like a jeweled badminton birdie across the stars, but instead saw no comet, no miracle, only fogbanks hunkering below the town's deceitful sky.

So many memories. Their weight, making my body weak. But soon I'd be home again; soon I'd sit beside the bed and tell her everything I'd learned.

The old man and old woman.

Their two grandchildren.

Warren and Donna.

Ahead, to the left of the snowy road, was KSIR, the prison where she'd once worked: its solemn walls and towers, its saw-toothed coils of razor wire. I thought of the *True Detective* magazines she'd always smuggled home; of the handcuffs she'd saved and later used for the boy's slender wrists. And I thought of weekend afternoons when I was young, sixteen, with my first car, when I'd drive to KSIR to surprise my mother. I'd idle in the street below the walls, radio blaring, and then I'd squint skyward to confirm my mother was on tower duty. Eventually, she'd look down and see her son, grinning from the window of the car, waving.

It was during those same days, too, that I first discovered Carey Park. It was less than a mile away. So many afternoons or evenings, I'd innocently wave to my mother, only to speed unobserved toward that forbidden scene of drugs and sex. Once more, I recalled Dolores's voice as I'd left the house: *Do the things you did when you were young. Go out and be a kid again.*

The sky was dimming with the threat of snow. I reminded myself of the day's sole priority, and knew I should return home. But, ultimately, the withdrawal was overwhelming.

The possibility of scoring drugs, however remote, lured me through the gates and onto the park's narrow road.

My heartbeat was rushing, my palms slick on the wheel. I passed the duck pond, the nine-hole golf course, and the stark, neglected playground with its broken swings and corroded corkscrew slides. And lastly, in the glowing headlights, the familiar stretch of woods. I could see another car, parked in the adjacent playground lot. *Don't stop,* I thought, *just go back home.* But I eased behind the car; I shut the engine and stepped outside.

The woods were dark and cold. I could hear the swallows, bickering unseen from the cottonwood trees: the exclamating air; the weird din of them. The snow had melted in patches, revealing a muddy path peppered here and there with tiny glittering stones. I followed its downward slope, silent as a shepherd, watching for any nearby movement. Farther into the trees, along the softly slapping river.

Even in the twilight, I could see the footprints, the heavy tracks of boots. I trailed them through the tangled scrub, pushing deeper into the trees, but I saw no other soul. Gradually, the footprints faded in the mud. I began to think I'd dreamed the car in the playground lot, even dreamed, perhaps, these woods, this desolate park. Soon the guilt was swelling inside me: I'd chosen to cruise this place, hoping for drugs or sex, while my mother lay sleeping in the hospice bed. I dared myself to allow the words: *her deathbed.*

To the left, I heard a rustle, a hesitant cough. Someone was standing in the shadows of the trees.

As I neared, I saw the figure was a teenage boy. He wore paint-spattered combat boots and a long black coat. A silver hoop through each earlobe; another through the crook of his bottom lip. Beneath the coat was a black T-shirt; on the front, glowing white, a smiling skull.

Littered among the leaves at his feet were wadded tissues, ripped condom wrappers, unrolled condoms. I stepped close enough to touch, to prove the boy was real. "About *time* somebody showed up," he said.

His eyes were dark, his skin pale as paper. He smelled like the spice cologne my mother had bought for me once, some long-ago birthday. I could see he wasn't here for drugs; he only wanted sex. He leaned against one of the trees, then rubbed the fly of his jeans, daring me to put my hand there too. How rough and disarrayed must I seem to him, how desperate? I thought of myself at his age, my trips to this same secret curve of Carey Park, and I remembered how I'd loved it when older men fixed their attention on me. Back then I'd owned a similar pair of combat boots. Back then I had equally blue eyes, equally pale hands, and I'd bait all the lonesome, leering men by rubbing the front of my pants.

The boy was waiting for my response. I placed a hand on his shoulder. *I know how you feel,* I wanted to say. *Twenty years ago I leaned against that same tree and smiled that smile.* I knew I should have been aroused; surely he expected me to unzip his jeans or dart my tongue into his mouth. But I was hollow. What I thought I'd wanted, when I parked beside the woods, was no longer possible, incapable of piercing through this husk. When the boy reached for me at last, I could only shake my head in rejection.

"At least kiss me or something," he said.

I clasped the back of his neck, drawing his face closer to mine. The cologne was strong but I caught an undersmell—not from his T-shirt or coat, but deeper—perhaps from the skin beneath, musty and muddy, as though he'd spent nights lying in the earth. And I kissed him. The mouth was hard and very cold, as though I'd leaned into glass to kiss my reflection.

The boy slid both hands down my back. I deflected, lowering my head to his neck, grazing the skin beneath his ear. We must have looked like dancers. If I squinted through the gaps in the trees, I could see the empty golf course; an isolate edge of the prison's towers. The wind was blowing the year's last leaves; the snow was melting to the river with a sharp, silver trickle. It was the same river that wound through Reno County, the flatlands and sandy-soiled basins, along to smaller towns like Haven; it was the same wind that flowed southeast, over the roof and house, over the bed where she lay.

The boy persisted. He slipped his fingers under my belt, trying to get inside my jeans. But I pushed his shoulder and shuffled away. He bent his eyebrows in protest and reached for me, ripping the name tag from my shirt.

I watched his hand crush the square of paper. Then I looked back to his face. And I realized.

"Oh, it's *you*," I said. "It's finally you."

I pictured him at the side of the road, the defiant and pugilistic boy, his scratches and flecks of blood. Yes, these were the same thin but powerful arms. These were the muscles that had hurled the tomatoes, swift, tantrumy fire, to strike our truck.

"These past few days, I've been wondering if you were only a dream. Something we'd created, just because we needed you."

He shook his head, stuffing his hands in his coat pockets. I smelled his buried smell. I stared at the image on his shirt: his face had the same angles, the same grin, as the skull.

"Please come home with us again," I said. "Just one last time. She'll be so glad to see you. And we can tell her together. Hurry now, before she's gone."

The boy backed farther against the tree, clearly puzzled by my words. And then, loudly, he began to laugh. He canted his head, offering the noise to the trees and sky, the muscles taut in his throat. Now I could see he wasn't Allen, wasn't Otis, after all. He wasn't Henry or Evan or Warren. He was just an anonymous teenage Hutchinson boy, lonely and frantic for love, playing the role I'd once played.

When I realized my mistake, I stumbled backward, nearly slipping in the mud. Then I turned and ran. I shot through the frozen branches—fast, exquisite snags at my skin and clothes—but I didn't look back, didn't stop, until I reached the truck.

My breathing was staggered and raw. I waited for my heartbeat to steady. The branches had cut my ear and one corner of my mouth, and I dabbed at the blood with my sleeve, watching the path and the line of trees, checking to see if the boy had followed. But there was only silence.

Once again it began to snow. I turned the key and backed out of the lot, retracing the route past the playground and pond and welcome sign. I tried to forget the boy, his wild eyes, the melody of his laugh. I tried focusing solely on my mother, the quiet bed in the quiet room. Hopefully the designated pastor had come and gone. Hopefully he'd withdrawn his futile persuasions, his attempts at stuffing her with heaven. By now, Mary had finished her duties; Dolores would be ready for a rest.

Just before the highway exit stood the edge-of-town McDonald's, its lights blurred and ashen through the snow. In recent weeks, Dolores and I had visited once or twice a day, routinely ordering strawberry milkshakes. My mother had loved their sweet berry bite; she'd loved the way they chilled her hand. Although I knew she could no longer drink them, no longer hold the plastic cup, I turned onto the street, I steered toward the drive-through window.

The employee was a young girl with smudged mascara and a stained gold visor. I ordered the extra-large size, the thirty-two ounce, as though its volume could reflect my mercy or love. The girl bagged my order, walked to the window, and delivered it into my trembling hand. Without thinking, I took a drink: the chalky, puddled pink of it; the familiar clown-colored straw.

Frowning, the girl stared into the pickup, then announced the total amount. I reached for my wallet to pay her. But my jeans were empty. I tried the pockets of John's jacket. I tried the seat; the floor of the truck. The wallet was gone.

Perhaps I'd lost the wallet while sprinting back through the trees. More likely, I knew, the boy from the woods had stolen it. The last remaining bills from Dolores. All my photographs and credit cards; my proofs and identifications. The girl was holding out her hand, but I could only give a pathetic shrug. I had nothing to give her. I'd finally faded away.

TWELVE

AND THEN THE snow turned to ice, sealing the phone lines and weathervanes, the black limbs of trees. The wind rang the church bells. In front of the phantom house, a branch had cracked and collapsed in the street.

I came inside from the cold, waking Dolores from her nap. She'd turned on the rotating fan, but had switched off all the lamps. On the tray of the antique high chair was a half-filled tumbler of bourbon. I saw her staring uneasily at the cuts on my face, but she didn't speak.

"There's so much I have to tell her," I said.

More blood had dried on my mother's lips, flaked red as though she'd chewed a crayon. Her breathing had changed once again. I listened as her lungs struggled with air. Following each exhalation was a wet, gurgling sound, and then an awful, sustained silence.

Dolores stood from the rocking chair. "If you want to be alone, I'll leave for a while."

"No. I want you to hear everything, too."

Dolores suggested we bathe her. In the bathroom, we found the sponge Mary had brought. It was round and dimpled and pink, so thick I needed both hands to hold it. We also found a bar of sandalwood soap, a gift last Christmas from Alice, saved in the medicine cabinet but never unwrapped. "That's such a wonderful scent," Dolores said. "Your mother loves that scent." I looked at her under the bathroom light, and for the first time noticed her lipstick, eye shadow, and carefully styled hair. She'd tried to make herself pretty for tonight, for my mother.

We brushed aside the blankets. We dipped our hands into the water and washed her face, her scalp, and the back of her neck, taking extra care around the bruises, the scar from her fall. "There now," Dolores whispered, "doesn't that feel nice?" We tried not to spill the water or dampen the gown. We dabbed at her ankles, up to her thighs (*there now, there now*), the skin around the catheter tube and drainage bag. Then we finished by running the sponge along her breasts, her arms, her hands.

Now my mother was glistening white. We were panting feverishly, as though we'd ascended a steep hill. I began moving through the house, locking doors, closing curtains. It seemed necessary to cordon us off, to reject the rest of the world. When I returned, Dolores was sitting in the rocking chair. I took my seat at the end of the bed. I placed my mother's feet in my lap, and, as always, warmed them with my hands. Softly, I began to speak.

I don't know the entire story. I suppose there's no way of ever knowing all of it. Some of its parts are presumably facts, or at least the facts as reported by the *Hutchinson News*. Other parts came from Pammy Sporn, from all her years in Sterling. And the rest I've colored here and there, adding the plausible pieces, making connections, embellishing the places and names. Just as my mother and I had done before, with our tales of the missing.

I know that on the afternoon of May 9, 1950, a tornado ripped across Rice and McPherson counties in central Kansas. A total of twenty people were killed. One of the dead was Margaret Anders of Sterling, a twenty-eight-year-old widow with two children. The older child was a nine-year-old boy named Jesse; the younger a girl of six, named Jill. The newspapers don't say much about Mr. Anders—perhaps their father died from a farm accident or influenza; perhaps he was killed in the war—but I can safely say that Margaret was raising the boy and girl on her own.

When the tornado hit, the Anders children had been at school—Sterling Elementary, third grade and first—and their mother, Margaret, was across town, assistant teller at the local bank. The warning sirens began blaring, and I can picture the students filing hastily into the hall: crouching low to the floor, their hands safeguarding the backs of their bowed heads. But at the bank, Margaret and the other employees ignored the sirens and continued working. I wonder about the locomotive roar as it approached. I wonder what she saw that crippling instant when the roof tore away and she faced the erupting air.

(It's possible my mother already knew these details. She'd visited the library; copied photographs; researched the micro-film reels. The information was there. So it's likely she'd learned about the storm and Margaret's death. Likely she knew what I would say next.)

After the funeral, the children went to stay with their mother's parents. Adele and Raymond Crowhurst lived south-west of town, at the Triple Crown stable, in one of the ranch hands' cabins. Adele was a housewife and seamstress, who taught Sunday school and played the organ at the Congregational church, and Raymond, a horse trainer and part-time mechanic.

I can only imagine the family's grief. It must have been so difficult for Adele. Over a decade had passed since she'd last had a child in the house—after Margaret, there was no one else—and now the rooms were restless with the pair of them, two youths filled with uncertainties and defiances and fears. It's possible she fought hard to keep Raymond away from the whiskey. It's possible she persuaded them to stay faithful to their church, saving Sunday afternoons for cemetery visits, cutting lilacs from her garden to place on Margaret's grave.

And poor Raymond. The storm that killed his daughter had also wrecked the Triple Crown, where he'd lived and worked for decades. It had ravaged the stables and maimed three of the Huntleys' champion horses. Throughout that year, Raymond must have thought of his daughter as he helped rebuild, as he stoically trained the new palominos. Did he carve her name into some discreet rafter of the stable? Did he use the bridle that Margaret had used when he'd taught her to ride, all those years ago?

But, surely, during these long months of sorrow, there were happy times, too. I imagine them hosting pony-riding parties for the children on the Huntleys' manicured lawn. When Jill and Jesse grew restless, Adele must have searched the hall closet for Chinese checkers or one of Margaret's old board games. Indians and Cowboys; Chutes and Ladders. They'd play the records she'd played as a teenager: Jesse's favorite was "Jeepers, Creepers," and Jill liked "Don't Sit Under the Apple Tree."

(I'm certain my mother, too, had obsessed about these months. What additional details had she invented? How had her elaborations differed from mine? Maybe she'd decided that Raymond and Adele had bought the grandchildren a kitten; maybe a sad-eyed cocker spaniel puppy. Maybe they'd taken the kids for countryside drives in the family Imperial, or watched them ride ponies with young Rebecca Huntley. Maybe they'd enjoyed long walks through wintry Sterling Park.)

For the first eight months of 1951, I can only guess. The newspapers don't mention the family at all. Spring, and then summer . . . the loss and the resulting grief . . . the progression of healing. And then, September.

The reports claim that the fire started just before midnight, while everyone was sleeping. The reports don't, however, mention a definite cause. In fact, I found it difficult to uncover many of the necessary details; Pammy Sporn had been right when she'd claimed the papers had centered solely on the death of Mrs. Huntley. But it's clear that Raymond tried to save her. It's clear he didn't see the danger to his own adjoining home until the wind shifted toward the east and the fire quickly, unexpectedly, spread. By then, it was too late.

I don't know why they couldn't escape. *Engulfed* was the word Pammy Sporn had used. But I try not to think about the fire. I try not to hear the children's screams.

From the stories my mother had told about her kidnapping, I know that four years passed between the night of the Triple Crown tragedy and that afternoon she'd sat in the playground grass, calmly coloring the dinosaurs in her book. In my searches through the *Hutchinson News*, I could only find a single article about Adele and Raymond from that time. Five weeks after the fire, it was reported that Raymond Crowhurst, sixty-five, had finally been released from Hutchinson Hospital. The article doesn't describe his disfiguring third-degree burns. It calls him "the valiant man who had pulled Martin Huntley and young Rebecca to safety." It calls him "the hero who had tried in vain to save Katherine."

The article makes no mention of Jesse or Jill.

There's so much I still want to know. What happened to Adele and Raymond Crowhurst during those intervening four years? In what small, unassuming house did the elderly couple choose to rebuild their lives? Did they stay close to Sterling? Did they find a peaceful acre of land near a peach orchard?

Did Adele resume her duties as organist for the church, and did she take solace in the countless Christian hymns? Did Raymond eventually return to work at the stables, even after the Lockridges purchased the land and began to rebuild?

I can almost hear her soprano, raised toward her greedy god, trying to bless their little souls. Her prayers, her hymns. *Strange songs,* my mother had called them, *with strange, sad melodies. And she'd watch us like she was going to cry.*

I can almost see the gloves on his hands, and his scarlet, puckered scars. *He always wore something over his face, like a scarf or sometimes some kind of mask.*

At what point did their despair grow insurmountable? Did they speak of their plan in whispers; did they speak of it at all?

Was it her idea? His?

How long before they bought replacements for the lost games and records, before they stockpiled boxes of candy bars, before they began preparing the basement?

And when did they start taking the Imperial for secret, wordless drives? How many miles did they have to travel until they found a boy who looked like Jesse? Until they found their surrogate Jill?

Dolores listened closely as I spoke, at first rocking slowly in the chair, and then hardly moving at all. My mother remained motionless, her breaths now sudden and wet, like hiccups. We could hear the telltale rattling and we knew that it was really happening, that this was the night. After I stopped speaking, I was silent for a long time. I had no awareness of my withdrawal or sickness. My only focus was my mother. Foolishly, I wanted her to wake, to open her eyes one last time, to look into my face and see me. Not Otis, not Warren, but me. But of course she couldn't wake. After a while, I stood from the end of the bed, and Dolores brought the bottle of morphine.

We moved closer and dropped the liquid on her tongue. Her mouth did nothing with it, and we had to wipe her wounded lips. From outside we heard the indifferent snow against the house. Dolores took my mother's left hand, and I took the right. I told her I was sorry we couldn't give her more answers. I was sorry we hadn't found Warren. And I told her that I understood. I knew why she'd kept silent, all those years, about the Crowhursts, about her disappearance. *They'd loved you so much. But in the end, it was a misplaced love. You weren't their Jill, and they had to take you home.*

Beside me, Dolores was saying beautiful things in a beautiful voice. *It'll be more peaceful soon. We're here with you, just let it go.* My mother's hand was small and cold. She was very clean, almost glowing. We'd shut the lamps in the room, but I could sense a halo from her, a light. We hovered over it, waiting.

Then the rattle in her throat became too much and I could fight no longer. In a rush, I moved myself onto the bed, lifting my leg over the rickety slats, fitting my body next to hers. I put my head on her shoulder. I wrapped an arm around her, like a shield. I could feel her belly and the striate edge of the port in her chest. Her legs and arms were so cold, but I could still feel some heat, some final warmth within her. There, below my ear, where her heart made its tired plod. I could still hear it, my mother's heart. I tried to wrap her in my arms. I wondered how we must have looked, all those years ago, our positions reversed, my mother holding the infant Scott.

Dimly I sensed Dolores leaving the room, shuffling toward the kitchen. I'll let you have this time alone, she said. I heard her empty the water and sponge in the sink, and then I heard the back door, the hinges creaking as she stepped outside.

Now our world had narrowed; there was only mother and son. I ran my hands along her face, touching the remaining hairs on her head, the stubble around the scar. I would remember all of it, every bony angle of her shoulders, the loose flesh of her upper arms. Her elbows, her elegant hands, the ridges and whorls of her fingerprints. Had a stranger entered the darkening room, he might have thought my mother was telling a precious secret, and I was straining to hear. He might have thought us soundly sleeping, or that both of us, not just the mother but also the son, had slipped forever, that together we'd entered that nothingness.

My mother. My junk-shop bargainer, my field trespasser. The Tired to my Wired. My sponsor and cook and chauffeur, my confidante, my prison guard. My morning alarm and bedtime story. Magnet and tape; scrapbook and scissors. My iced tea, my Tennessee whiskey. My farmhouse on the hill. My quiet Haven house at the end of the street. My vitamins and steroids, my Neupogen and Anzemet, disease and remission. Doll and rabbit and carousel horse. My yellow leaf, fallen in her hair. My scarf and my wig, my big switch and small switch, my Cherry Mash, my clawfoot bathtub, my thousand chandeliers. My pretty little pigeon. My Hansel and my Gretel, my plot at Rayl's Hill, my newspaper headline, my photo and my story.

And then only blankness, a sealing of sound. I squeezed her hand, but there was nothing. I looked up into her face and, slowly, my mother's eyes opened and I dropped the hand.

The room was darker now. I stayed with the body, curled against its chill. Eventually, I stood and arranged her arms at her sides. I brought the hands up to fold them over her heart. She looked more peaceful this way.

When I left the room, I went to the backyard garden to find Dolores. She was sitting in the snow, her back hunched, her hands nimbly working. Somehow I knew that she knew. "It's over," I said. She didn't turn her head, but only sat, as focused as a bootblack, concentrating on some critical task. As I neared, I saw the thread and scissors and scraps of cloth: she was sewing one of my mother's unfinished scarves.

After a pause, she glanced up from her work. "So that's the way it happened, then? Everything you said is the truth?"

"I don't know. Probably not everything. But I hope so. I hope it's as close as I've imagined it."

"I wonder how much she'd learned for herself. And how much she kept secret."

I looked away, shaking my head. Perhaps we would never know. Dolores stood, picking the thread and scissors and scraps of cloth from the snow; I could feel her gathering the strength to go inside.

"There's one more thing that still confuses me," I said. "The stories she told you and Alice were so outlandish and false. But it seems the story she told me was real."

"I don't think she necessarily *wanted* us to believe her. Not me, and not Alice."

"But why, then? Why only me?"

"You really don't know? I think it's obvious."

"Tell me."

Dolores looked down at my hands, at my tired body, and then back to my face. "With you, she had so much at stake."

She smiled then, and suddenly I understood her meaning. My mother had hoped I would immerse myself: to step away from my world, the depression and drugs, to enter the mystery and join in her pursuit.

"Your mother wanted to save you," Dolores said.

Now the wind had changed direction, wheeling along the streets in a secretive hush, the snow falling in thick, ashen lumps. We realized we hadn't dressed warmly enough. Dolores began walking back to the house. Before reaching the door, she turned to let me know she would make the necessary telephone calls: first Alice, and then Kaufman, Mary McVickers, and the funeral home. And then, she said, she wanted a few minutes alone with my mother.

Dolores closed the door; through the glass, I watched her shaking the snow from her boots. I remembered her words: *My best friend in this whole damn world.* I saw her take a deep breath and make her way through the kitchen, toward the bed.

I don't know how long I stood there, watching the snow. I don't recall the thoughts that weighed heavy in my head. But after a time, Dolores opened the door again. With a wave, she beckoned me back inside.

I followed her into the kitchen, but saw instantly that the room wasn't the same. The walls were entirely bare. The photographs—every face from the refrigerator door, from the space above the sink, from the sides of the antique telephone and cabinets and stove—had dropped and scattered across the floor.

"Look what she's done," Dolores said.

We stood and studied the room. I remembered the night I'd arrived home, the scrapbook I'd bumped and the pictures I'd strewn on her bed, how I'd drifted to sleep amid the miss- ing. And I remembered sitting together with Otis—*Allen*— talking and talking, the photos spread around us in careless hills. Had it all been a dream? What had happened to that boy? Had I loosed him conclusively into the world? Was he brooding inside me still?

I knelt, and Dolores knelt. Our bodies touched at the stain where my mother had fallen and spilled her blood. And once again we joined hands. Their pictures were all around us: each ripped from its tape or tack or pin; each lying face-up on the floor. We remained like this for a long, soundless time, staring down at the photographs, all their last lost faces, until we heard the black car in the drive, the footsteps on the walk, the knock at the door.

(FADE)

FOR A WHILE, after everything was over and
I'd returned to New York, Dolores tried to learn more. She
spent random spring days driving to Sterling, alone, taking
the winding, abandoned back roads in her car. She searched
through thirty-two separate Kansas phone books—she kept
a list of them, in a yellow notepad from my mother's house—

and one night, after too much bourbon, called all the families named Crowhurst, the families named Anders. But no one gave the answers she needed.

Another drunken night, Dolores returned to the Triple Crown stables. When she confessed this over the phone, she giggled like a teenage girl. Apparently, she spent two hours trespassing across the place. Then Pat Claussen's husband, watching from a second-floor window, saw her stumbling through the backyard grass, the land where the fire had once burned. He waited until Dolores unlatched one of the stable doors and went inside. Then he woke his wife, and together they walked out with a flashlight and a cup of hot coffee. After an hour calmly chatting in the hay-scented dark, the Claussens sent Dolores home.

I'm certain my mother never behaved this way. I'm still not sure why she didn't.

On my birthday, I receive a card from Dolores; inside is a handwritten note and a photograph of her new Manx kitten. Her stationery smells of the perfume she'd worn that night when she retrieved me from the bus station, when she forewarned me about my mother's health.

In the note, Dolores claims she's giving up her search. *It happened too many years ago,* she says. *No one will ever know the answers. Any final secrets were lost when we lost your mom.*

The autumn passes. I go to meetings, I relapse, and I go to more meetings. I call Alice twice a week, and I reveal the details of Pammy Sporn, the Crowhursts, the tornado and the fire and Jesse and Jill. One night, I even divulge everything I can remember about the boy in the basement. The burned ditch, just outside Sterling . . . the handcuffs and cot and cramped storage room . . . the hallucination in the woods at Carey Park. At first, Alice laughs uneasily, certain I'm telling an extravagant joke. But then she remains silent, only making the occasional nervous murmur, until my story is finished.

For days I'd been preparing this speech, brooding carefully over the wording of my questions. I ask Alice if she believes the boy was real. Perhaps he was only a dream, created by our mother to represent a past she wanted to reclaim. Alice thinks before she answers. Then she says, "Of course the boy was real. He *must* have been. Remember, she wasn't the only one who experienced him. You did, too. Why would *you* invent him? What did he represent for *you*?"

October, November. Nearly a year after my mother's death. Throughout these months, I hear nothing from Dolores. And then, one day, as I sit behind my desk at Pen & Ink, she calls again.

It seems that Pammy Sporn has tracked Dolores down. She's been asking questions around Sterling, learning secrets we might have missed. She gives directions to an abandoned graveyard, two miles from Sterling's cemetery, an hour's drive from my mother's stone at Rayl's Hill. "You and Donna's son might want to go there someday," Pammy says. "I think you'll be content with what you find."

Naturally, Dolores couldn't wait. She has located the graveyard without me. A dreary, treeless plot of land: a field of wheat on the left, field of milo on the right. If she hadn't been driving that dusty road to specifically find the graves, she'd never know they were there.

It seems that Raymond wasn't able to afford headstones. There are only markers, chipped square plaques obscured by the tangled, frozen weeds. But Raymond assured their names were proudly listed. Their birthdays, the dates of their deaths. Dolores has made charcoal rubbings of Margaret's stone, of the smaller markers for Jesse and Jill. She will send them to me in the mail.

I ask her to read the words on the stones. It's just as I expected: Jill's birthday in February, and Jesse's in September. I remember Adele's ring from my mother's stories, the violet amethyst and blue sapphire, the birthstones of her lost grandchildren.

And there's more, Dolores says. In an antique store five miles east of Sterling, she has found a copy of *Hansel and Gretel* with page after page of illustrations, like my mother had requested. Dolores can't wait to show me. She will keep it on her bookshelf in her little house. It isn't clear who previously owned the book. But of course we imagine Adele. We see her holding it in her sturdy hands, lamplight spilling across its pages, as she reads to Jesse and Jill, and, later, to Warren and my mother.

And finally, Dolores has been searching the library. In the microfilm reels, from the years before and after my mother's disappearance, she has found recurring classified ads for a business called "Adele's Kitchen" that specialized in "pickling/canning." A number with a Sterling prefix is listed, but there is no address. Would we be wrong to assume it's the same Adele?

We picture the woman in the kitchen, channeling her grief. She must have gotten so good at it. The jars of pearl onions, the cloved apples, the jellies of mulberry and sandhill plum. And, of course, her famous peaches. We like to imagine Raymond secretly entering them in the county fair. Maybe they won Adele the first-prize ribbon. Row after row on the basement shelves, buoyed in their jars like the slumbering heads of babies. Peach preserves stirred into the breakfast oatmeal. Spiced peaches for dessert, served warm with scoops of ice cream, taken to the basement for Warren and Donna in matching blue bowls.

But of course this all is speculation. One of many things we may never know. We've never found the peach orchard. We've never found Warren.

How comforting it would be, after all these years, to know the truth. The deliverance. The utter peace of it.

Insights,
Interviews
& More . . .

Meet Scott Heim

Scott Heim was born and raised in central Kansas. In the town of Little River, he was one of twenty-five people in his graduating high school class. He obtained degrees in English literature and art history at the University of Kansas in Lawrence, and moved to New York City in 1991 to attend Columbia University's MFA program. He finished his first novel, *Mysterious Skin*, as his master's thesis; it was published by HarperCollins in 1995. A second novel, *In Awe*, followed in 1997.

Heim has won fellowships to the Sundance Screenwriters Lab and the London Arts Board's International Writer-in-Residence program. In 1995, the *New York Times Magazine* named him "one of thirty artists and writers under the age of thirty to change the culture in the next thirty years." He is also the author of a book of poems, *Saved From Drowning*. His stories, articles, and reviews have appeared in *Interview*, the *Village Voice*, *Out*, *Paper*, *Time Out New York*, *The Advocate*, Nerve.com, and many literary journals, as well as in the anthologies *Boys Like Us*, *Obsessed*, *Hot Spots: The Best Erotic Writing in Modern Fiction*, *Circa 2000*, *Best American*

Gay Fiction 1996, *Waves*, and *Personals: Dreams and Nightmares from the Lives of 20 Young Writers*.

Besides his career as a novelist, he also has worked as a copyeditor, a high-school textbook writer, a clerk at an independent record store, a waterslide park ticket-taker, a librarian, a salesperson at a watermelon stand, an assistant to a literary agent, an English tutor to foreign students, a security guard at a college dormitory, and an announcer and scorekeeper at the Midwest's largest softball complex. In college, he played drums for two separate rock bands. (At the time, he was uncertain whether to pursue writing or music, but the theft of his drum set settled the matter.)

After living in New York for eleven years, Heim moved to Boston in 2002. Playwright Prince Gomolvilas's stage adaptation of *Mysterious Skin* debuted at San Francisco's New Conservatory Theatre in 2003. Director Gregg Araki's film version, starring Elisabeth Shue, Joseph Gordon-Levitt, and Brady Corbet, was released worldwide in 2005. The film appeared on more than fifty critics' top-ten lists for that year.

Heim's interests include thrift stores, roller coasters, documentaries and horror films, and collecting records. His favorite foods are sushi, cherries, and pickled beets. He really likes gin. He lives in Boston with his partner, Michael Lowenthal, and is working on a screenplay and a new novel. His website (and accompanying blog) can be found at www.scottheim.com. ∾

> ❝ [Heim] was uncertain whether to pursue writing or music, but the theft of his drum set settled the matter. ❞

3

A Conversation with Scott Heim

What were some of your favorite books when you were young?

I read *The Boxcar Children*, by Gertrude Chandler Warner, twenty or thirty times. It concerns four recently orphaned kids and their dog who run away and live in an abandoned boxcar in the woods. My edition had terrific black-and-white silhouetted drawings that only added to the whole magical quality of everything. Warner wrote a bunch of books about these characters, mostly mysteries, and I devoured them all. Apparently there's a museum in Connecticut now, in honor of the author and this series. I'm surprised no one's ever made a film from this book.

Back then, was there any hint that you would eventually become a writer?

I loved ghost stories and horror novels, and I loved scary "urban myth" stories—things like "The Hook Man" and "What Licked Her Hand?"—stories you can easily find on the Internet now. At school, I'd tell these to anyone who wanted to hear, huddled under a tree somewhere at recess time. Later I started writing them down, and then started creating short horror stories of my own. I'd enter them in the annual *Read Magazine* writing contest, but I never won an award.

> ❝ I loved scary 'urban myth' stories—things like 'The Hook Man' and 'What Licked Her Hand?'—stories you can easily find on the Internet now. ❞

Who were some of the novelists who influenced you or books that made you want to become a writer?

I didn't start writing seriously until I started reading the Confessional poets—Sexton, Lowell, Berryman, and Plath. I wrote strictly poetry for a long time, pretty horrible, simpering stuff. It gradually got more and more narrative, with longer lines and fuller story lines. When I was eighteen, I read a lot of Southern Gothic writers, and then I read people like Dennis Cooper and Kathy Acker and Kevin Killian.

Talk about the process of writing Mysterious Skin.

The book was my master's thesis at Columbia University. Coming from Kansas and studying next to a lot of Ivy League kids made me very competitive, and I wanted to publish my novel before my classmates did. While I was turning in chapters of the book to my professors, I was also meeting with six or seven peers once every two weeks, showing them the progress. After I'd finished half the book, my professor (and onetime HarperCollins editor) Ted Solotaroff read it and gave me great feedback; he told me that when I finished, I should send the book to Robert Jones at Harper. So I shut myself away for three months and went crazy and finished the last hundred pages of the novel. And luckily, Robert Jones was eventually the editor who bought it. ▶

> ❝ I wrote strictly poetry for a long time, pretty horrible, simpering stuff. ❞

A Conversation with Scott Heim (*continued*)

Are you still that disciplined and focused?

Not at all. It's sounds horrible to say this, but now I almost despise writing. It's excruciating—sitting there for hours, totally alone, working and reworking the same page, the same paragraph, same sentence.

All of your novels—your first two, and now We Disappear—*are set in the small-town Kansas settings where you grew up. For the past sixteen years, however, you've lived in cities like New York and Boston. In the future, do you plan to write about places other than Kansas?*

I think I still have Kansas material to write. I suppose my geographical background sets me apart from other writers. There are already so many novels set in New York or Boston, and I get such a powerful emotional response from the Kansas setting, so I'll very likely continue to write about it.

At the end of Mysterious Skin, *your character Neil says, "Hollywood would never make a movie about us." The characters, however, were later immortalized in a 2005 film directed by Gregg Araki. When you wrote the novel, did you ever think this was truly possible? What were your experiences with this book-into-film process?*

I didn't think the book had even the slightest chance of becoming a movie.

66 There are already so many novels set in New York or Boston, and I get such a powerful emotional response from the Kansas setting, so I'll very likely continue to write about it. 99

I knew that very few people get their books published, even fewer get them optioned for film, and still fewer are lucky enough to have them produced. So I'm really lucky for having the film come to fruition. But the film didn't happen overnight. It was first optioned in 1997 by a totally different company, and I wrote my own screenplay based on the book. This version was never made, and that project was shelved. But during that time, Gregg read the novel and eventually contacted me. We became friends, and he shared his ideas for his vision of the ultimate film. And I think I knew that he was the right person for the project—that if the film was ever made, it would be Gregg, and no one else, who could do it.

Were you actually involved in the making of the film?

Yes and no. I wasn't around for the majority of the filming (except for the few scenes in New York—you can actually see my blurry form in the background of one of the subway scenes). But I spoke with Gregg a lot, before and during. Since this was a low-budget independent film, it was a labor of love for everyone involved— no one got rich; everyone was doing it because they believed in the project. I made close friends with the producer, and a lot of folks on the crew, and many of the actors; I even returned to Kansas with Joseph Gordon-Levitt to usher ▶

66 Since [*Mysterious Skin*] was a low-budget independent film, it was a labor of love for everyone involved. 99

A Conversation with Scott Heim *(continued)*

him around the cities and towns and houses and ball fields where the book is set. He met my mom not long before she died, and I know that was very special for her. And he, my sister, and I made a short film together, which is still floating around online.

Did the film version of Mysterious Skin *help in any way with your productivity and inspiration to finish* We Disappear?

Very much so. It had been years since I'd published my two books, and I think I'd given up hope that I'd ever finish my third. I'd wanted to finish it for my mother, but she'd passed away; I'd moved from New York and was content with just entering a new phase of my life that probably wouldn't include a writing career. But then the movie happened, and I was extremely satisfied with it. And my publisher reissued the novel as a tie-in with the movie, and I began receiving positive letters and e-mails again. This all inspired me to return to *We Disappear* and explore ways to rejuvenate the story, to make it exciting once again for me to endure the long process of writing. ∾

❝ I even returned to Kansas with [*Mysterious Skin* star] Joseph Gordon-Levitt to usher him around the cities and towns and houses and ball fields where the book is set. ❞

A Purging of Demons
Writing *We Disappear*

WHEN I PUBLISHED my first novel, *Mysterious Skin*, in 1995, I was unprepared for the sort of questions I'd hear when I gave readings or interviews. *How autobiographical is your story? Which character's experience is based on yours?* And worst of all: *Were you molested like the boys in your book?*

These questions made me uncomfortable. I learned that any answer was the wrong one. If I claimed that the events in my novel were merely fiction, people seemed disgruntled, as though creating characters and scenes solely from imagination made me a liar and cheat (and an especially degenerate one, considering the sex and violence in the book). Conversely, if I hinted that the characters' trials and traumas were indeed my own, some people seemed to discount my craft as a storyteller, as though a writer is less skilled if he or she creates solely from personal experience.

Eventually I became vague, dodging these types of weighty questions as though I were a political candidate. I remember telling a friend, not long after my first book tour, that I would never again write a novel that resembled my own life. In my second book, *In Awe*, I again used my home state of Kansas, and certainly I based several scenes, characters, and emotions on my own experience. But I purposefully distanced myself by using a third-person point of view, by focusing on two female lead ▶

> ❝ I remember telling a friend, not long after my first book tour, that I would never again write a novel that resembled my own life. ❞

9

A Purging of Demons *(continued)*

characters, and by adding elements of horror and melodrama to the plot.

In 1999—four years after *Mysterious Skin* and two after *In Awe*—I showed my editor the first 120 pages of a new book I was writing, a novel called *We Disappear.* The plot was radically different than its present state, and it strayed even further from any personal experience I'd had. It concerned a troubled Kansas family and the ghost of a young girl buried in their peach orchard. My editor found the book intriguing but potentially difficult to sell and decided to wait until I finished before deciding whether to buy it. He recommended I continue working on the story. So I went back to writing.

Or rather, I *tried* to go back to writing. Around this time, I became disillusioned with the world of publishing. Novels in general weren't selling as well as they once had, and as a result, some of my writer friends were losing their book contracts. My agent changed careers, and my editor passed away. I felt stranded. I went to London for five months, and began to develop a pretty severe case of writer's block. Problems in my personal life led to a major depression. I put *We Disappear* away. Occasionally I'd try and return to it, but the story never held my interest for long. I simply didn't care about books anymore, especially my own.

The years passed. In 2003, I went home to Kansas to care for my mother, who was dying after a long battle with cancer. Suddenly nothing else in my world seemed important. The final weeks with my mother turned out to be the most harrowing, intimate, strange, beautiful, and profound time of my life. Occasionally, when she was sleeping—in her hospital bed or, in the last days, at home—I would find myself scribbling notes in a notebook. Soon I realized that I was actually revising my novel again—but this time, I disregarded my onetime vow to "never write a book that resembled my life." I changed the setting and events to resemble my own immediate world; I even renamed my characters "Donna" and "Scott." Fictionalizing our experiences helped me make sense of my mother's death, gave my emotions a certain legitimacy that never before existed in earlier versions of the book.

Now that my novel is finished, I realize that readers will once again focus on the "truth" behind the words, the autobiographical elements of the story. I know I will be asked about my mother's illness and death. I know I will face questions about my depression and admittedly disreputable past. But this time these questions won't bother me. Writing *We Disappear* was a bit like therapy: both a purging of demons and a creative reconstruction of the past. My only regret is that I took so long to complete the novel. It's an ode to my mother, ultimately, and I wish she could see the finished product. If she were here, I'd tell her I'm sorry.

> 66 Fictionalizing our experiences helped me make sense of my mother's death, gave my emotions a certain legitimacy that never before existed in earlier versions of the book. 99

Author's Picks
Further Reading
and Listening

MOST PEOPLE I meet have never been to
Kansas. Others have only driven through
the state once or twice, on their way
toward somewhere with skyscrapers
or mountains or beaches. Still others
only recognize Kansas as the setting
from two classic books: Truman Capote's
In Cold Blood and L. Frank Baum's
The Wonderful Wizard of Oz.
    I read both these books when I was
young, and they remain among my all-
time favorites. (Moreover, my mother,
sister, and I once made a pilgrimage to
Holcomb, miles and miles to the west,
to visit the town of Capote's book, and
watching the Technicolor MGM film
version of Baum's story was a once-a-
year event I never skipped.)
    But there are more great novels set
completely or partially in Kansas. Here's
a list of some. Evan Connell's classic
Mrs. Bridge actually takes place in Kansas
City, Missouri, but that's close enough.
Particularly special to me are Kellie
Wells's *Skin*—Kellie went to school
with me at KU and has always been a
dear friend—and Geoff Ryman's *Was*,
which takes the familiar Wizard of Oz
story and gives it a wholly innovative,
gorgeous reinvention.

1. Evan S. Connell, *Mrs. Bridge*
2. Robert Day, *The Last Cattle Drive*

3. David Anthony Durham,
   Gabriel's Story
4. Laura Moriarty,
   The Center of Everything
5. Antonya Nelson, *Living to Tell*
6. Dale Peck, *Martin and John*
7. Scott Phillips, *The Ice Harvest*
8. Nancy Pickard,
   The Virgin of Small Plains
9. Geoff Ryman, *Was*
10. Kellie Wells, *Skin*
11. Daniel Woodrell, *Woe to Live On*

My writer friends think I'm nuts because I often listen to music when I work. I wish I could create a soundtrack for my books: certain sounds and textures and atmospheres that could accompany the reader's experience of the narrative. Although I listen to a pretty wide variety of music, there's a certain type that I play the most when I write. It's often instrumental; it's often dreamy, eerie, or sad. Some of the album titles even illustrate the mood of the music: *A Strangely Isolated Place; Music to Submerge In or Disappear Through.* Below, I've made an alphabetical list of the recordings I listened to the most during the years I was working on *We Disappear*.

Amp, *Astralmoonbeamprojections*
Aphex Twin, *Selected Ambient Works,
   Vol. 2*
Angelo Badalamenti, *Twin Peaks:
   Fire Walk with Me* (Motion
   Picture Soundtrack)
Bark Psychosis, *Codename: Dustsucker* ▶

> ❝ I wish I could create a soundtrack for my books: certain sounds and textures and atmospheres that could accompany the reader's experience of the narrative. ❞

Author's Picks *(continued)*

Bed, *Spacebox*
Boards of Canada, *Music Has the Right to Children*
Harold Budd and Brian Eno, *The Pearl*
Cindytalk, *In This World*
Clock DVA, *Digital Soundtracks*
Cocteau Twins, *Victorialand*
Coil, *Musick to Play in the Dark*
Cyann & Ben, *Spring*
Dif Juz, *Soundpool*
Explosions in the Sky, *The Earth Is Not a Cold Dead Place*
Flying Saucer Attack, *Further*
Future Sound of London, *Lifeforms*
Peter Gabriel, *Passion: Music for* The Last Temptation of Christ
Jon Hassell and Brian Eno, *Fourth World, Vol. 1: Possible Musics*
Hood, *Outside Closer*
Hula, *1000 Hours*
In the Nursery, *Stormhorse*
Isan, *Meet Next Life*
Labradford, *Mi Media Naranja*
Liars, *Drum's Not Dead*
Low, *I Could Live In Hope*
M83, *Dead Cities, Red Seas & Lost Ghosts*
Main, *Motion Pool*
Mogwai, *Happy Songs for Happy People*
Movietone, *The Blossom Filled Streets*
Múm, *Finally We Are No One*
My Bloody Valentine, *Loveless*
Pieter Nooten and Michael Brook, *Sleeps with the Fishes*
Björn Olsson, *Instrumental Music . . . to Submerge in . . . or Disappear Through*
Ulrich Schnauss, *A Strangely Isolated Place*

Scorn, *Evanescence*
Seefeel, *Ch-Vox*
Sigur Rós, *( )*
Slowdive, *Pygmalion*
Stars of the Lid, *And Their Refinement of
    the Decline*
Talk Talk, *Laughing Stock*
The Third Eye Foundation, *Semtex*
This Mortal Coil, *Filigree and Shadow*
Windy and Carl, *Depths*

Have You Read?
More by Scott Heim

MYSTERIOUS SKIN

At the age of eight Brian Lackey is found bleeding under the crawl space of his house, having endured something so traumatic that he cannot remember an entire five-hour period of time. During the following years he slowly recalls details from that night, but these fragments are not enough to explain what happened to him, and he begins to believe that he may have been the victim of an alien encounter. Neil McCormick is fully aware of the events from that summer of 1981. Wise beyond his years, curious about his developing sexuality, Neil found what he perceived to be love and guidance from his baseball coach. Now, ten years later, he is a teenage hustler, a terrorist of sorts, unaware of the dangerous path his life is taking. His recklessness is governed by idealized memories of his coach, memories that unexpectedly change when Brian comes to Neil for help and, ultimately, the truth.

Originally published in 1995, Heim's debut novel was made into an award-winning, critically acclaimed film directed by Gregg Araki and starring Elisabeth Shue, Joseph Gordon-Levitt, and Brady Corbet.